THE DEVIL'S BACKBONE

TALES OF APPALACHIAN HORROR

RONALD KELLY, RED LAGOE, AND LAUREL HIGHTOWER

Book 13 in Crystal Lake's Dark Tide series

Let the world know:
#IGotMyCLPBook!

Crystal Lake Publishing
www.CrystalLakePub.com

Follow us on Amazon:

WELCOME
TO ANOTHER

CRYSTAL LAKE PUBLISHING
CREATION

AFOOT IN THE NETHERWILD

RONALD KELLY

MORGAN'S MILL, TENNESSEE
1880

CHAPTER ONE

THERE WERE THREE undeniable truths in the young lives of Nash and Anna Mae Ayres.

First and foremost, that their father, Bowden, was a good and decent man. Hardworking, honest, plain-spoken, and fair to those around him. He loved his children and did all in his power to keep them warmly clothed and their bellies full, which was more than some of the other young'uns in the mountain township of Morgan's Mill could say about their own folks.

Secondly, that their mother, Judith, was dead. She had succumbed to a nasty bout of scarlet fever shortly following Anna Mae's birth. Nash remembered little about the woman, except that her hair was jet black and her eyes were blue and kind. They visited her gravestone in the churchyard cemetery twice a year to pray and leave wildflowers, just to show that she had been cherished and not forgotten.

And third, that the earth beneath their feet could not be trusted.

Since their births, their father had told them tales of the Devil's Backbone; of its ways and dark inclinations. He'd told them that some of the earth they trod upon were acres wrought of Paradise, while other places could not be depended upon to bring anything but sorrow and misery.

According to their father, the Backbone ran at a slant across the chain of the Appalachians, starting just southeast of Lexington, Kentucky, cutting through the southwest tip of Virginia, and descending into northeast Tennessee, ending near the town of Elizabethton. The Backbone was lonesome, mountainous territory and desolate of human habitation for miles at a time, but bountiful in its resources and beauty. Its bones were sturdy and strong, spiking to cloud-draped peaks, then descending steeply to deep, lush valleys in between.

True, the spine of the Backbone itself was healthy and dependable. However, it was the marrow deep within that was unfavorable. Wrought with a dark cancer—poisonous—pure evil, through and through. For the most part, it remained mercifully hidden. But when it decided to venture forth into the world they knew and loved . . . it was a terrifying and troubling thing to behold.

CHAPTER TWO

IT WAS A late afternoon in the autumn of 1880, when the dark nature of the Backbone was fully revealed to them.

"Quit your straggling, Anna Mae!" Nash Ayres called back to his sister. "Let's fetch that water and get back before Papa gets home."

The two children traveled the narrow footpath that stretched from the back porch of their two-room house, through thick bramble and tall pines, to the twisted backwoods branch of Silver Dollar Creek. The time was a half hour or so from dusk and the sun had dropped past the tops of the trees. Already, the shadows of the grove were beginning to deepen and sap the day of color and light.

The little girl, blond and cherub-faced, lugged the heavy wooden bucket they took to draw spring water. The pail was much too heavy for her limited strength, but Nash was in a particularly unruly mood that day and forced her to tote it out of pure spite, or that's what she suspected. Her brother could be like that when their father was absent. Often, she figured that he resented the fact that he was forced to spend the majority of his day—a day that could be spent fishing, hunting, or wandering—watching over her and keeping her out of mischief.

"I'm a-coming!" she snapped, dragging the bucket over stones in the pathway. "We'd get there a mite faster if you'd haul this heavy, old thing yourself!"

"Stop your bitching and come on!"

Anna Mae's eyes narrowed. "I'm gonna tell Papa you cussed at me. He'll likely take a hickory switch to you for it, too!"

"You keep your tongue behind your teeth!" Nash warned her. "You tattle and I'll lay a switch to your legs my ownself."

The five-year-old hushed up. Her brother was four years her elder and a good half foot taller, and he was liable to do what he threatened if she crossed him.

A few minutes later, they arrived at their destination. Silver Dollar Creek wound through the forest ahead of them, bordered by banks heavy with green moss and ferns. The branch was named for the pale, white stones that were scattered along the length and breadth of its channel; stones that gleamed like silver coins in dappled sunlight or the pale glow of a Tennessee moon.

When they neared the water's edge, Nash spotted a gray squirrel perched on a fallen log across the way. Silently, he crouched, located a choice stone on the pathway, and chucked it with all his might. The rock overshot the critter, spooking the squirrel and sending it scurrying up the trunk of a sugar maple.

"Knew you weren't gonna hit it," the girl said with a grin.

Nash only had to glower at her to shut her up. "Give me that pail and we'll fill 'er and get back to the house." He thought of their father, who had spent the day at Traver's lumbermill, dividing pine, hickory, and cedar into boards and railroad ties against the spinning teeth of the big, circular saw. Depending on the size of the order and the hardness of the wood involved, Papa would likely be plumb tuckered out and hungry enough to eat a bear, if there was one skinned, cooked, and laid out on his plate. One of Nash and Anna Mae's many chores was the supper-cooking, and they were already an hour late in fixing it. No bear to speak of . . . just salt pork, white beans, and corn pone. The water they were fetching was for washing and brewing coffee, which Bowden Ayres insisted on having with all his meals.

Anna Mae hefted the bucket and handed it to her brother. The boy took the wooden pail and began to lean forward to dip out a generous amount. Halfway there he stopped, as though his bones had seized up and his muscles had frozen.

"What are you . . . ?"

The girl saw then that he was looking at something. Following his gaze, she turned her eyes to the far side of the creek.

Standing there was a tall figure dressed from head to toe in black. It was a woman clad in a long dress of lace and taffeta and a dark mourning veil. Her hands were slender and as pale as the underbelly of a fish. Her face shone, just as white and bloodless, behind the ebony sheer.

For a long moment, they simply stared at her and she stared back. Then the woman raised her white hands like two, heaven-bound doves and slowly lifted her veil.

"My loves."

Nash gasped and dropped the bucket. It struck the stones of the creek with a splash that neither child heard.

"Mama?"

Anna Mae had been far too young to have remembered her mother, but she had heard tales about her all her life. She studied the woman's gaunt face. It was lovely, but the cheeks were sunken and the pits beneath her brows were cast in shadow. The eyes that peered at them were kind and as blue as a cloudless sky. Or wild blueberries, or the wing feathers of a jaybird.

The woman extended a pale hand. "Come."

Without hesitation, Nash took a step forward.

Anna Mae latched onto his sleeve. "Stop! We don't know her . . ."

Her brother pulled away. He glanced over his shoulder at her. His face frightened her. His eyes were glazed and unfocused, like someone lost in a dream who walked in their sleep. "Yes," he told her flatly. "We do. It's Judith. It's our mother."

Our mother is dead, thought the girl, but refrained from uttering the words out loud. For she herself couldn't truly say for sure.

The tall woman stepped into the creek and held out both hands. "My darlings. I've missed you so."

Nash began to cry. "Oh, Mama!" He reached out and took her right hand.

Anna Mae stared at the nimble fingers of the left, protruding from the sleeve of black lace and cloth. *But what about the tombstone in the cemetery?* she wondered. *The flowers? The prayers upon the grave?* She found herself reaching out, but only because her brother had. Because she trusted his judgment.

Then the hand closed around hers and she knew they had been deceived. The grasp was cold and inescapable. She pulled back but could not break the hold. She felt like a muskrat or weasel caught in a steel trap, frightened and yearning for freedom. Then the coldness radiated through her small bones and the flesh that surrounded them, and her thoughts grew muddled and confused.

As the woman led them across Silver Dollar Creek to the bank just beyond, all thoughts of the bucket, the squirrel, the rickety house a hundred yards up the pathway behind them, began to fade. Papa no longer seemed to matter, as well.

There was only *her* and an encompassing sense of belonging.

As the sun sank lower and the woods grew darker, Anna Mae looked up into the face of the one who possessed them.

Her eyes were no longer blue.

Neither were they kind.

In fact, she had no eyes at all.

CHAPTER THREE

ON ABOUT MIDNIGHT, a pine knot in the fire popped loudly, ringing throughout the cabin like the brittle crack of a rifle shot.

Startled, he sat up from where he lay on his corn husk pallet, ears keen, eyes staring intently into the darkness. His heart beat wildly, thundering in his shallow chest like a horse that had broken its tether and taken to the hills. Deep breaths settled the organ and returned it to its natural rhythm, but his spirit remained troubled.

With a sigh, he flung aside a patchwork quilt his grandmother had sewn nearly a hundred years ago. Standing on bare feet, the lanky man walked to the stone hearth at the far side of the cabin's single room. The chill of the night dissipated the closer he neared the fireplace.

It wasn't warmth that he sought, however, but knowledge.

He sat on a wooden bench before the fire and leaned forward, hands upon his knees, watching the dancing flames. It took a moment before he found what he was looking for. From the ash and cinder of the charred wood drifted three shadows. Each was caught in the heat of the fire for a brief moment, before rising up the sooty channel of the stone chimney.

Two small forms and one larger . . . gaunt and willowy, malevolent.

A chain of emotions coursed through him, jolting and harsh, like ice water in his veins. Surprise, confusion, hopefulness, acceptance. Then fear and regret. Something unseen pressed against the calloused flesh of his palms and entwined his fingers. A cadaver's caress. His hands grew cold, then numb. Quickly, he pulled his eyes from the flames. Instantly, the sensation vanished.

He sat silently for a short while and ruminated on the vision. Then, with a grunt, rose from the bench. He considered what he must do and soon, purpose overshadowed the uneasiness and confusion that had plagued him moments before. He walked to one of the cabin's four windows and stood there, peering into the night. An owl hooted somewhere beyond the frosty panes. He waited for the call to come again, but it never did.

The man yawned and stretched until the bones of his spine crackled. Then he went to a cupboard next to the hearth, took a leather knapsack from a nail on the wall, and began to prepare all that he would, and might possibly, need.

CHAPTER FOUR

BOWDEN AYRES STUMBLED through the forest, exhausted, wrought with fright and despair. A heavy mist stood amid the trunks of the trees, making it difficult to see a yard or so ahead of him. The paleness of dawn had come an hour earlier, but the morning was still young and the wildlife of the Backbone—birds, squirrels, rabbits, and such—still slept soundly in their nests and burrows.

Bowden felt as though he were the only man alive in the world at that moment in time. The big woodsman—tall and broad-shouldered—clutched a long rifle of blued steel and polished curly maple tightly in his huge hands, primed and ready to fire. A revolver—one of those new-fangled Sam Colt pistols that loaded with brass cartridges—was stuck in his belt, the curved butt angled across his belly.

As he trudged through ankle-deep kudzu, he kept his eyes sharp for signs of things he'd just soon not dwell upon in his mind. Blood on leaves and the trunks of trees, tatters of clothing, pale forms, limp and twisted. So far, he had been fortunate enough not to come across such harbingers of tragedy.

"Nash!" he hollered, putting every bit of force and volume he could into it. "Anna Mae!" Bowden paused for a second and listened to his voice echo throughout the forest, hoarse and edged with trepidation. There was no reply.

He was trudging up a slope toward the rim of a rocky ridge, when he heard a fallen branch snap beneath the weight of a footfall. Heart pounding like a smithy's mallet, Bowden whirled, instinctively raising the stock plate of the fifty-caliber to his shoulder and thumbing back the hammer. The firearm was heavy—a good twelve pounds from the muzzle of its octagon barrel to the crescent moon end of its stock—but he held the sights steady and squared, unwavering.

"Who goes there?" he demanded. He heard a crack of fear in his voice, as well as an underlying weakness, and he hated himself for it. But it couldn't be helped.

At first, he saw nothing. Just pale gray mist hanging between the close-grown trees. Then a form slowly emerged and made itself known.

"It's only me, Bowden Ayres."

The man was tall and rawboned in nature—perhaps six-and-a-half feet in height—narrow in the shoulders and lanky in the arms and legs. He wore woolen britches, a dingy cotton shirt, heavy canvas coat, and mule-eared boots that looked to have walked a thousand miles or more. He toted no rifle or scattergun, just a long, hickory staff, pert near as long as he was tall. He wore a shapeless gray hat upon his head and his hair was shaved close to the scalp, the same salt and pepper hue as the unruly beard that graced his cheeks and chin.

A couple of things about the fellow distinguished him from other men in Morgan's Mill or thereabouts. One was his eyes, the irises of which were so pale blue in color to be nearly mistaken for white. The other was a dark port wine birthmark of deep burgundy that completely engulfed the right side of his face.

Bowden didn't have to study on him for more than a second to know precisely who he was.

"Uriah Coldcreek," he muttered, lowering the barrel of his rifle. "What in tarnation are you doing here?"

"Looking for you," the tall man told him. "Have you been out all night?"

Ayres nodded. "That I have. My young'uns . . . my son and daughter . . . they're . . . "

"Missing," finished Uriah with a curt nod. "Or most likely, *taken*."

A sensation like a cold stone settled in the pit of Bowden's stomach and he felt sickness threaten to overcome him. "How do you know of it? I took off searching by myself, without alerting another soul."

"I saw it happen," the man replied. "In my own way."

Bowden didn't question him further, for he knew who Coldcreek was and, more importantly, *what* he was. Everyone around Morgan's Mill and the Tennessee region of the Devil's Backbone, knew that Uriah was a man of talents; talents that few possessed or wished to possess. He was known to be the seventh son of a seventh son, who had never laid eyes upon his daddy since birth. Folks said he was a conjurer of mountain magic and concocter of potions and salves, some with healing properties, some as poisonous as the strike of a timber rattler. He could divine for water, track by sight and smell like a bluetick hound, and cure a baby of the thrush by breathing into its mouth five times. He was a quiet and stoic man who pretty much kept to himself . . . until he was needed.

"Found any sign of them so far?" Uriah asked him.

"Nary a one," Bowden said, dejected. "It's as though the earth just cracked open and swallowed them whole."

A wry grin crossed Uriah's bearded face, one that failed to match the sternness of his eyes. "Let's be hoping that isn't the case."

Both knew such things had happened before on the Backbone. Either from unforeseen sinkholes . . . or things more sinister in nature.

"Let's head back to your place," the lean man suggested. "We'll see if we can get a bearing on what became of them."

Bowden breathed in a lungful of cool mountain air and released it, fighting to settle his nerves. He nodded and turned in the direction from where he'd started. "Follow me."

CHAPTER FIVE

A SHORT WHILE LATER, they stood on the western bank of Silver Dollar Creek.

The wooden pail lay on its side at the edge of the creek. A gray toad sat atop the bucket, pale throat throbbing, but it leaped away as Uriah reached down and lifted the container from the stream.

It was at that moment that Bowden noticed that the hand that held it was the same dark hue as his face. "Not to offend . . . but are you like that all the way down?"

Uriah nodded, undisturbed by the man's observation. "From scalp to sole." He turned the bucket over in his hands, sniffed the damp wood, then tossed it into a bed of ferns at the water's edge. Then he crouched and pointed to the earth. Two pairs of tracks. One smaller than the other. Toes pointed toward the far side of the creek. Deep enough to tell that they stood there for long moment, staring across the stream.

"What do you reckon they saw?"

The tall man shook his head slowly. "Can't rightly say for sure. But whatever it was, it wasn't of a benevolent nature." He took several broad steps across the creek and stood on the other side. Footprints again. The larger walking evenly, while the other dragged the earth, as though attempting to resist. "Maybe it seemed to be such at first, but not after they took the bait."

"Who made off with 'em?" Bowden asked. "Can you tell that by sign?"

"No. Because there's none to be found. Whatever took them left no tracks." Uriah stood and looked off into the woods. "As though it never touched the earth at all."

The confusion on Bowden Ayres broad face slowly bled away and alarm filled his eyes. "What the hell was it that they came across?"

Uriah hesitated, then turned and looked him squarely in the eyes. "Have you ever heard tell of the Coveter?"

The name didn't ease the anxiety Bowden felt. Just the opposite. The dread within him seemed to increase tenfold. "Just stories my ma told me when I was a young'un. Tales to frighten my mischief and ill manners away. She'd say if I wasn't good, it'd come and steal me away, never to be seen again."

"Being good or bad has nothing to do with it," Uriah told him. "But other than that, I'd say your mama's stories were right on the money."

"But, hell, there ain't such—"

The mountain man raised his burgundy-hued hand, halting Bowden in mid-sentence. "If'n you want my help, you'll not be doubting or denying. To get your children back, you'll need to depend on me and the things I dabble in. And that includes believing things you might think foolish or beyond belief. Do you understand that?"

Bowden said no more and simply nodded. He followed Uriah down the opposite pathway, away from the Ayers homestead. The forest grew thicker and wilder the farther they traveled. A hundred yards or so from the creek, they found something lying upon the earth.

Uriah picked it up. It was a rag doll with button eyes and hair of yellow yarn. "Is this your girl's?"

"It is. Anna Mae totes it everywhere. Keeps it in her apron pocket."

Rather than hand the play-pretty to the missing girl's father, Uriah opened the flap of his knapsack and placed it inside. "We may have need of it later."

As they headed southeast, Bowden couldn't help but voice what was preying on his mind. "Where has this thing—this Coveter— taken my children?"

Coldcreek turned and regarded him. His bearded face was as solemn and still as a gravestone, and his eyes were unflinching and devoid of emotion.

"To the Netherwild," he simply answered. "Now, stop jawing and get to walking. We've got a far piece to go before nightfall."

CHAPTER SIX

A S MORNING DREW into mid-day, the two men ascended into the high country of the Devil's Backbone.

The sun was bright, warming their shoulders and the crowns of their hats, and intensifying the brilliant hues of autumn around them. The leaves of the trees seemed painted in bold strokes of crimson, orange, and gold. But something about the foliage seemed inherently wrong. Not so much beautiful as visceral in nature, like the violent cutting open of flesh and the spilling of blood fresh from the vein. Bowden attributed the unsettling observation to his nerves being pulled taut by fear and worry.

But as they continued upward along a narrow deer path, the thoughts continued to plague him. The stones upon the ground grew jagged and difficult to tread upon, and scattered among them were the denuded bones of small animals. Once, while squeezing between the stone walls of two high bluffs, they came upon a woodchuck. It had not been bitten in half but torn asunder. And it had not happened very long ago, either. Uriah had crouched and laid a hand upon the animal's broken back, just behind its head.

"Still warm to the touch," he said. Standing, he tightened his grip on the hickory staff until his knuckles grew pale with strain. He looked toward the narrow gap between the cliffs several dozen feet ahead of them, then peered into the darkness above them.

Bowden looked into the shadows as well, but saw nothing. The fine hairs on the nape of his neck tingled, however, and he was thankful to be away from there when Uriah led the way onward.

Halfway through the afternoon, they paused and sat upon limestone boulders, partaking of venison jerky and tepid water from a canteen the seventh son had brought along.

"So," said Bowden, "this Netherwild. What is it exactly? Can't rightly say I've ever heard it mentioned before."

"That's because few know of it and those who do had just soon not speak of it." Uriah wished to leave it at that, but the big man's gaze, intent and unflinching, made that impossible. "It's a dark and dreadful place beneath the crust of the earth itself."

"A cave?"

"In a way, I reckon, and in a way not. It's said that there is acre upon acre of black forest and treacherous bramble there, as well as critters as pale as a winter's snowfall, blind and colorless, for lack of sunlight. It's also the realm of the Coveter."

"Have you been there before?" Bowden asked.

"No. I wouldn't be going there now, if not for the lives of your children. Man has been blessed with God-given free will. Most of the time he has choices of what to do and not, but sometimes he finds he has no choice at all. And when I awoke in the dead of night and looked upon those flames in the hearth, my mission was made clear to me. There was no casting it from my mind and returning to sleep. I was bound, body and soul, to search you out and begin this journey."

Bowden nodded humbly. "And I'm obliged to you."

"Save your gratitude for when the two are safely at home in their beds," Coldcreek told him gravely. "Until then, the matter hasn't been settled or sealed."

After taking nourishment, they continued up the pathway and found themselves nearing the highest point of the Backbone. Lucifer's Mount rose ominously overhead, dense with spruce, black oak, and longleaf pine. Amid the trees grew blackberry bramble and honeysuckle vine so heavy it was nearly impenetrable.

"Looks like a bastard to break through," said Bowden. "Is there another way over or around?"

"Not that I'm aware of." Uriah withdrew a long knife from a leather sheath on his hip—an Arkansas Toothpick with a Damascus steel blade a foot in length and haft of polished chestnut. He took it firmly in his wine-hued fist and, swinging his lanky arm, hacked and cleaved the vegetation away as they continued onward.

CHAPTER SEVEN

ON ABOUT SUNDOWN, as the western sky deepened into hues of violet and crimson, they stopped and camped for the night.

While Bowden gathered branches and fuel for a fire, Uriah stepped into a copse of birch and maple, and high-stepped through a dense growth of kudzu that blanketed the earth. The tall man paused for an instant, listening, then reached beneath the vegetation, his hand as quick and sure as a rattler's strike. He hauled a good-sized possum into view and brought it back to the campsite, paralyzed with fear and playing dead. A quarter-hour later, the critter was done-in, skinned, and impaled on a spit above the fire.

The two men ate in silence. That day's hike had been lengthy and trying on the muscles and bones, and both were weary and ravenous. After every last shred of cooked flesh was devoured, they settled down for the night. Bowden took a patch of cloth and oil from his possibles bag and cleaned the blued steel of his rifle and pistol. The seventh son filled the bowl of a corncob pipe with store-bought tobacco, lit it, and began to smoke.

For a while, they said nothing. The only sounds they heard were the chirring of crickets in the woods about them and the distant call of a lonesome whip-poor-will.

Uriah looked up at the dark sky beyond the treetops. "What do you see up there, Bow?"

The man studied the night and shrugged. "Stars. The moon, if the weather is favorable."

"God?"

"I reckon. I'm not a church-going man, but I believe."

Uriah seemed to contemplate his companion's answer. His gaze sharpened, as though attempting to stare past the stars into the blackness in between. "Do you suppose there's only one? God, I mean?"

Bowden laughed. "Of course there is. The Bible claims so and it's the Book."

"But men wrote it, didn't they? Every last word."

"My ma used to say it was written by Moses and others but inspired by the Lord."

Uriah nodded. "I've heard the same. But inspired by a truthful god or a lying one?"

"So, you're saying there's more than one?" The turn of conversation perturbed Bowden a little. "Wouldn't have thought that of you, Uriah . . . considering your ways and the good that come from them."

The man's lean face shone in the flicker of firelight, one side light, the other dark. The wine-hued birthmark looked as thick as old blood in the campfire's glow. "I do believe in the Lord, but could be there are others . . . maybe less benevolent, maybe even older than the Creator. Sometimes I have dreams. Dreams of otherworldly beings, not in other worlds, but in our own." He paused for a moment, took a long draw on his pipe and allowed the smoke to curl from his nostrils. "Some could be right here on the Backbone. Or deep down within."

"What do you mean?"

"My grandpappy Coldcreek believed that pieces of places unknown once dropped from the deepest, darkest depths of the heavens and fell to Earth," Uriah mused. "That these pieces held iniquity and evil the likes that mortal man could scarcely perceive. Said they hit ground with enough force to buckle shale and granite, push them upward, and form the peaks of the Backbone. And under the soil and stone, that wickedness made itself a new home . . . festering, flourishing, feeding off the creatures that dwelled above it. At first, it was content with simple life . . . birds, squirrels, deer, bear. Then man braved the wilderness and settled into the mountains and the valleys between, and it found more nourishing and satisfying game."

"Sounds like your grandpa was a mite tetched in the head," Bowden told him flatly. "Don't tell me you believe in what he told you."

"I do, indeed. For there's places and things out yonder that can't rightly be explained," Uriah said. He drew on the pipe, then let the smoke roll from his nostrils. "Not only here, but in other places along the Backbone, as well. An evil held at bay by a coven of whiskey-brewing witches in Kentucky. A pool known as the Bathtub in Virginia, where folks go to seek forbidden knowledge and reap madness instead. Just different branches of the same damnable root revealing itself in various ways."

"Do you think this thing that took my young'uns—this Coveter—is one of them?"

"Can't rightly say that it is or isn't. But one thing is for sure. It ain't one of our kind and its hungers and desires are far from what we consider to be reasonable and sane."

"A thing from Hell, you mean?" countered Bowden.

Uriah smiled, but his eyes held no such humor. "Perhaps. Or somewhere much worse."

The father stared into the flames of the fire, silent, thinking. When he spoke, his voice wavered. "Do you reckon it'll do them harm?"

Uriah's brow furrowed and he frowned. "Well, it didn't take 'em for a picnic and a pony ride."

The remark angered Bowden. "You funning me, or just being a smart ass?"

"Neither. But you'd not like what I really think. So, I suppose I'd best keep it to myself." The lanky man rose from where he sat. He reached into his leather bag and withdrew a Mason jar. Inside was a grainy powder like sand, but yellow, like sulfur. "We'd best catch some shut-eye and commence to walking with the dawn." He unscrewed the cap, then walked the perimeter of the campsite, sprinkling a liberal amount in a broad circle around them.

"What is that?"

"A precaution," Uriah told him. "Not against this thing we search for, but others. Like I said, the Backbone is plentiful with vile and evil critters. Abominations. Obscenities against humankind. No need to take risks if'n you don't have to. Right?"

"I suppose you know more concerning these things than I do," said Bowden Ayres, and felt grateful for that mercy.

Uriah Coldcreek took a twig from the ground and dipped it in the fire, catching a flame on the tip. He touched it to the powder. The two men watched as blue fire caught hold and encircled them. It ebbed and flowed only across the yellow powder, however, and neglected to stray beyond.

The seventh son nodded in satisfaction, knocked the ash from his pipe on a stone, and stuck it in the breast pocket of his shirt. "Now we shall rest easy with no worry of interlopers."

"Where are we headed tomorrow?" Bowden asked him.

"You've heard of Mockingbird Ridge before?"

"Once or twice. What business do we have there?"

"I've heard tell of someone there who may be able to help. An old granny woman with intimate knowledge of the fiend we seek." Uriah took a woolen blanket from his pack and laid it upon the ground. "Sleep well, Bow."

"Yessir. And you, as well."

But even as Bowden settled into his own bedding, he knew that slumber would come slow and fitfully. Despite his heathenness, he said a short prayer for Nash and Anna Mae, then lay there for a long while, pestered by his thoughts and fears, and the uncertainty of the darkness beyond the protection of the blue flame.

CHAPTER EIGHT

THE FOLLOWING DAY, three hours hiking took them to the uppermost reach of Mockingbird Ridge.

They approached the old shack carefully, knowing very well that some who lived in the mountains shot trespassers on sight, without asking who, what, or why. Could be that the old woman was of the same disposition. When they were an acre's length away, Uriah cupped his hands to his mouth and shouted. "Hello, the house!"

For a moment the structure, all gray, weathered boards and rusty sheet tin roofing, stood silent and devoid of motion. Then the door opened and a gaunt form stepped out into the morning sunlight. "Y'all come on up," she called back.

When they reached the wooden stairs leading to the high porch, they found her sitting in a rocking chair, awaiting their arrival. The granny woman was ancient; perhaps in her late nineties, maybe even past a hundred years in age. Up close, she was even thinner in stature than she had seemed from a distance. Her hair was cotton white and thin, showing the flesh of her scalp underneath, and her face was severely wrinkled and puckered, like a peeled apple that had been left in the sun to dry. Her eyes were as green as spring clover, though, and as sharp as the edge of a shaving razor. She wore a blue calico dress that was threadbare and faded with age and her skinny shoulders and arms were cloaked with a knitted shawl of white cotton. The woman wore no shoes. Her feet—darkly veined and yellow nailed—rested upon the boards of the porch, the calloused skin underneath appearing as thick and tough as a miner's boot soles.

The seventh son mounted the steps and stopped halfway. "Would you be Granny?"

"That I be," she said. Her toothless mouth worked on a plug of tobacco like a cow chewing its cud. "And you'd be Uriah Coldcreek."

Uriah was surprised. "You've heard of me before?"

"Everyone along the Backbone has, I suppose. Me, in particular, since our life's work is of mutual practice and benefit." She appraised him and nodded to herself. "Besides, no one else—perhaps not of this world—resembles a mid-month's moon . . . half-dark and half-light. Just saying that as a fact, not as a slight or slander."

"No offense taken at all, ma'am. This here's Bowden Ayres. We hail from the way of Morgan's Mill."

Granny nodded. "I'm aware of the place. Never been there before." She studied the two men sagely. "You came wanting to ask or know something of me. What lays heavy on your minds?"

"My children—Nash and Anna Mae—they've been taken," Bowden said, speaking up.

The elderly woman seemed to sense the fear in his eyes and urgency in his voice. She sent a spritz of tobacco juice past her thin lips and over the porch railing. "By the Coveter."

"That seems to be the case," Uriah replied. "I've heard that you know of the thing and its ways."

"I know of many a sorry and sadistic thing in these mountains, Mr. Coldcreek," she told him. "The Coveter is but one."

"We aim to find my young'uns and fetch them back to where they belong," Bowden said resolutely.

Granny let out a phlegmy chuckle. "You do, do you? Well, that's bound to be a daunting task indeed." She was quiet for a long moment, then, bracing her spidery hands against the armrests of the rocker, hauled herself slowly to her feet.

"It's nearly noon. Come inside and we'll talk over vittles."

The two men followed her into the ramshackle house. There was only one room in the place. It sported an eating table and chairs, a hearth constructed of gray stones mortared with red clay, and a narrow bed in a far corner. All manner of medicinal plants and animal hides dangled from the rafters overhead. The structure smelled of woodsmoke, tobacco, coffee beans, and the earthy aroma of roots dug from the ground and hung to dry; ginseng, burdock, dandelion, and valerian. There were other odors as well; some holding the muskiness of animal pelts, while some were faintly reptilian in nature.

"Take a load off and sit," she instructed. Taking her time, she went to the hearth, lifted the lid off a boiling pot, and ladled speckled beans and ham into three wooden bowls. She set the servings before them, along with a skillet of cornbread. "Whiskey?"

The men nodded. She brought over a clay jug, pulled the cork, and set it in the middle of the table. Each of them took a long pull from the liquor before commencing to eat or talk.

"So," said the granny woman, "you intend to confront the Coveter, do you?"

"Yes'm," said Uriah. "It's Bowden's duty as a father, and my mission, according to my heritage and upbringing."

"You'll be heading into the Netherwild then. You got any idea where it is?"

Uriah reached inside his coat and withdrew a small book. Its binding was ancient and deteriorating, and the pages in between were as yellow as parchment. He opened it, thumbed through its contents, and laid a crudely drawn map before her. "I reckon it hasn't changed location since this was drawn a hundred years or so ago. Not that it couldn't happen. Such shiftings have been known to take place from time to time on the Backbone."

Granny leaned forward and studied the etching. "It's still where it's always been but getting there has changed course." She pointed to a spot in the trail, three or four miles past Mockingbird Ridge. "There was a rock slide several winters ago, so the way is impassable here." She traced a broad loop to the south with the tip of a jagged fingernail. "This route will serve you much better. But halfway there will be a heavy grove of ancient oaks . . . perhaps the tallest trees on the Backbone. As you pass through, keep your eyes centered straight ahead and take rein on your nerves. Don't look into the treetops, no matter what. Just concentrate on getting past the lightning-struck boulder on the far side and you'll be safe and back on the path again."

"Much obliged," said Uriah, returning the book to his coat. "Have you been there before, Granny? The Netherwild?"

The elderly woman's eyes were distant as she nodded. "Once. And for the same reason as you."

"To save a young'un?" asked Bowden.

"Yes. One of my own. A daughter by the name of Ophelia."

Uriah hesitated to ask, but he did so anyhow. "Were you successful in getting her back?"

Granny reached over and hefted the jug. She took not one

lingering swallow, but two. She returned the flask to the tabletop with a thud, wearily, as though surrendering a heavy burden. "No. I was ignorant of the Coveter's ways and left empty-handed." She grinned bitterly. "Its love to barter is nearly as strong as its jealousy and greed."

"Barter?" asked Bowden. "What could we possibly trade for the lives of two children?"

Granny stared through the dirty panes of a front window; her gaze dreamy. "Oh, I possess that which it truly desires. I didn't know it back then, but I do now."

"And what would that be?" asked Uriah.

"We'll finish our meal first. Then I'll prepare it for you."

They sat and ate and drank for a while longer, silent and contemplative. Then, when the bowls and skillet were clean, and the clay jug sat half empty, the old woman rose from her chair and walked across the wooden floor. She stopped a foot or so from the base of the fireplace and slowly dropped to her knees.

Yellowed fingernails hooked around the cracks of a loose board and pried it free.

The two men watched as she lifted something from the cobwebbed darkness beneath the floorboards. It looked to be a glass jar shrouded with a soft black cloth and secured around the neck with a length of coarse twine.

Granny brought it to the table and set it there. Together, they looked at it. There was something about the shrouded container that was both mysterious and ominous.

"Do you have one of the children's possessions?" she asked grimly.

Uriah opened his knapsack and withdrew the rag doll with yarn hair. He handed it to her.

"Yes," she said softly. "This will do nicely."

They watched as she walked to a wooden chest at the foot of the bed and rummaged through its contents. She returned with a pair of sewing scissors, a needle, and a spool of thread. Without hesitation, she snipped the seams along the doll's back and pulled open the cloth. The soft ticking from a pillow showed in the hollow within.

Bowden Ayres eyed the urn covered in ebony cloth. "What's inside the jar?"

"Do you really desire to know?" she asked.

The big man squared his shoulders. "I do!"

"A piece of Heaven, a bit of Hell," the old woman told him. "High from the sky, deep from the earth, and in between." She reached into the deep pocket of her apron and withdrew two black patches; the sort that hid the eye when it was injured or blind. "There's one thing for damn sure. It's not to be looked upon. If one chances a glimpse, the wonder of it, the sheer vastness of what it holds, will drive a soul plumb raving mad."

She cradled the open-backed doll between her knees, then slipped a patch over each aged eye, tying them tightly in place with the strings attached to them. "You two best step back yonder beside the door. Keep your eyes tightly shut and don't open them till I say so. You get the urge to look and there will be no saving you."

The two men did as they were told. In the darkness behind their eyelids, they waited and listened. Soon, there came the rustle of cloth drawn away from the body of the jar, the grating noise of the lid being unscrewed, then a rasping fumble as narrow fingers dipped inside and withdrew something from the hollow within.

Abruptly, they were overcome with a strange and frightening sensation. A spinning bout of dizziness seized them, as though the backwoods cabin had risen from its stone foundation and flipped, floor over rafters, and was continuing to flip at an alarming pace. After that, there was an impression of being propelled at great speed toward a destination beyond the Devil's Backbone, beyond Tennessee, beyond the very Earth itself. Uriah and Bow felt their muscles seize and lock, their bones ache, and the flesh that encased their innards stretch to the point of splitting. There was a smell in the stale air of the cabin . . . or a combination of smells. The molten hot odor of a blacksmith's furnace. The nostril-scorching reek of a spot where lightning had touched ground or split tree wood an instant before. The ancient stench of moldering graves, of the yellowed pages of forgotten books, of demon's breath, foul and fresh with the ichor of the defeated and the damned.

Uriah heard a low, keening cry rise from beside him. It was Bowden, pushed past the normalcy of all he had ever known; terrified, but tempted to look upon all that vexed him at that moment. The seventh son reached over blindly, found the woodsman's contorted face, and clamped his wine-stained hand tightly over his eyes. "Don't!" he warned harshly, hoping— praying—that the man would take heed.

Before Bowden could surrender, the sensations, the smells, the chaos and confusion that gripped them, suddenly vanished. Disoriented, they rocked on their heels and steadied themselves. Although they had never left their spot on the cabin floor, they felt as though they had traveled a million miles or more in the span of a heartbeat.

"You can look now," Granny told them.

Uriah opened his eyes. The old woman still had her patches in place, but she deftly sewed the back of the rag doll up with needle and thread, as though she had done the deed once or twice before. Bowden Ayres didn't fair quite as well. With a groan, he turned and staggered out the open door to the railing of the front porch. The man leaned outward toward the yard and violently voided the contents of his stomach.

"What happened here, Granny?" asked Uriah, both distraught and amazed.

"You teetered on the precipice of dark knowledge," she told him. "Of things and places humankind has no inkling of . . . nor should ever yearn to comprehend." She finished her sewing, tightened and knotted the thread, then handed the doll to the lanky mountain man. "There's your ware to barter with. When you make the trade, I advise you to grab the wee ones and get the hell out of there. And, for God's sake, don't look back."

Uriah nodded and stashed the button-eyed doll in the folds of his leather bag. "And what do we owe you?"

Granny shucked the black patches away, her green eyes sparkling. "I'll collect my fee at a later date," she assured him. "When I'm in need of something that only you can provide."

"Fair enough." Uriah walked to the wooden table, took Bowden's rifle and possible bag, and joined the big man on the porch. He laid a hand upon Ayres' broad shoulder and felt a tremble beneath his palm. "You alright?"

"Let's get on with it," grumbled Bowden, as though wishing to depart the mountain cabin and the moment's worth of mortification that had inflicted him. Then he took his bag and firearm in hand and headed down the steep steps and across the rocky ground toward the tall grove of pine and spruce just beyond.

As Uriah Coldcreek followed, he heard Granny's voice call out to him from behind. "You'd best watch over him," she said sternly. "You and I have gifts and understandings that he could never hope to grasp. You may do everything right and true from this point onward, but one misstep by an unschooled fool could kill you both . . . as well as those you seek to deliver."

Uriah simply nodded and lifted a hand in thanks. Then he slung the leather pack across his back and headed into the wilderness, feeling as though the doll that he toted was a thing partly of salvation and partly of dormant catastrophe.

CHAPTER NINE

AFTER LEAVING THE SHACK on Mockingbird Ridge, they continued onward for several more hours, aware that daylight would bleed into twilight before long.

All signs of civilization fell behind and wilderness crowded about them. The path they trod was the only trace that others had traveled there before. The forest on either side of them grew heavy, darkening with shadow as the branches of the trees overlapped, leaving only random dapples of sunlight upon the trail. The faces of the stone cliffs and outcroppings they came across grew steeper and more serrated in nature. The terrain, as a whole, became a wild and untamed thing unto itself, indifferent and unaccommodating to the needs and comforts of mortal man.

They soon reached the spot in the trail that the granny woman had indicated on the map. A wall of earth and stone blocked their progress, and it was clear to see that there would be no scaling the barricade the avalanche had wrought.

"This way," said Uriah, remembering the route Granny had suggested. Together, he and Bowden Ayres departed the trail and moved southeastward, picking their way through the heavy woods that stood upon the precarious slope of the Backbone.

Dusk was nearly upon them when they approached the dense forest of oaks the old woman had warned them of. From a distance, the trees seemed to stretch to the heavens, as though attempting to cast shade upon the throne of God Himself. As they grew nearer, they became aware of the silence that surrounded them. Nary a bird sang in the branches or squirrel scuttled across the coarse bark of the ancient trunks. It was as though all life had been driven away . . . or utterly consumed by the darkness of the heavy foliage high overhead.

"Remember what she said," Uriah told Bowden quietly.

"Straight ahead with your eyes on the far side of the grove." He saw the man's fists tighten about the maple wood stock of the mountain rifle. "And, unless you're absolutely in fear for your life, refrain from firing your longarm. Do you hear me?"

Bowden Ayres was not a man accustomed to taking orders or relinquishing control, but he did so then. "I do," he replied. To show that he was favorable to Uriah's instructions, he slung the rifle over his shoulder until he had need of it. But unseen by the seventh son, his right hand remained only inches away from the .45-caliber pistol that jutted from his waistband.

They entered the forest and silently made their way through the grove of towering trees. Again, the oppressive absence of sound struck them. It was not a comforting or peaceful quietude, but one that weighed heavily on their thoughts and sent a creeping sense of dark dread through both body and mind.

Halfway through the thicket, the silence was broken. A low wail echoed from the uppermost branches of the trees, slowly growing in volume and intensity until the shrillness of it cut through the ears of the two travelers like shards of broken glass. Bowden ducked his head and covered his ears with the palms of his hands.

"What the hell was—?"

Uriah turned from where he had walked point and locked eyes with the man. The warning on his double-hued face was irrefutable. *Shut your mouth and keep walking!* Then he returned to the trek, his gaze centered straight ahead, focused between the dark columns of the oaks at the far edge of the woods, a quarter mile away.

The strange cry came again, but this time at a distance from an entirely different direction. It was followed by another, and yet another. They could sense movement in the leafy foliage overhead, and every now and then, fallen leaves and dislodged branches fell around them. Although they dared not look, they could imagine dark forms—neither bird nor mammal—leaping from limb to limb and tree to tree. There seemed to be some playful mischief to the unseen creatures, but one bearing the potential for malice and misfortune. *Don't look into the treetops, no matter what,* the old woman had forewarned them. Both men held her words as gospel as they slowly and purposefully made their way through the grove of age-old trees and the thick bramble that grew plentifully in between.

It seemed to take an eternity, but they eventually made it to the opposite end of the stand of oaks. The two men were thankful when they reached the limestone boulder, a good fifteen feet in height, which had been split in half by heavenly fury. The last few yards of the detour had been nerve-rattling, to say the least, for both Uriah and Bowden were certain that whatever the things in the trees were, they had clung to the branches scarcely a dozen feet from their heads, ready to pounce if fearful eyes were cast upon them.

The travelers stepped through the forked portal of the cleaved stone and found themselves scarcely twenty paces from the original pathway. Quickly, they left the thicket and continued down the trail. The sun had begun to set and the sky overhead was the colors of bruised, torn flesh . . . dark violet and garish blood red. Normally, the brilliant hues of dusk were looked upon with wonder. But, that evening, they saw only ugliness and uneasy foreboding. It was more an omen of somber things to come, rather than the promise of a tranquil night and a bright and cheerful day ahead.

CHAPTER TEN

STORM CLOUDS BEGAN to roll in from the east before nightfall, casting deep shadows upon the trail and the forest around it, slowing their progress. The wind picked up in speed, growing strong and blustery. Every now and then, they heard the deep rolling of distant thunder. They decided to camp for the night and chanced upon a cliffside hollow beneath a sandstone ledge before the heavens decided to surrender and open up.

They huddled in the shallow cave, neglecting to light a fire. Their worrisome hike through the oak forest had revealed that things dwelled in that stretch of the Backbone that was not fond of human company. A campfire may have warded them away, but also would have revealed their whereabouts. So, they sat with their backs to the stone wall, talking quietly and sharing a cold supper of venison jerky and dry sourdough.

"When should we get there?" Bowden asked after a while.

"The Netherwild?" Uriah took his pipe from his pocket, then thinking better of it, returned it to its rightful place. The smell of tobacco smoke could draw undesirable critters to them just as easily as a fire might. "Probably before noon tomorrow. According to the map in my book, we have five or six miles more to go."

"That book of yours . . . is it a diary?"

"No, more like a bible for folks such as me," the seventh son told him. "Mountain history . . . mostly concerning the Backbone . . . as well as spells and incantations, and recipes for potions and poultices."

"Dark magic, then?"

Uriah could feel the man's eyes upon him in the gloom, regarding him with disapproval. "A little, I reckon. Enough to fight the ones who hold such evil things dear to their heart . . . or what passes as one." He raised his wine-hued hand and tapped his forehead. "There's a sight more knowledge up here than there is in those pages . . . knowledge that shouldn't be written down or read by those who have no business being privy to it. When I'm gone, it's gone. I don't relish my demise, but there's some comfort in the certainty of that."

Ayres sat and chewed on the jerked meat. "There was something you said earlier . . . about the Coveter appearing favorable to my young'uns before they were abducted. What did you mean by that?"

Thunder rumbled overhead as the rain continued to fall steadily beyond the lip of the outcropping. "It's said that it can take the form of those its victim loves most. A father or mother . . . husband or wife, mostly those who are no longer among us. It takes that love, grief, and longing and hooks its prey, like a barb in a catfish. It draws the ones it covets to it, and once it takes hold of them, they no longer have any say-so on whether they stay or go."

Bowden nodded. "Then it would be their mother—or the likeness of her—that tricked them into going." He peered into the wet darkness beyond the cave and shuddered. "Judith."

"Could very well be," agreed Uriah.

"She was a good woman and I miss her sorely. If she'd appeared to me, I'd likely done the very same thing they did." He was silent for a long moment. "Were you ever married, Uriah?"

The man beside him was so quiet and still that he could have been sitting there stone, cold dead . . . or not there at all. "I was."

"What was her name?"

When he spoke it there was no feeling to the word. No pain, no regret.

"Lorraine."

"Did she pass?" Bowden asked him. "Of sickness or misfortune?"

"No, I can't rightly say what happened to her. I woke up one morning and she was gone. Her side of the bed was empty and cold to the touch." The lanky man sighed. It was like the essence of his soul was attempting escape betwixt his teeth . . . eager to take wings and flee in search of her. "There was one thing I can't deny. I loved her dearly and she loved me. So, simply abandoning me was not a thing to be considered. Everything she owned . . . clothes, keepsakes, all that held value to her . . . remained in that cabin where it had been the evening before."

"How long ago was this?"

"Fifteen years. Maybe more."

"Did you search for her?"

Silence again. Long and lonesome. "I still do."

After the jerky and bread had been devoured, they prepared to bed down for the night. The storm increased in its fury, sending whipcracks of lightning across the southern sky. During one such burst of brilliance, they spotted the dark silhouette of leafless trees across the trail from where they had sought shelter. Perched among the branches of those trees were dark forms. Hunched, motionless, patient.

Slowly, Uriah Coldcreek reached into his satchel and withdrew the jar of fine, yellow powder. He crept to the edge of the opening in the cliff, poured a line of the substance from one end to the other, and lit it. Blue flame leaped into life as it had around the backwoods clearing the night before.

Startled, the things let out a low mournful cry, then lifted into the wind and rain of the storm and were gone.

"They'll not bother us again tonight," said Uriah.

"Were they the ones we encountered a while back?" Bowden asked. "The ones atop the oaks?"

"Could be. Or others with the same direful nature. No need to worry. Just settle in and get some rest."

Bowden grunted doubtfully. "Seems that every time you say that, I can't catch a wink."

"Well, I'd sure do my best, if'n I were you," Uriah told him flatly. "'Cause tomorrow we leave this world and enter another. And we're gonna need every last bit of strength and fortitude we can muster."

CHAPTER ELEVEN

ARLY THE FOLLOWING MORNING, they prepared to complete the first leg of their journey along the Devil's Backbone.

As they climbed from the shallow cave and stepped onto the trail, they were grateful to find the skies clear and no sign of the storm that had raged so violently the night before. The leafless trees where the dark forms had roosted were utterly barren. There was no sign that the creatures—whatever they were—had been there at all. The only evidence that what they had witnessed had not been their imaginations was a scattering of fresh droppings around the base of the trees. They were as dark as coal and stank of sulfur and decay.

The two men continued down the trail, silently, lost in their own troubled thoughts. As far as they knew, they were the only ones who had ever trekked to the Netherwild to retrieve that which had been stolen from them. Except for Granny, that was, and she had come away defeated, robbed of the child named Ophelia. They thought of the rag doll in the knapsack and the dark magic that had been sewn inside and hoped that what they had to offer would be enough to deliver young Nash and Anna Mae from the possession of the one known as the Coveter.

At about mid-morning, they reached a lofty pinnacle of gray limestone and scrubby vegetation known as the Cathedral. Thankfully, the pathway skirted the base of the mountain, and they weren't forced to scale its steep slope to the crest and over. The way they traveled was treacherous and darkly ominous, however. Tall stands of thorny bramble rose on each side, devoid of greenery, the jagged barbs as black as pitch. Every so often, they would see small creatures entangled amid the thicket, impaled on the wicked barbs; squirrels, rabbits, sometimes a raccoon or possum. They squirmed in agony and fear, unable to break free, while ebony crows sat amid the tangled underbrush, picking away at soft flesh and sinew, then devouring it with quick snaps of their ravenous beaks.

It was nearly noon when the trail began to descend into the pit of an overcast valley. The path twisted and turned, sometimes disappearing entirely, before revealing itself again several yards ahead. A strange, gray mist rose up from what lay down below and Uriah and Bowden soon found themselves engulfed in a heavy fog. Tiny droplets of moisture within the vapor settled upon their hats and clothing, soddening the material and chilling them to the bone. The condensation had an oily quality to it and held a rancid odor that stank like shed snakeskin.

Downward they journeyed, their eyes and ears keen, attempting to detect any menace that might befall them within the thick haze. But there was nothing to be seen or heard. There was only the swirling mist about them and complete and utter silence.

Then, abruptly, out of nowhere, they found the large opening of a cave yawning before them. The rocky portal was fringed with dark ivy and a strange black vine with violet flowers the size of a man's hand. It was a plant they had never set eyes on before that moment. As they stood there, they watched as a pale-winged moth fluttered from out of the fog and lit on the petals of a bloom. Savagely, the flower folded up and ensnarled the insect, pulling it deeply within the hollow of its funnel. Within the folds of the plant, the moth struggled, but soon grew still and surrendered to its fate.

"Well, I reckon this is it," said Bowden somberly. "Where we go in."

"I'd say so," replied Uriah. He turned and studied the man's broad face, shadowed with two days' worth of stubble. He searched for fear and reluctance but found only resolve in his expression. "Stay behind me and do as I say. And don't make use of that rifle or pistol unless it's absolutely necessary to do so."

"I understand."

Uriah studied the open maw of the cave. It was as dark as any he had come across and knew there would be no light within to guide their way. He found a dead tree branch lying at the side of the pathway. Taking an old shirt from his knapsack, he tore it into strips and wound them tightly around one end of the stick. Then he took the jar and coated the cloth liberally with the yellow powder. He lit the bundle and it blazed with brilliant blue light. Holding it ahead of him, he entered the mouth of the passageway with Bowden Ayres following closely behind him.

CHAPTER TWELVE

FOR WHAT SEEMED to be hours, they walked through the narrow tunnel that descended into the depths of the Netherwild.

The shaft twisted in sharp, steep curves like the blade of a corkscrew. The walls were wet with the oily substance that had hung in the moisture of the mist and, every now and then, the blue flame of Uriah's torch would gleam off thick veins of quartz and amethyst. There were also small holes in the stone—the burrows of unknown creatures. Tiny eyes sparkled within the hollows, watching them as they passed. They could not tell whether the inhabitants were fearful or malevolent. They clung inside the shadows of the holes and did not reveal themselves.

At one point, Bowden placed a hand firmly on the seventh son's shoulder. "How far down to you figure we are?" he whispered.

"Half a mile perhaps, maybe deeper," Uriah told him. "But we'll soon be there."

"How do you know?"

"The tunnel isn't nearly as steep as it was. It's beginning to level out."

Bowden was surprised to realize that the marked man was right. The floor of the passageway no longer sloped sharply. He found no comfort in the fact. Rather, he gripped his rifle tightly and braced himself for what was to come.

They walked a while longer and, suddenly, the stone walls of the tunnel were no longer around them.

The two men found themselves standing on the edge of a dark forest that stretched as far as their limited vision could see. The trees were charcoal black and completely devoid of leaves, like ones that had been struck by lightning and charred to the root. Dark-leaved thicket grew heavily in between. Amid its concealment, they could hear things scurrying through the vines and bramble. The blue light revealed tiny creatures as pale as a mourning dove. Some were the size of chipmunks, others as big as a bobcat. All watched them warily from the underbrush, as though resentful of them being there.

The stone floor of the tunnel continued through the center of the wilderness. As they walked onward, Uriah and Bowden became aware that what they trod upon had become a narrow roadway cobbled with black stone. The thoroughfare looked ancient and, at the wayside was evidence of those who had labored to pave their way. They couldn't tell whether the small bones were those of animals or children.

Uriah removed his hat and stuck it in the pack over his shoulder. He lifted his head and peered upward. A vast expanse of eternal night yawned over them. Unlike the world they knew, this one had no nocturnal illumination to speak of. Nary a star or sliver of moon could be seen. Curiously, Uriah brought the end of his staff down sharply upon the stones of the walkway. The report echoed for several long seconds, reverberating off the unseen walls and towering ceiling of the underground cavern around them.

"Let's go," Uriah said in a low voice. "But take care and keep your wits about you."

Together, they made their way into the heart of the Netherwild.

CHAPTER THIRTEEN

A S ONE HOUR PASSED, and then another, Bowden Ayres felt his nerves begin to fray and his confidence slip a notch or two.

Uriah Coldcreek blazed the trail ahead of him, standing tall and resolute, holding the blue-flamed torch aloft like some medieval wizard in a book of fairy tales. Every now and then, he would pause and survey their surroundings, or consult the small leather-bound book by torchlight. Then they would continue onward. The entire time, they felt as though they were being watched, from both the thicket and the gnarled branches of the dark trees, or even followed at a steady, creeping pace, like prey stalked by an unknown predator.

Once, a great shambling creature crossed their pathway at a distance. It was albino in nature, its coarse fur as white as snow and its angular face, ears, and hairless tail as pink as a newborn babe. After a moment, they realized that it was a hellish hybrid of possum and bear. The brute stopped, caught scent of them, and turned its massive head. Its blind eyes flashed with hostility. It bared long, yellow fangs as long as a shoemaker's awl and its fleshy paws clenched and unclenched, scoring the stones of the path with hooked claws.

Bowden raised his rifle and thumbed back the curved hammer, ready to take aim. However, Uriah took hold of the barrel and gently pushed the muzzle earthward. "Uncock your piece, Bow," he told him. "You could put lead square betwixt its eyes, and it'd still be upon you before you could load another."

The woodsman knew that his companion was right. He slowly eased the hammer down and canted the gun to his shoulder. The pale beast paused for a moment longer, then disappeared into the black forest on the opposite side of the trail.

They continued onward. It had been cool in the tunnel leading to the Netherwild, but the subterranean land they now traveled was much colder. Frosty plumes of mist drifted from their nostrils with each breath they took as they gathered their coats closely about them. A few minutes later, Uriah spotted something lying in the pathway. He crouched and showed it to Bowden. It was a boy's hat.

"That belongs to Nash," the man told him.

"Then we must be getting nearer."

Uriah handed him the hat. Bowden's hand trembled as he took it. "Do you think he's—?"

"We'll find out soon enough, I'm a-thinking." As they turned to continue onward, a shriek echoed overhead. They lifted their eyes, and above the tops of the skeletal trees flew a flock of white-fleshed creatures. The blue glow of Uriah's torch failed to reveal them fully, but they seemed to possess the wings of bats and the slender bodies of weasels.

"What manner of Hell is this that we've come to?" Bowden asked.

The seventh son said nothing at first. He watched as the pale critters soared to the uppermost reaches of the underground cavern and vanished from sight. "Let's find the ones we came for and be away from this damnable place."

Together, they continued their journey into the stygian wilderness that lay before them.

CHAPTER FOURTEEN

AS IT TURNED OUT, they were closer than they realized.

The forest of dark trees and thorny bramble began to dwindle and grow sparse as the footpath slowly descended into a broad basin. Soon, there were only tall pinnacles of gray stone and rocky mounds of earth around them.

Abruptly, Uriah Coldcreek halted, raising his hand. "Listen!"

Up ahead, they could hear the distant voices of children. Their tone was flat and emotionless, not excited or cheerful or anxious as normal youngsters might sound. The two men strained their ears to identify what was being uttered. It was a song; an old Appalachian folk ditty that most of the youth along the Backbone had been taught since birth.

> *"My old hen's a good old hen,*
> *She lays eggs for railroad men.*
> *Sometimes eight, sometimes ten,*
> *She lays eggs for railroad men.*

The song was one of the Ayres children's favorites. Bowden recalled that the tune tickled him and made him laugh every time Nash and Anna Mae sang it. But the way it was sung at that moment, low, monotonous, and devoid of humor or joy, made the big man's blood run cold.

> *Cluck old hen, cluck and squall*
> *Ain't laid an egg since late last fall.*
> *Cluck old hen, cluck and sing*
> *Ain't laid an egg since late last spring.*

As they moved forward toward the noise, they prepared themselves for what they would find. But no matter how wildly they might imagine, they could never have readied themselves for the grim tableau that the blue-flamed torch cast its flickering glow upon.

Sitting in a circle upon the dark earth were a dozen children. They were boys and girls of various sizes and ages. The gathering sat cross-legged in the dust, their heads bowed, playing with makeshift toys constructed of stone, wood, and bone. As the two men grew nearer, they saw that the youngsters' flesh was sickly and pale, and their hair was bleached as white as baking flour, as though every speck of color had been bled from them. Their eyes were glazed and their pupils gray. As they sang the Old Hen song, their heads bobbed slowly, and their fingers fumbled aimlessly with the play-pretties that their capturer had constructed for them.

"Good Lord!" rasped Bowden beneath his breath.

Solemnly, Uriah studied the youthful congregation. "Do you see yours among them?"

Bowden shifted his gaze from one child to another. His attention settled on two sitting side by side. A boy of nine and a girl of five. The sight of them terrified him. They seemed thin and emaciated, not at all the healthy young'uns he had last seen just three days ago. "That pair yonder."

When the man made a move toward them, Uriah reached out and grabbed his arm firmly. "In this place and time, they no longer belong to you," he told Bowden. "Not until we bargain with the fiend who stole them."

At that moment, the coldness around them seemed to intensify. Bowden was shocked to see fine crystals of ice begin to creep down the blued barrel of his hunting rifle. The firearm grew so frigid in his bare hands that he could hardly keep hold of it. The same was true for Uriah's hickory staff. The length of wood became covered with a thin coating of white frost.

Low hollow laughter rang not only in their ears, but their minds, as well. It was a dark and disturbing sound, edged with scorn and supremacy. Like a giant that casts its eyes contemptuously upon the lowly ant.

Then, come. Come forth and show me the pittance that you have to offer.

They looked beyond the circle and saw a dark form sitting in a great stone chair. Ancient symbols were carved deeply into the supports, back, and armrests of the throne, for in that awful creature's realm that was precisely what it was.

Runes, thought Uriah, *or something like them.*

The one who sat there was tall and slender, and as black as the inside of a casket six feet under. At that moment, it looked to be neither male nor female. Its face was long and gaunt, the cheeks and eyeholes dark and deeply sunken. It possessed no mouth that they could detect. But it spoke nonetheless, in a way that reverberated clearly through their minds.

Don't dawdle! it commanded. Suddenly, the voice had altered, taking on an unmistakably female resonance. *I know that you would not have come here without something valuable to barter with . . . now would you, dear Uriah?*

The seventh son watched breathlessly as the lean form contorted, the inky blackness taking on texture and detail. A moment later, its narrow head sprouted pale hair and its face became that of a woman. It was a face that Uriah knew intimately.

"Lorraine."

Do you mourn my absence, husband? the thing said slyly. *Do you weep tears of loss and regret in the dark and lonesome hours of the night? Do you yearn for death to ease your pain?*

Anger flared in Uriah Coldcreek's colorless eyes. He wished to step forward and curse the creature, to demand that it refrain from defiling the memory of his beloved. But he stood his ground and held his tongue. The lives of the two Ayres children depended on his discretion and restraint.

Slowly, he slipped the leather sack from his shoulders and opened the flap. "This is what we have brought in trade." He pulled the rag doll from the belly of the bag and held it out to the Coveter.

The fiend rose from its seat and stood. The thing that resembled Lorraine Coldcreek stretched almost sensuously, its height doubling as its arms and legs lengthened to frightful proportions. The hazel green eyes that Uriah had once fallen in love with sank into shadowy pits and from the darkness gleamed twin lights like winter moonlight on graveyard marble. There was a glee in those otherworldly orbs, and yes, a hunger, as well. A hunger for things other than what it had been forced to accept and partake of for countless centuries, exiled from those of its own kind.

Uriah held the doll out and the Coveter's long arms extended outward, impossibly lean and long. The delicate fingers of Lorraine crackled and grew as long as the knife sheathed at the mountain man's hip. Soon, the nightmarish hands had wrapped around the object of cloth and yarn, drawing its prize away from his grasp.

It looked down at the rag doll but did not see it at all. Rather, it was the thing *inside*—the unknown object placed there by the granny woman—that it craved.

Take them and go, it simply said in dismissal.

Without hesitation, Uriah turned and, grabbing Bowden Ayres, shoved the man toward the circle of children. "Fetch your young'uns and let's get the hell out of here."

Bowden did as he was told. He shouldered his rifle and walked swiftly to the boy and girl who sat hunched at the far side of the pen. Lifting their heads from the makeshift toys, the two regarded the man with puzzlement for a moment, then slowly recognized him for who he was. Bowden lifted Anna Mae into his arms with no resistance at all, but Nash was of a different mind.

"No!" the boy protested, attempting to wrestle his arm from his father's hold. "It's Mama! I can't bear to lose her again, Pa. I just *can't!*"

"Nash . . . son! It ain't her!" Bowden said helplessly.

"It *is* her! She came to us at the creek. Said that she missed us . . . loved us!"

Aware that time was wasting, Uriah stepped forward, grabbed the boy by his shoulders, and pointed him directly at the dark thing that clutched the rag doll. "Look a-there, boy! Is that your ma? Is that the one who gave birth to you and loved you with all her heart and soul?"

The boy looked upon the true form of the one who had brought him and his sister there and he wailed in terror. The delicate, feminine face of a moment before was gone and, in its place, was the sunken black countenance of the Coveter. He watched as its face split open and a gaping hole appeared, even deeper and darker than the blackness around it. Inside the maw writhed ungodly things . . . slick, ebony, eternally hungry for what awaited it inside the hollow of Uriah's offering.

Nash wept bitterly and buried his face in his father's side. Sadly, Bowden regarded the others in the circle. "What about them?"

"We came for yours alone," Uriah told him, although he

seemed pained to say so. "The trade has been settled. We'd best go before we regret tarrying!"

They looked in the direction of the Coveter. The long, spindly fingers of the entity tenderly caressed the doll. Then they tore at the fabric, rending cloth and breaking the seal of the seams. From the awful orifice of its altered face a long, black tongue of jagged scales and pulsating barbs extended, eager to accept the sustenance that was hidden within.

"Turn your eyes away!" yelled Uriah. "For God's sake, turn away and *run*!"

CHAPTER FIFTEEN

THEY WERE MIDWAY across the field of stones, heading toward the edge of the forest, when the Coveter claimed the essence of what the granny woman of Mockingbird Ridge had concealed within the doll.

The release of some vast and untethered force seemed to rise and spread throughout the height and breadth of the Netherwild. Uriah felt himself lifted off his feet and hurled toward the dark tangle of the undergrowth. In his mind's eye, he could imagine the Coveter taking the contents of what had been in Granny's jar—perhaps something ancient and unfathomable from another world—examining it, breaking it apart, and lifting it to the gaping cavity of its ghastly face to devour.

At the same instant, he experienced what had taken place at Granny's mountain shack, but five times more potent. Uriah felt the ligaments and muscles of his body stretch taut, so much so that they threatened to tear from their moorings. His blood boiled, his organs fought to retain their function, and his brain ached and throbbed, as though on the verge of vomiting up every childhood fear and adult nightmare he had suffered during the span of his forty-five years. As his body hit the ground forcefully enough to dig a shallow ditch behind him, the lids of his eyes cracked open, and he looked toward the towering ceiling of the underground cavern.

Blackness no longer loomed there. Yawning before him was a spiraling expanse of strange colors of an unknown spectrum and violent, clashing rays of energy stronger than any lightning bolt or cyclone he had ever known. Dread and mortification assaulted his mind and he screamed. Clinching his eyes tightly shut, he felt as though he were being turned inside-out, again and again.

When he came to his senses, the maelstrom had passed. He felt strong hands on his shoulders, shaking him roughly.

"Uriah!" said Bowden Ayres, crouching above him. The big man's eyes were full of fright and concern. "Snap out of it, man!"

Exhausted, the seventh son sat up from where he was lying on the stony earth. Every bone in his body ached and every muscle felt sore and bruised. "What happened?"

"You looked upon the . . . hell, I can't rightly say what it was! But the way you were bucking and howling, we were certain it had driven you plumb mad!"

Nash Ayres walked over and handed Uriah his hickory staff. With some effort, the man used it to pull himself to his feet and steady his balance. He turned and looked in the direction where the circle of stolen children and their hideous captor had resided. There was only a dense pall of choking black mist in their place. A stench like brimstone and charred flesh stung his nostrils. It was how the hottest and most foul pits of Hell must reek.

Uriah looked around and, a few yards away, saw the blue-flamed torch lying discarded upon the bare earth. He ran over and snatched it up, gripping it firmly in his left hand.

"Come on," he told Bowden and the two children. "Let's get through the woods and to the tunnel." From far away, he heard the ear-piercing shriek of flying aberrations. Their cries were full of agony and anger. He realized that they were on the hunt, blindly in search of someone to inflict their dreadful rage upon.

Quickly, the four made their way along the cobbled path, into the black heart of the underground wilderness. In the thicket on either side of the trail, the pale creatures who had once cowered and kept their distance, now stalked them. Boldly, they snapped and snarled, reaching through the thorny bramble savagely to rip clothing or pierce tender flesh with jagged claws.

"How much farther do we have to go?" Bowden asked. His voice was edged in desperation. He clearly feared for the lives of his children, if not his own.

"It's difficult to say," Uriah replied truthfully. He stared ahead, but the blue glow of the torch was limited in its reach. "I reckon we'll know when we get there."

They were deep into the thicket of the Netherwild, when the winged weasels abruptly descended from above the treetops and attacked. More out of instinct than skill, Uriah swung his staff and knocked one of the flying monstrosities from the air. It crashed to the ground and flailed frantically. Its pale flesh had been stripped away by the blistering force of the Coveter's prize, leaving only raw, bloody muscle and sinew and protruding bone. Its eyes were deranged. It was clear to see that the creature and the others of the flock had been completely stripped of their cunning and sanity.

He brought the end of the cane down sharply upon the weasel's head, shattering its skull. Others attempted to swoop down but lead from Bowden's revolver either brought them down or chased them away. Young Anna Mae squealed as one landed upon her back and attacked her. Uriah drew the Arkansas Toothpick and cleaved its malformed head from its slender neck, then flung its winged body away from the child.

Time seemed to alter and stretch into an eternity as they stumbled down the stone pathway. Every time they thought they were nearing the end of the nocturnal forest, it only thickened and grew more dense. Several times, they feared that they had taken a wrong turn somewhere and were hopelessly lost.

Suddenly, Nash pointed excitedly. "Ahead!" called the boy. "The tunnel!"

Uriah was relieved to see that Nash Ayres was right. The shadowy portal of the passageway entrance was scarcely a hundred feet away. "Quickly!" the seventh son instructed. "Get inside!"

Bowden, Nash, and Anna Mae were soon entering the mouth of the tunnel. Uriah joined them, then groped through the contents of the knapsack and found the jar of yellow powder. He looked toward the dark forest of the Netherwild and spied a massive beast three times the size of the possum-bear they had encountered earlier. It lowered its enormous, horned head and galloped swiftly toward them.

Uriah didn't hesitate. He cast the jar to the earth at the entrance of the tunnel, shattering it and scattering its contents upon the ground. With no chance to dig a sulfur match from his coat, he flung the torch upon the golden residue. A wall of brilliant blue flame leaped upward, barring the way and halting the behemoth's assault.

"Let's get going!" he said, taking the lead. The father and his young'uns followed silently, aware that their survival depended on the man marked with the crimson stain.

For what seemed to be hours, they traveled in utter darkness with no means with which to light their way. The climb was steep and treacherous. The two children, weakened by their capture and imprisonment, struggled to keep pace. Before long, Bowden carried Nash, while Uriah toted Anna Mae.

Eventually, they saw the walls and floor of the passageway illuminated before them and they stumbled from the mouth of the cave into the crimson and violet glow of early sunset. Wearily, they dropped to the ground and sat there, breathing in the crisp mountain air.

They looked back at the entranceway to the Netherwild.

The dark flowers that had grown lush and plentiful around the rim of the opening were dead. Something had caused them to wilt and waste away.

CHAPTER SIXTEEN

A DAY-AND-A-HALF'S HIKING found them back on the wooded crest of Mockingbird Ridge.

From a distance, they could see the old house. Uriah cupped his hands around his mouth to warn the old woman of their approach, but he stopped before he could do so. There was something odd about the place. The day was chilly and there was no sign of woodsmoke drifting from the gray stone chimney. As they grew nearer, they were confounded to discover that the pitch of the roof sagged sharply in the center and there was nary a pane of glass left in the structure's windows.

"I swear this is the same place, Uriah," Bowden said. "Or am I mistaken?"

"It is for sure," the tall man replied. "Let's go take a look."

When they mounted the rickety steps to the high porch, they knew that the old shack was deserted. The weathered door hung loosely from rusted hinges and the wood and timbers of the structure smelled of age and neglect. They stepped inside and found that no one was there. It appeared to be abandoned and looked like it had been for several decades. All that furnished the old house was a single wooden bench in front of the empty stone hearth and a set of rusty bedsprings discarded in the far corner of the single room. The rafters were laced with dust and old cobwebs, and bare of the hides and dried plants that had hung there several days ago. In fact, there was not a single nail in the wooden studs that might have sustained such.

"I don't understand," said Bowden. "What's become of the old woman?"

Uriah had no words of explanation. He walked over to the hearth, knelt, and attempted to lift the loose board where the cloaked jar had been concealed. The length of wood held firm. It was nailed securely in place.

"We broke bread and drank with her. She sat right there in that spot and prepared the doll for the trade." Bowden shook his head, bumfuzzled by the state of their discovery. "Now it's almost as though . . . "

"She never existed?" Uriah stood near an open window and stared into the lonesome stretch of woods that surrounded the cabin. "It's a perplexing thing to dwell upon, ain't it?"

Bowden saw the liquor jug sitting on the flagstones of the hearth. The urn was cracked and yellowed. He watched as a fiddleback spider crept from the open spout and skittered swiftly to the floor.

"Does it really matter?" the seventh son asked him. "You have your children back, safe and sound. I'd say we accomplished what we set out to do."

"I reckon so," agreed the big man. "And I'm much obliged to you for it."

Uriah nodded and said nothing. He simply walked out onto the porch and waited for the others to follow.

As Bowden, Nash, and Anna Mae descended the steps, eager to make their way home, Uriah Coldcreek stood a moment longer at the porch railing. He took his pipe from his coat pocket, lit it, and smoked as he surveyed the lonesome stretch of forest. At the edge of the tree line stood a couple of objects nearly hidden from sight. The markers of two graves wreathed by fallen autumn leaves.

One was large, the other much smaller in size. From where Uriah stood, he couldn't read the names chiseled into the mottled stones, but there was really no purpose in trying.

Although it was beyond his understanding, there was no doubt in his mind exactly who they belonged to.

SPIRIT COVEN

LAUREL HIGHTOWER

CHAPTER ONE

LES WILLIAMS WOKE early to the smell of woodsmoke, his nostrils flaring at its acrid warmth. He sat up, heart pounding, sleep far behind him. Smoke meant fire, and as there was no one else in his cabin to build one in the stone fireplace, it also meant danger.

He threw the frayed quilt from his legs and swung out of bed, went to his darkened window. It looked out on the back part of his property where it hugged the swollen banks of the river. The ceaseless rain threatened to spill the water from its confines, but for the first time since it started to fall weeks ago, Williams was glad of it. Every flammable surface should be too soaked to catch, yet the smoke was pervasive, the smell seeping in from the sealed edges of the glass.

He parted the heavy curtains that shut out the light on the rare mornings he slept in, eyes widening when he saw two bright flames. They looked small from his vantage point. He squinted, trying to gauge where the fire was—his woodshed? The truck? There were no close neighbors, so whatever burned in the night, it was his responsibility.

All at once his gaze focused closer in and he saw the lines of a silhouette he was intimately familiar with. It had been twenty years since he'd last seen his wife's face, but he couldn't mistake the gentle slope of her nose, the determined set of her chin, and the bow of her upper lip. His heart thudding, he put a hand to the glass but pulled it back swiftly when intense heat stung his calloused fingers.

"Maggie?" he croaked, but the figure in the window was still. He studied the face, hungry for the sight of her in a way that had faded steadily in the intervening decades. Then the two flames winked out and almost immediately returned, and he knew what he was looking at.

He stumbled back from the window, raising his arm to cover his face, though from what he couldn't say. When he looked again his wife's face was gone, and with it the smell of smoke, and her bottomless, fire-bright eyes.

CHAPTER TWO

PEPPER CLARK LEANED beside the softly lit window of the dress shop and watched the bitter, halting procession of three coffins down the mud-clogged main thoroughfare of Arnett, Kentucky. She glanced over her shoulder and squinted through the glass, but Tabitha didn't so much as look her way, her sister's attention focused on the handsome shop assistant. Pepper sighed and turned back to the street, narrowing her eyes under the dripping brim of her hat, clamping the fragrant cigarillo she'd rolled herself between her front teeth. Three was a hell of a lot of deaths for a town their size, especially after the lawyer drowned last week. At least whoever it was hadn't been found on the sisters' land. She cringed at the heartless thought, but it didn't make it any less true. The coven was never more vulnerable than when people needed a scapegoat.

Fewer folks than she would have expected followed behind the two-horse funeral wagon, the wheels of which got stuck in the mire every ten or so steps and had to be coaxed loose by young Arthur. The undertaker's apprentice seemed to be on his own; Myron Patrick, who owned Arnett's only funeral home, was nowhere in sight. Pepper's gaze narrowed farther and she scanned the far side of the street, her vision hampered by torrents of rain.

"Ms. Clark," came a voice beside her. She didn't need to look to know who it was—she'd yet to venture into Arnett without running into the man. He wasn't interested in her, though, so she didn't mind.

"Mr. Williams." She cast a glance over her shoulder and saw the shopkeeper's stocky build, rain dripping from his nose and beard, his clothes as soaked as her own.

"What happened there?" she asked after a minute or so of silence, nodding in the direction of the coffins, which had yet to make it past her.

The man sighed and shook his head. "Whole family died together. Almost all of 'em, anyway."

Pepper sucked in a breath. "Hell."

Williams nodded, his mouth twisted. "Drowned, all three of 'em. Father and two kids—the Helstroms."

Tears stung Pepper's eyes and she cast her angry gaze at her boots. She barely knew the family, why the hell did she always have to cry at the slightest provocation? Without thinking she sought the ragged straggle of mourners for who might be left. "Wife didn't die?"

He shook his head. "Wasn't with 'em. People say she's lucky, but . . . " He trailed off on another heavy sigh.

Pepper found who she was looking for—a bedraggled woman in a faded print dress that had seen better days, her shoes not meant for this kind of weather. She stared straight ahead, her hand limp in the Pastor's hold. At least she had someone to walk beside her, thought Pepper. What a hellish damn thing, to be the only one left.

She cleared her throat, blinking back tears. "Boating accident?"

Williams pursed his lips, still not looking at her. "Not that I've heard. No one saw what happened, anyway, and Helstrom wasn't known to be a boating man."

No, thought Pepper, he was known for being a drunk, but she'd be the last person to cast stones at him for that. She felt the familiar desire creep over her, her jaws aching as her salivary glands reacted to a phantom burn. She closed her eyes and bit down harder on the cigarillo. She'd been saving it for the drive back, but she needed something to take the edge off. Trading one addiction for another, but at least smoking didn't have much chance of hurting someone else.

Williams coughed and Pepper looked up. The man's jaw was thrust out, his eyes staring past her. Now she was looking, it was impossible to miss the man's darkened eyes, the whites riddled with red veins. His strong cheekbones seemed sharper above a face thinned since the last time she'd seen him.

"You okay?" she asked. "You don't look so good."

He lifted a shoulder and gave a brief smile. "Just tired. Haven't been sleeping so well the last week or so."

Pepper nodded. "This rain'll do that to ya. Want a remedy? We got plenty that'll help with that."

He shook his head. "Thanking you kindly, but no. It'll settle out."

"Suit yourself."

Williams cleared his throat, cast a glance at the mountain looming behind them. "Don't suppose y'all have . . . heard anything, up there? Seen anything unusual?"

Her shoulders tightened and she lifted her chin, met his gaze. "Not me. Not anyone else, far as I know."

"Hm. What about Jude?"

Pepper pursed her lips against a smile. It might take him a while, but he always came around to Jude in the end. "She hasn't said anything about it. Not sure why she would—we only knew about Mr. Gross because the sheriff came to talk to us."

Williams grunted. "Because he was on your land?"

Pepper sighed. "Thereabouts. Before you ask, we don't know what happened there, either. Could just be the rain—everything's washed out and the creek's higher than ever."

He looked away. "I heard he was . . . that there were some injuries, to his face and one of his legs. Foot was damn near detached."

She frowned. "We didn't hear that part—didn't see the body, either."

He nodded. "Sorry if that sounded like an accusation—it wasn't."

She could tell he wasn't done and waited him out in silence.

"So, you haven't seen anyone who's—who shouldn't be there?"

Pepper stared. "What the hell does that mean?"

"Or smelled, I dunno, smoke? Fire, maybe?"

She cocked her head. "You mean beyond the ones in the house?"

He nodded.

"I don't understand. What are you wanting to know, specifically?"

He sighed. "Nothing, I guess. Never mind. I think I'm just too tired."

Pepper shrugged and returned her attention to the walking wake. She was startled to find the widow's gaze upon her. The woman's eyes were dark, lifeless, her face slack as it had been when Pepper saw her a minute ago, but in a flash it changed. Her lips came together, pinched tight, and her eyes blazed to life with fury.

She had reason to be angry, thought Pepper, and offered the woman a nod of sympathy. She knew better than most how much difference it could make, knowing you weren't alone.

The widow didn't return her nod, instead twisting her mouth into a sneer and lifting her finger to point at Pepper.

"Wretched woman!" screeched the widow, grinding the procession to a halt. "You dare to show your face after what's happened? After what you *did*?"

A cold feeling washed over Pepper and she straightened, her focus pulling in, vision clearing. This could turn bad, fast, and she was already running three steps ahead of herself. She'd need to get Tabby, drag her from the store if need be. Get to the car, crank up the engine, and hope it didn't get stuck. All of that without drawing more attention to herself or seeming like she was running away. Mobs formed quick and easy in times of stress and could be as dangerous as any wild animal. Survival depended on the same principles—don't make eye contact, and don't run.

"Easy, Pep," breathed Williams beside her, sliding into the fatherly role he sometimes assumed. As though Jude being the "mother" figure meant he was the dad, but this time she didn't mind. She could use whatever help he offered.

The widow's screeches grew in volume, spittle flying from lips that split as she got more agitated, blood trickling to her chin. "You awful, awful women. Bringing *sin* to this town, day after day, not even having the decency to hide yourselves. Flaunting it, *proud* of it." She drew in a breath and spat.

It didn't come close to hitting Pepper, but she flinched all the same. She had no illusions of how some of the populous viewed her and the rest of the sisters—she and Tabby needed out, now.

She lifted her hands, palms out, and dredged up a smile she hoped was the right mix of sorrowful and placating. "Got no plans to upset you, ma'am. I surely meant no harm, but if it'll ease your heart, I'll go."

Pastor Rockfort blinked rain from his eyes and made an effort to calm the woman. "Beth, my child, this anger does you no good. Ms. Clark is not to blame for what happened to your family, but I understand your pain. Come, let us keep walking, get your children in out of the rain."

The woman rounded on him. "Out of the *rain?* They drowned—do you think a little water can bother a corpse?" She burst into tears and Pepper backed up a step, put her knuckles to the glass storefront behind her and knocked. Prayed Tabby would hear her and make an unobtrusive exit.

Williams stepped in front of Pepper, blocking her from sight. "Go on, then, this is a good time to get," he said softly.

With the widow's attention on the hapless Pastor, they might have made it, if the damned shop door hadn't had that jangling little bell. Tabby stepped out, the door swung wide, pushing to Pepper's side with a swagger. "Just what the hell's goin' on out here?" she asked in a voice that penetrated both the rain and Beth Helstrom's bitter sobs.

Pepper gritted her teeth and took Tabby's wrist. "Nothing we need to concern ourselves with. Let's go and leave these folks in peace."

The widow straightened and whipped around, hungry for a new focus for her ire. As targets went, Tabby Newsome was a good one. Young, lovely, flirtatious, and outspoken, Pepper had seen it many times before. Worse than that, she never walked away from a fight, never turned the other cheek to an injustice.

"So you brought the whole *coven* down for the show, did you?" seethed Beth. "One of you not enough?"

Tabitha pulled her wrist from Pepper's grip, her hand drifting to her hip where Pepper knew she carried a gun. "You got something to say to my sister?"

Williams tried to move himself in front of her as well, block both women from view as though that would stop what was about to happen. Tabby pushed him out of the way.

"Your *sister?*" Beth shrieked, shoving away from the Pastor with enough force that he toppled over and landed in the mud. Beth was a strong woman, a farmer's wife—she'd had to fight for everything she'd ever had, which made her both admirable and dangerous.

"You talk like you're a bunch of nuns up there on that godforsaken mountain, that you're doing the Lord's work, as if you were a convent. We all know different." Her voice thickened with tears and her shoulders shook. "We know what you are."

Pepper grabbed Tabby again, hissing in her ear. "The woman's lost her whole family. She's not thinking straight, so let's not make it worse. We have nothing to prove here."

Tabby shook her off and stepped to the edge of the wooden walkway, impervious to the sodden coffins sinking toward the mud as the ugly scene played out. "What is it exactly you're accusing us of? Gonna speak it or just hint around it?"

Pepper bit her lip and briefly considered leaving Tabby to her fate. She didn't much care for turning tail and running, either, but she knew the risks too well. Pride wasn't worth dying over, especially not dying hard.

Beth Helstrom straightened, her soaked dress clinging to her skinny shoulders and chest. She raised her finger once more and pointed at each of the sisters in turn. "Whore," she spat at Tabitha, her lip curling. "*Witch,*" she hissed at Pepper and drew the sign of the cross on her chest.

More bystanders had crept from behind closed doors to see what the commotion was, and at the woman's words, the town held their collective breaths. There it was, out in the open, the word that floated around the sisters without ever quite touching them. This wasn't Salem in the 1600's, but that didn't much matter, once mob mentality took over.

"You take that *back,*" Tabitha ground out, advancing from the walkway onto the mud-covered street. Her hand was by her hip but not on the butt of the gun, and Pepper hoped it stayed that way. She followed close behind, ready to pull Tabby from the scene by force, but at their approach, one of the horses drawing the funeral wagon gave a shrill neigh and made an attempt to rear.

Hampered by its traces, it didn't get far, but the motion was enough to jar the wagon and one of the plain pine boxes slid out of place and toppled to the ground. It wobbled for a precarious moment that stretched Pepper's nerves, its head resting on one of the wagon wheels, the foot sinking fast into the mud. *Please be nailed down tight.*

Maybe God couldn't hear above the downpour. The coffin's weight shifted again and the head hit the ground with a squelch, the impact enough to pry off the sodden wooden top. Pepper held her breath, her grip tight on Tabby, the whole world frozen around them. A dripping head of dirty blonde hair flopped into the rain, the little girl's mouth a slack and gaping void. One eye was open, milky and sightless, the other swollen shut above a nose missing half its flesh. Mud packed the ear Pepper could see, and trailed from the corners of the girl's lipless mouth. Even in the open air and at this distance, Pepper could smell the putrid rot of the child's flesh, and her gorge rose as fast as her panic.

Tabby stepped back, a hand over her mouth and nose, her gun forgotten.

"Jesus, Mary and Joseph," she breathed.

No one spoke for long seconds, then a keening wail Pepper felt in her marrow filled the air. The widow collapsed where she stood and crawled her way through the deepening muck to reach her daughter's side. Her hands pressed against the dead girl's cheeks with shaking tenderness, then she laid her head back and sobbed to the heavens.

Pepper felt a light touch on her shoulder and nearly jumped out of her skin. Williams stood behind her, his grim gaze on her instead of the scene in the street.

"Now. Go, while you can."

Pepper nodded absently. He was right, but she couldn't silence the part of herself that saw a grieving soul in need and wanted to sink into the mire beside her, hold her shoulders and add her screams to the widow's.

She shook it off and took a firm hold of her sister's arm. It wouldn't help—nothing Pepper could do would help, beyond removing herself from the woman's sight. Tabby didn't fight her this time, and they made their unobtrusive way to the side street where they'd left their car.

When Pepper slid into the driver's seat, Williams put an arm on her window, his expression unreadable. "Be safe now, girls."

"We will," promised Pepper, antsy to get out of town before anything else went wrong. Still he kept hold of the vehicle and she looked at him, impatient.

"Tell Jude . . . " He sighed, broke off. Stepped back from the car and patted the hood.

"I will," she said again. For all the good it would do.

CHAPTER THREE

ON HER KNEES before the darkened water, Jude waited, her consciousness floating somewhere beneath the surface. Without eyes to see or ears to hear, she swayed in the stillness, cold surrounded by the cold. Her mind only dimly perceived the ache in her joints, the press of sharp rocks into her tender flesh. She was too old for this, yet too young to hand over the reins, even if she could. These troubles, too, were distant, unable to penetrate her communion.

Lacking senses, her astral self still felt the approach in the stirring of the water. There was no bottom to the cavern's pool—none she'd ever seen, nor likely would in her lifetime. Only once she'd passed over, added her power to the mountain and become one with the Devil's Backbone, would she see what waited below. But whether she saw it or not, something shared the water with her.

She felt the wrongness of it first—a dizzying sense of being off-kilter, her mind tilting this way and that, the world spinning by too fast for her to grasp. She fought a wave of nausea, struggled to right herself, bring things back into focus, but whichever way she moved set her twisting again. Though she had no limbs in her current state, or stomach for that matter, she still felt the slide of silt against her feet. She jerked back, felt the weight of water pressing her down. She'd never come this far before, and panic filled her at the idea she might not make it back.

The silt slid against her, shifting away, sucked like sand with the tide, and the ground beneath her was gone again in the space of seconds. The dark water was peaceful no longer—things were as bad as she'd feared. Something took hold of her, closed around her throat, and she struggled to breathe.

The smell of smoke brought her fully awake, nose wrinkling

against the sting, lungs burning as she coughed. Her throat burned and the screaming ache of her knees came back to her. She groaned and tumbled on her ass, sucking in a breath that set her to coughing again.

It took her several minutes to right herself, and once she had, the smell of smoke was gone. She frowned over it, another worry setting up residence in her subconscious—fire wasn't to be taken lightly, particularly all the way up here, but of greater concern for Jude was what she'd seen and felt in the pool.

She dragged herself close to the edge again, stared at her reflection. Waited to see if someone else's would take its place, but it never did. Not yet.

"I'm sorry," she whispered to the empty cave. "I'm trying, I swear it. I feel what's happening, but not *where*."

There was no answer, and Jude straightened her back. "I'll try harder. I'm not letting this happen—not again." Her voice softened; she cupped her hand against the freezing surface of the water as though it were a lover's cheek. "You won't hurt again." The smell of smoke was gone as though it had never been. It should have been a relief, but nothing about any of this was a coincidence. Before she could consider what it meant, the sound of tires on gravel set her heart racing. A strange feeling of shame washed over her—her cheeks burned and her mouth was dry, though that was likely a result of imbibing the special sort. She searched for the bottle, a third or so of the amber liquid left, and assured herself the cork was safely in. The supply was dwindling and she couldn't afford to lose a single drop.

She pushed to her feet slowly, her knees moving stiffly, one foot numb from the way she'd been sitting. It wouldn't do to let Pepper see her like this—the other woman worried enough as it was. She didn't understand yet what promises she'd made when she came to live here. What promises they all made, and the heavy cost of breaking them.

Putting her shoulders back and working the kinks out of her legs, she neither saw nor sensed what watched her from the darkness with fury in its heart.

CHAPTER FOUR

JUDE COULD TELL before Pepper stopped the engine things had gone wrong. It was written in Tabby's wild eyes and Pepper's slumped shoulders.

Jude sighed. "Well?" she asked.

Tabby was already climbing from her seat, spilling out like the whirlwind she was. "Wasn't our fault," she said, glaring at Jude.

"Didn't say it was." She turned to Pepper. "How bad?"

The younger woman sighed, her arms draped over the steering wheel. "Three more dead. A family. Father and two kids."

Jude sucked in a breath and closed her eyes. Kids—that was bad. She cast a glance over her shoulder at the dark opening to the cavern, then back at Pepper. She'd be feeling it worse than any of them, given her own losses. Jude leaned in the window and put a hand on her sister's shoulder, gave it a squeeze until Pepper looked at her. There were shadows under her pale eyes, hurt there that went beyond mere reminders.

"What?" Jude asked softly.

Pepper looked away. "There was a procession. The widow—she caught sight of us."

"Of you," said Tabby, her tone sullen.

Jude ignored the younger girl. "What'd she do?"

"Blamed us. There was a bit of a scene—she said it was our fault her family died, because we were there bringing sin to town."

"Called me a whore, and Pepper a witch. Widow or not, I'd have given her a black eye for talkin' like that." Tabby had a quick temper, the fire in her belly not yet doused by years of swallowing hurt. The girl couldn't help it, but it made her dangerous at times. Women like them had to know when to walk soft. "'Sides which, that *sin* she's so happy to condemn keeps half that town from killing the other half, on top of the other cures. We don't bring

66

anything but what they want. Most folks in this country would kill for us to bring 'em liquor."

Jude didn't answer, though she knew the girl spoke truth. Five years since prohibition passed in a wave of outrage and hypocrisy, politicians voting to keep alcohol out of the hands of the populous, smug in the knowledge they'd always be able to exercise the rights they stripped from the rest of the country. She couldn't think about it too hard or she'd give in to her temper, so instead she kept her eyes on Pepper. "Who was it?"

"The Helstroms," she said in a flat tone.

"Which just goes to show—her husband bought more bottles off us than he could afford," fumed Tabby.

"I'd imagine that's part of the problem," said Jude dryly.

Pepper frowned, tapping one finger on the wheel.

"What is it?" Jude asked.

The woman looked at her, lips pursed. "Helstrom barely had two pennies to rub together."

Tabby put her hands on her hips. "Yeah, I just said that, didn't I?"

Jude kept her eyes on Pepper. "What are you thinking?"

Pepper bit her lip. "I hadn't thought much about it before, but the last month or two, he's bought a hell of a lot more off us, every time we're in town."

Jude raised an eyebrow. "You didn't give him anything on credit, did you?"

Pepper shook her head. "I don't do that—not for folks just drinking. Only for people that *need* it."

"So he had the money?"

She nodded slowly. "Georgie's increased her order, too. Said she's had trouble keeping the bottles on the shelves. I'd chalked that up to all this rain, folks not having enough to do, but Arnett isn't a money town, not since the mine closed." She glanced over her shoulder, down in the direction of the defunct mine's entrance. She'd never asked Jude why they'd bought the land, after what had happened there, and she didn't ask now. "And Georgie doesn't give credit, either." She turned back and raised her eyes to Jude's, her own dark with trouble. "Hadn't put it together before, but . . ."

"But now you're wondering where he got the money," said Jude.

Pepper nodded again. "Man wasn't working, far as I could tell."

Jude felt a trickle of unease in her belly, something catching at the back of her mind. Another worry, but one she couldn't quite articulate. Not yet.

"Who cares where he got the money? Still doesn't make it our fault," Tabby said, her temper exacerbated by the conversation.

"Doesn't it, though?" asked Pepper, still in that flat, empty tone.

Jude searched her face. "How'd it happen? Was he drunk?"

She shrugged. "Don't know. Seems likely, though—he usually was."

"But they're not sure what killed 'em?"

"Drowned, like the lawyer."

Jude sucked in a breath between her teeth, tightening her grip on the car to keep from swaying as her vision wobbled. "Exactly like the lawyer?" she asked.

"That was all Williams knew." Pepper looked down at her lap, her mouth turned down. "But one of the coffins busted open, and I saw the girl. She was . . ." She put a hand to her mouth.

"Injured?" pressed Jude, feeling the weight of the open mine.

"Hard to say. If she hit her head, that'd account for it, and also explain how she drowned. For the rest . . . fish mighta got at her."

Tabitha paled and looked down, crossed her arms over her belly.

"But?" Jude pressed.

Pepper shrugged again. "There was . . . mud. A lot of it, I think. They'd cleaned her up some, but it was kinda leaking." She swallowed hard.

"What's happening?" Tabby asked in a soft voice. She sounded so young.

Jude saw both sets of eyes upon her, expecting her to have the answers. That was only natural—she was the elder sister. She'd never counted on stepping into that role so unprepared, and cursed Angie silently for the hundredth time. Her predecessor had no damn business dying so young, her sacrifice wasted through no fault of her own. "I don't know," she answered finally.

Tabby stepped closer, leaned in. "Is it the magic?" she whispered, though no one was around to hear. "Is it going bad?"

Jude ignored the heightened pain, the way the Backbone pulled at her. She straightened, let go of the car and moved aside. "Come on outta there, Pep. No use moping, Jessica could use your help—she's been at the stills all morning, must be close to out of what she needs."

Pepper obeyed, moving slow, but at least she was moving. Exercise would do her good.

Tabby wasn't done yet. "That ain't an answer."

Jude rounded on her, temper frayed by worry. "It's not the magic. Magic doesn't 'go bad'—it's people that do that. What's here on this mountain, it simply is. It's all in how you use it, whether you show the proper respect for balance." She tightened her arms around herself, looked past the girl to the woods beyond.

Tabby looked down and scuffed her boot in the mud. "How would I know? You won't let me near it. How am I supposed to learn if you keep it all to yourself?"

Jude looked at her again, exhaustion hitting her all at once. The strain of struggling to understand, to restore the balance every second of every day, was catching up to her, and there wasn't a thing she could do about it. "That right there is how I know you're not ready. I don't *keep it to myself*, because it's not a thing anyone can own. But in the same way I wouldn't hand a three-year-old a rifle, I'm not bringing you in until you show you're capable of the respect you need." When the girl turned away, Jude took her arm. "That's for your safety more than anyone else's."

"Sure," said Tabby, pulling away and kicking her way up the trail.

Pepper hesitated, her gaze on Jude. "You okay?" she asked, her voice too soft for Tabby to hear. "You don't look so good. You get any rest at all last night?"

Jude gave her a tight smile. She couldn't remember the last time she'd slept through the night, or spent even half of it in her bed. "I'm fine."

Pepper's gaze narrowed and she stepped closer, raised a hand and skimmed a finger over Jude's throat. "What happened here?" she asked.

Jude coughed and put a hand to her neck, her scalp prickling at the feel of raised flesh beneath her fingers. It was sore, too, abraded in a few spots, and went all the way around. She hunched her shoulders like it had a chance in hell of hiding what was almost certainly a rope burn that hadn't been there before she entered the cavern. "It's nothing," she said, turning away and heading up to the house. "Probably just heat rash." She wished she could believe it. She'd experienced pain like that before, after her sessions, but the injuries had never manifested on the outside. What that meant, she didn't know, but she wouldn't drag Pepper into it.

When she didn't hear the other woman move, she pursed her lips. "Best catch up to her, Pep. Heaven knows what Tabby might do in a temper." She didn't turn, but a second later heard the squelch of Pepper's boots on the muddy ground. Jude sighed and allowed her shoulders to drop, casting one last glance back at the pool's cavern.

"Time," she said softly, her hand back at her aching throat. "I need a little more time."

A crack of thunder sounded overhead, echoing through the mountain, and the sky increased its weeping, rain pelting down with the force of hail. Jude hurried to the house, hoping like hell that wasn't her answer.

CHAPTER FIVE

"I DON'T GET IT. She has all that power at her fingertips, and she don't do nothin' with it."

Pepper sighed but didn't look back, her shoulders aching from the weight of the cask she carried. "And what exactly is it you'd do?"

"More than just make liquor and drink myself silly, I'll tell you that."

Pepper closed her eyes briefly against the onslaught of want, the phantom taste of whiskey on her tongue. "It's not just liquor, and you know that. Jude heals people."

Tabby huffed. "*She* doesn't do it at all. When was the last time Jude even worked the still, or helped with the cures?"

"She don't need to. She taught the rest of us, and she's the reason any of us can do what we do, so all of it is down to her. I'd like to see a doctor with half the success rate she's got. And drinking—that's part of it. But name one time you've seen her drunk."

Tabby ran ahead to open the barn door, peering into the darkness. "That's small stuff, and she don't get any credit for it."

Pepper smiled. "You mean *you* don't get any credit for it. Jude doesn't care about that shit."

Tabby helped her set the cask down gently, one of the last for this year's batch. "Is it so bad to want people to like me? Us? Wouldn't it be nice to walk into town and not feel all those eyes on you? Not wonder if this'll be the time the tide turns?"

Pepper grunted as she scooted the cask into place, checking the barrel head. Tried not to breathe deep of the fumes in the barn, but it was a heady place to be. "And you think you can, what? Cast a spell to make people like you?"

"No, that's not it. But if we did something bigger, something people had to take notice of, and they knew it was us? They'd change their minds, don't you think?"

Pepper shrugged and headed for the door, stopping to pick up a woven basket with a wrapped handle and two large glass bottles. When she held them up, Tabby grimaced and grabbed the bottles. Pepper put the basket over her arm and headed out into the rain once more. "Maybe. Or maybe they'd take it as the proof they've been looking for and come burn us out. History doesn't take kindly to women who step out of line. You think all those folks down there would feel comfortable, seeing a display of power like that? You saw how mad that widow was today, just because we were there. If we did something bigger, shoved it in their faces, what we do up here? You think that'll make people trust us?"

Tabby jogged to catch up. "They'd have to. If it was something good, that helped them, they'd respect us, wouldn't they?"

"Maybe. Maybe not," said Pepper, slowing her pace, searching for the opening that led to the biggest of the wheat fields. "But remember, Jude's been doing this a lot longer than you. She knows the stories of the Backbone, the oral history of it. There were some bad times. Real bad."

"I know, but that was back then. Things are different now."

"Not different enough. Ah, here we go." The path to take her to the field was almost washed out, nearly impossible to see beyond the impediment of heavy rain.

Tabby moved around to stand in front of her. "What if we *had* saved those kids? You don't think people would be happy with us?"

Pepper sighed. "I'm sure they would. But we didn't, because we didn't know a damn thing about it."

"But we could've, right? If we'd asked the right questions, drunk the right mix, or whatever it is Jude does to know what she knows? I mean, why *didn't* she know?"

Pepper's voice hardened. "It ain't her fault, and don't you go sayin' it is. She ain't an oracle. And she spends too much time and energy on this mountain as it is."

Tabby wouldn't let up. "But she could be. She's done it before."

"And how the hell would you know that? You've been here a whopping two years, think you know everything about the place."

The girl rolled her eyes. "Don't play dumb. Everybody knows she can. Steph told me—she knew about the cave-in before it happened, didn't she?"

Pepper set her jaw and moved past the girl. "Don't hold those bottles in the same hand—you'll crack the lips."

Tabby sighed. "So what? Ain't like we don't have buckets and such. And I don't understand why we can't just use the well water from the house. It's the same damn thing."

Pepper shook her head and grabbed a low-hanging branch so she could swing over deadfall blocking the path. "That right there's another reason Jude knows you're not ready. It's *not* the same, not by a long shot."

"What the hell does it matter? The well water pulls from the mountain, too, so it ain't like there's much difference."

"Except there is. Jude knows what sources are best for what cures. It's not just scooping up water from wherever you happen to see it, storing it in some dirty old bucket. She blesses those bottles, and she has very precise rituals. You can't just skip over all that."

Tabby snorted. "Oh, please. How's that different from the bullshit the Pastor does? Acting like it matters where a person talks to God, or what kinda prayer they make. Why can't we just drink the same stuff Jude does, and figure out what's been going on down there? If Jude doesn't want to, how about you and me?"

Pepper breathed out slowly, pushing away the insidious slide of her will. Sometimes all it needed was someone else's suggestion, and all her hard work threatened to fall away. She didn't have to say anything—Tabby realized her mistake almost immediately.

"Okay, so not you, but why not me? Didn't you tell me Jude wasn't much older than I am now when she took over from the last sister?"

Pepper swallowed the want, dragged her attention back to the matter at hand. "That's right. She was young—*too* young, as she'll be the first to say. When you start practicing, you'll have Jude to teach you, look out for what you're doing. You'll have me, and Jess and Steph, too. But Jude had *no one*. Angie died, and left Jude in charge, and she had no one to ask or learn from. You don't see how that's different?"

Tabby stopped and wrinkled her brow. "I guess. But if it's that hard for her, if she's overwhelmed as it is, then why not let us help? Why not share the burden? I can't understand why she doesn't want to help the town." Her gaze narrowed and she lowered her voice, though no one could have heard her over the rain beating down on the trees. "Do you think she already knows something about those people?"

Pepper turned on the girl, her jaw set. "Meaning what, exactly?"

Tabby dropped her gaze and took a step back. "I guess I just wondered . . . she talks about balance all the time, sacrifice. Giving back to the mountain in the same amount as what we take."

"And?"

"So what if she's talking about human sacrifice? What if she took those people to restore the balance?"

Pepper tried to keep her breathing even, put a stopper in the rage that threatened to spill over. She wasn't that person anymore—couldn't afford to be. "I'll pretend, just this once, that I didn't hear that. Jude's a damn good person, and she'd never do a thing like that. You oughta be ashamed of yourself for saying it. Now go to the spot we went last week and fill those bottles. Mind, get it *only* from that spot, and don't forget the prayer, okay?"

Tabby seethed but didn't move, letting Pepper leave her behind. When she was sure the older woman was out of sight, she turned back toward the house. To hell with the water. If no one else was going to help the people of Arnett, she would.

CHAPTER SIX

TILLY MCPHERSON SAT on her covered porch, watching the endless rain and worrying. Her gaze took in her acres, the forty-one of them she and Ralph had scraped and saved to buy, to make their own go of things once the mine shut down. They'd worked their fingers to the bone, both of them, but for Tilly it was worth it. The land was theirs, free and clear, and aside from the monetary possibilities, it made her feel free. They'd never have to pay rent or tithes of crops again, and no one could make them leave. Then Ralph had gone and screwed all that up.

"It's still our land," he told her, his lower jaw jutting out like it did when he got pig-headed. "What do we care about a hole dug here or there? Won't bother us none. It's free money, and about damn time something went our way."

Ralph hadn't seen the mine closing the same way Tilly had. For her, it was a blessing she remembered daily, that he'd come out of that black hole in the earth, that he hadn't died in there along with the thirty-five men he'd worked alongside. The fear of that day, the certainty of loss as soon as her sister brought her the news, it was indelibly stamped on her heart and mind. She didn't know how to hope, so she started grieving, and when her husband returned to her, bruised, cut up and lungs full of coal dust, but so miraculously *alive*—the relief burned everything else away. But for Ralph, the mine closure meant the humiliation of losing his job. A third-generation miner, it was all he'd known, and he counted on the money. He resented the way they'd had to struggle since then, that his wife had to get her hands dirty. He'd promised her the day he asked her to marry him that he'd provide for her and hadn't much listened when she told him she didn't need that. So when a too good to be true opportunity came along, Ralph only saw the good part, or claimed to, anyway. The fact he'd exercised his will over hers, sold rights to their land without so much as asking her—Tilly knew her husband too well to believe he truly saw no reason for worry.

Her anger at him aside, Tilly couldn't shake the feeling he'd sold their souls out from under them. He might think such a fancy was silly, but Tilly learned long ago to trust her gut, and that morning, her gut was tied in knots. They weren't the only ones who'd sold those minerals—she'd noticed quite a few folks seeming plumper in the pocket lately, and it only made her worry more. It didn't feel right, cutting up the land like that. Things seemed like they'd gotten worse as soon as that awful Boots man came back.

"C'mon you stubborn old mule, get your ass home," she muttered under her breath, pacing the length of the porch for the fiftieth time that day. Why the hell Ralph needed to fish in the pouring rain, when he knew the creek's banks would be swollen as hell, she'd never understand. Except, of course, she did—it was enough for that man to want something, and next thing she knew he expected to have it. His ma was most to blame for that, Tilly thought sourly, but even so. He was old enough to know better—a person can't just tell Mother Nature what's what and expect it to go their way.

Her reminders of the four deaths Arnett suffered did nothing to change his mind.

"Hell, Ralph, that lawyer died doing *just* what you're planning to do yourself. Drowned while fishing, and that doesn't give you pause?"

Ralph laughed it off. "Branden Gross was three sheets to the wind every damn time he got in that creek. It's a loss, what happened to him, but not a surprise."

She'd raised an eyebrow. "And that wasn't one of the sisters' bottles I saw poking out the top of your satchel?"

He got sharp with her after that, so she'd had no choice but to let him go. But he'd left at the crack of dawn, and ought to be home by now. She hoped he hadn't drunk too much just to spite her.

She chewed a thumbnail, already bitten down to the quick. Blood beaded from the torn flesh and filled her mouth with the taste of copper. She wondered again how long she ought to give it before going to retrieve him. Wished she could enjoy the quiet of an empty house without letting anxiety ruin her peace.

The rain made it hard to see much farther than her front yard, but as she squinted at the horizon, relief bloomed in her chest. Someone was coming her way, and a second or two later, she could make out the blurred outline of her husband, his fishing rod over one shoulder.

"Thank Christ, you stubborn man," she muttered, anger settling in place of her worry. She fought the urge to run to him, instead keeping dry on the porch. She wouldn't even move to the stairs to greet him and take charge of his day's catch, clutching the railing and standing firm.

She felt the vibration in her fingers first. She frowned, looking down at the way her hand trembled on the wood, but it wasn't just her hand, it was the whole porch. Next it came through her boots, rushing up her body, shaking things loose inside her. Her chest nearly itched with it, and her stomach roiled uneasily. Was it thunder? They got some bad storms here in the valley, and it wasn't unusual for thunder to shake the whole house. But she'd heard nothing aside from the rain, and still the land shook beneath her.

Dread spread its tendrils in her chest and her breath came faster. She looked out once more, saw her husband running in her direction, the fishing pole flopping side to side behind him. His hands were empty, reaching toward her though he was still a hundred yards away. Was he running for the safety of the house? Or running to get her out of it?

She took a step toward the stairs but made it no farther. The porch rose beneath her feet and she wrapped her arms around the rail tight to keep her balance.

"Tilly!" came her husband's cry, muted by the torrents from the sky.

"Ralph!" she called back. She had no intention of waiting on the man, instead crouching to swing her legs beneath the rail and drop to the ground below. The house shifted again, as though the back of it were driving into the ground, and her hip got wedged between the rail and the planks. "Oh hell," she muttered, looking up. Ralph was within a few yards now, his hands still outstretched, and Tilly made herself wait for him. She couldn't picture what the hell was happening, how the porch kept rising or what else might be going on: best to let him help.

The ground trembled again, and between breaths, her husband disappeared from sight. Tilly gasped, twisted herself as best she could to see where he'd gone—surely he'd tripped, would get to his feet in a moment and come back into view. But plenty of moments passed and still he was gone.

"Ralph?" she cried, struggling to free herself. Using all her might and scraping off a sizable portion of flesh from her hip, Tilly managed to get loose and back herself onto the porch planks once more. "Ralph!"

"Tilly," came his voice, but it was muffled, sounding much farther away than he should be.

She managed to pull herself upright again, though she had to hold tight to the railing. Peering over the edge, vertigo knocked her sideways.

What she saw made no sense. Or rather, what she didn't see. There was no ground, no grass or stone walkway leading to their home. The porch stairs protruded into the air, and beneath them was a blackness as endless as the rain. She couldn't understand it, her mind struggling for purchase as fruitlessly as her body.

"Tilly!"

"Ralph?" He sounded so far away from her, and she heaved herself up with all her might, managed to get eyes on the sides of the gaping hole in the world. A fishing pole stuck up from the darkness, and after squinting down, she was able to make out the top of her husband's head. He turned his face to hers, his hands locked tight around a sharp rock protruding from the mud.

"Tilly, help me," he called weakly. Before she could take a step, his wet hands slid from the rock and he dropped, soundlessly, into the deep nothing.

Tilly's heart stood still, her chest locked, body tight with the insistence she still had time to save him. It had only been a moment since he was there, and the abrupt and silent disappearance refused to register. "Ralph!" she screamed, the miracle of his return to her twenty years ago swept away by his loss. The earth wanted him. It had bided its time, but now at last it had swallowed him whole. Tilly's grief had no time to grow, snuffed out the moment she managed to throw herself over the tilting railing and follow her love into the maw.

CHAPTER SEVEN

JUDE LAY AWAKE listening to the rain, exhaustion pinning her to the mattress without gifting her unconsciousness. She was used to the misery of it by now. She'd spent hours in the cavern that night, not emerging for dinner and far too tired to eat once she finally gave it up. What was worse, more wounds had bloomed on her flesh—cuts all over, and one spot that felt like a bad burn. Luckily, they were all in places easily covered by her clothes, but they throbbed through the night.

She should be hungry, but instead her belly was a mess of anxiety, acid eating away at her stomach lining. The liquor didn't help, but she didn't have much choice. It was the best way, often the only way to commune with what dwelt in the deepest folds of the Devil's Backbone, but even that wasn't working anymore. She'd finished a whole bottle, reducing her dwindling supply even further, and though she was able to untether herself from her body, there'd been no answer from beneath. She had to face the truth: the source, the spirit of the magic, was gone. *She* was gone. Which meant things had gone too far for Jude to fix on her own. She'd have to ride it out, same as everyone else. The knowledge of what came next was a weight around her neck. Too tired for dread, she pushed that worry aside for another day.

She rolled over, thought about getting up. There was nothing else she could do, but there was no way she'd sleep anymore. She sighed and pushed up to sit on the edge of her bed. A despairing fatigue settled over her, the daily concession that there would be no more rest. She shoved it aside, turned her thoughts to the day ahead. Tried to start her sluggish brain working on the problems that beset her. Failed and gave it up.

When Jude stepped out onto the porch an hour later, hot coffee in hand, the sun was just coming over the horizon, half-obscured by heavy rain clouds. Night still clung to this part of the mountain, but light would make its appearance in its own time. Exhaustion held her in place, leaning against one of the porch supports, too tired to move, too afraid to sit down. If she did, she might never get back up, the way she felt this morning, and the steady thrum of rain only depressed her further. How long had it been since the sun had a chance to dry up the rising waters? With every inch the creek crept up, the risks to the people of Arnett grew higher. Despite the four recent deaths, she doubted the mountain was sated. She thought of mud leaking from every orifice and shuddered.

"Mornin', Miz Ersham."

Jude startled, spilling coffee on her hand. It should have burned, but the stuff was tepid, and she wondered if she'd fallen asleep on her feet. She set the cup down and looked up, squinting into the rain. "Who's there?"

"Sheriff Ison, Miz Ersham. Sorry to scare you, thought you heard me coming."

Jude blinked to clear her spotting vision and finally saw a horse ten or so feet from where she stood. She recognized the sheriff's Palomino mare, water running down her flanks as she stood with her head lowered, lipping at clumps of sodden grass. The sheriff stood close to the porch, the reins in his hand, not that he needed them. That mare was loyal to a fault and wouldn't be going anywhere.

"Must be all this rain," Ison said. "Loud on that roof, isn't it?"

Jude frowned. She should have noticed, anyway. She didn't like that he'd snuck up on her. "What's got you riding all the way up here in the wet, Sheriff?" she asked, setting down her mug.

The man hunched his shoulders, pulled his collar up. "Was hoping I could get your help on some things."

"What kinda things?" she asked, unease spreading through her gut. She was on good terms with the sheriff's office, but she knew better than to rely on that. Good will disappeared faster than a bourbon bottle drained.

Ison dipped his head and rain streamed from his hat to the muddy ground. "Awful wet out here, Miz Ersham. Could I come up there with you?"

Jude's instinct was to refuse, not to prolong his stay, but it was useless. He wasn't going away whether she agreed or not, so she crossed her arms and stepped back.

He wrapped the horse's reins loosely around the porch rail and climbed up beside her, shaking himself off a bit. She backed up a few more steps. He was a big man, too big to be standing as close as he was. She doubted it was a thing he gave any thought to, but she pressed her lips tight.

"So what'd you want to ask me?" she prodded when he stood staring out at her land instead of speaking.

Ison shook himself again and turned to face her. "Sorry. Almost drifted off—it's a peaceful place you've got here."

Jude kept her expression flat. "I've made sure of that."

He nodded. "I s'pose you've heard about the Helstrom family. Two of your girls were in town yesterday, got into a bit of an altercation with the widow."

She took a long breath before answering. Tabby might give in to her hot temper, but Jude couldn't afford to. "Way I heard it, the widow accosted them. All they did was exist in her presence." Temper or not, she couldn't stop the bitterness creeping into her voice.

Ison nodded. "From what I hear they conducted themselves well. Didn't mean to sound like they were in trouble—that's not why I'm here."

Jude allowed her shoulders to relax a bit. "Good. Mind telling me why, then?"

The sheriff looked out into the rain again, his gaze searching the mountain. "I wondered if you knew anything. About what happened to them—the Helstroms, I mean."

"I only know what Mr. Williams told Pepper while she was there. They drowned, right?"

"Mm hm. Mr. Williams. He speaks highly of you, you know."

Jude felt a rush of heat spread up her chest to her neck and hunched her shoulders but didn't answer. Ison was too young to remember how things were twenty years ago. He didn't know the history, the deep scar he picked at with his words.

When she didn't respond, he moved on. "They drowned, yes. Almost the same as the lawyer."

"How'd it happen? Boating accident or something?"

Ison frowned. "That's what we're having trouble with, to be honest. Mr. Helstrom didn't own a boat of any kind—he spent his money on other entertainment." He glanced at Jude and she pursed her lips.

"What people do with our products isn't our business, Sheriff."

"Oh, I know, I know. It was just odd. I can see the man drowning on his own—probably drunk as a skunk and lost his balance by the water, got carried downstream a ways. But I'm scratching my head over how those kids died. They were ten and twelve, old enough to take care of themselves."

Jude snorted. "You think ten and twelve is grown, do you?"

Ison raised his hands and sighed. "All I meant was they weren't little ones. Both strong swimmers from what we've heard. If they weren't out in the middle of the water, how'd it happen?"

She frowned. She'd been wondering that, too, since the previous afternoon. "You said they got carried downstream. Where were they found?"

"Washed up on the banks a good few miles from here. Laid out next to each other in a neat little row. Nature can be strange, can't it?"

Jude frowned and resisted the urge to cast a glance at the cavern, her tired brain beginning to spark. "It can."

Ison cleared his throat and sighed, put his hands on his hips. "Then there's the other folks."

Jude looked up. "What other folks? More dead?"

He shook his head. "Not that we know of—not yet, anyway, but I'll admit I'm worried. The way this rain's been . . . "

She nodded. "Dangerous. Who's missing?"

"Jake Michul. Rhonda and Timothy Ward. Julia Ritchie. Ben Carnes."

Jude sucked in a breath, her stomach dropping. Things were worse than she'd known. "Five?"

"For a start. There's also Ralph and Tilly Masters—went to check on 'em yesterday, since they're so close to the water, and the place was empty. Coffee cup laying on the porch, mud everywhere, but otherwise no sign."

"Hell," breathed Jude.

"Only thing that seems to tie 'em together . . . well, it's a weak link, even I can see that."

She frowned. She hadn't considered a connection before, yet another sign her mind was slipping. "What link?"

He shrugged. "Money. Seemed all of 'em had come into money in the last little bit."

Jude thought of what Pepper had said about Georgie's store.

Helstrom alone wouldn't have been able to empty the shelves of liquor—it made sense there'd be more. What the hell was happening down there?

"Then there's Mr. Boots."

Jude's brows drew together. "What about him?"

Ison rolled his neck till it cracked. "Ain't seen him in a week or so—his encampment's abandoned."

"Encampment? I thought he'd taken himself off when he didn't get what he wanted. Didn't realize he was back."

He nodded. "Yep. About a month now." He eyed her. "You telling me he hasn't been up here again, trying to buy that mine?"

Jude shook her head. "Haven't seen him. I can ask the other sisters, but I think they'd have mentioned it."

"That, and you never leave this mountain, do ya?"

Jude took a breath, let it out. Suspicion was natural to a man like Ison. "Not in quite some time. I have responsibilities up here."

He cast his gaze upward, studying the gray skies. "Shows how you can be mistaken—I thought for sure when he came back he'd take another swipe at it."

Her lips twisted. "He can take as many as he likes—the mine's not for sale. It ought never to have been built in the first damn place."

Ison offered no opinion on that. Like many people who hadn't lost anyone to the mine, he viewed its closing as a tragedy in itself. "So he wasn't a customer of yours? He didn't use your . . . medicines?"

She stiffened but kept her tone calm. "Not to my knowledge, but I don't have any way of knowing who buys it once Georgie has it on the shelves. No one comes up here direct, you know that."

"Like your privacy, huh? I can understand that."

"It's not just that. This place can be . . . dangerous for the uninitiated. The Backbone's no place to mess around."

He smiled. "Coming from someone else, a person might take that as a threat."

Jude sighed, stepped back to lean against the cabin's outer wall. "Well, it's not. Just the truth. And just so we can skip all the innuendos, I'll answer to your face what everyone else only asks behind our backs. We didn't have a grudge against Mr. Gross. We warned him off our land a few times, but we bore him no malice. It was for his own damn safety. Not for some silly land dispute—

hell, there's plenty of fish in that creek, we ain't in any danger of running out. He didn't come close enough to the homestead to bother us—if I could've, I'd have given the man an open invitation so he didn't embarrass himself thinking he was being subtle." She sighed, tightened her arms around herself and looked down at her scuffed and dirty boots. "It's not safe here. Not for folks who aren't familiar with it, or don't know how to respect what's been here since the Earth was new."

Ison's expression didn't change. "Did you know what was gonna happen to him?"

She raised her gaze again. "I was afraid of it. I didn't *know*."

The sheriff nodded, jutting out his lower jaw, looking like he was chewing the cud. "Would you object to me taking a look around up here?"

Jude's heart jolted, her face going hot. "What the hell for?"

His expression didn't change. "For the missing folks. You said it yourself; this mountain isn't a safe place to be. What if somebody came up here, maybe looking for you, and ran into trouble?"

"You mean Mr. Boots. You think he came up here and we did something to him."

Ison sighed heavily. "I didn't say that, and I don't think it. But these are our neighbors, Miz Ersham. Our friends in some cases. I want to make sure we're doing everything we can to find them. Maybe even figure out what's going on here, stop it from hurting anyone else."

For the first time Jude caught the desperation in his tone, the tremble in the man's hands still planted at his waist. He likely meant what he said, and she knew how it would look, refusing permission. Like she didn't care, or worse, like she was guilty. But it didn't change things.

"I can't allow that." She softened her tone as best she could. "I wish I could, and I promise you, we'll have a look around today. We find anything at all, you'll be the first to know. But it's not safe for your deputies."

His shoulders slumped but he nodded again, reached to unwrap the reins from the rail. "I guess I expected that." He eyed her. "You know I can get a warrant if I need to."

She swallowed, dread dropping her stomach like a stone. Time was shorter than she'd thought. "I hope you don't. We really will look, and that'll do more good than your people poking around up here. They don't know the place like we do."

Ison straightened his shoulders and tipped his hat to her. "I appreciate you talkin' to me this morning. Be seeing you."

She stayed to watch him ride back down the mountain, holding her breath when the mare stumbled once as the mud slid beneath her hooves. But she caught herself and stayed upright, and Jude was able to let the tension leave her shoulders.

She stayed on the porch a few minutes longer, evening her breath and working on her calm, a heavy ache in her chest and her pulse beating loud in her ears. She still felt like hell, but at least she knew what she needed to do next. She'd nearly convinced her body to get moving when the latch clicked on the door behind her, and she whirled to see who was there. The door was closed tight, and Jude realized with a sinking stomach someone had been listening, had heard her whole conversation with the sheriff. Depending on which sister it was, that could spell trouble.

CHAPTER EIGHT

WILLIAMS WIPED RAIN from his eyes with a sodden sleeve, doing little but moving the moisture around. His vision blurred from a week of broken sleep, and his body moved only by force of habit, muscle memory taking over where his mind stopped functioning. Good thing, too—even without the extra impediment of exhaustion, visibility was almost nil, and that was here in town. God knew how bad it was on the mountain.

He turned to squint over his shoulder at the looming presence to the east. The range ran from Tennessee all the way to Virginia, and cast its shadow over all of Arnett. The Devil's Backbone. He'd grown up with it, and despite its forbidding name, he felt it as a comfort, even after what happened with Maggie. It wasn't the mountain's fault any more than it was Jude's. He'd spent the last two decades trying to convince the stubborn woman, but she was determined to keep her hair shirt on.

Williams took a breath and refocused, pulled himself from the useless cycle of want and wish and regret he was all too used to. He bent to pull the last sack of gravel to the tailgate of his truck, the burlap weighted with the rain, when the ground trembled beneath his feet.

Williams straightened again, braced his hand against the outside wall of his general store. He frowned, his stomach dipping with the sense of movement, of fragility, as though the earth itself would slip out from under him. He hadn't imagined it—was still feeling it, though it dissipated by the second, as did the whiff of wood smoke he caught through the rain. Unease clutched his gut, and he thought of Maggie. He scanned the surrounding area, Main Street deserted in the downpour, but saw no signs of movement like an earthquake would cause. He turned to the mountain again, bracing for a rockslide or some such thing, but all he saw was a world gone gray with rain.

The sensation stopped, and something else sped into view, bouncing down the nearly washed-out road from on high. After a few seconds he recognized the sisters' car and sighed, fighting a useless hope and an equally useless worry. It wouldn't be Jude—it never was, but he'd yet to convince his heart of that. It didn't much matter who else it was beyond that—feelings were still raw from yesterday's debacle during the funeral march, and it was best the sisters stayed away for a bit. He'd expected them to understand that—Pepper certainly had. She erred on the side of caution, always, and the other women listened to her as a de facto aide de camp to Jude. If she was coming back, or had allowed one of the others to do so, things must be bad.

Williams left the gravel to soak a little longer and strode to the end of the planked walkway that ran along Arnett's small retail district, standing where he knew the car's driver must see him. He waited for it to draw abreast of him, raising a hand as it approached, but had to step back when the driver didn't so much as slow down, sending a sheet of muddy water up from the road. He cursed and raised an arm to protect his face from the worst of it, but had time to recognize Tabby in the driver's seat, her jaw set and eyebrows drawn. She was pissed about something, and taking it out on the car. Williams' worry turned to dread, his stomach sinking. Pep could keep the girl in line to an extent, but the passenger seat was empty.

Fuck. He stood at the edge of the walk again, hands on his hips, wondering where Tabby was going, and if he could head her off. She wasn't his responsibility: none of them were, and he doubted Jude appreciated his interference one way or another. But he still felt protective of them, all of them. Their position made them equally respected and feared, and it didn't take much of a breeze to blow public opinion from one side to the other.

The whine of the car's overtaxed engine cut off abruptly, a twisting wrench as Tabby turned the key none too gently. Williams started down the street, a sinking feeling in his belly. Things felt precarious in a way he couldn't pin down. He rounded the corner just in time to see her bang through the door to the sheriff's office, slamming it behind her. The car was parked crooked, the hood nosing the side of the building, tires sunk several inches in the mud. He frowned and picked up speed, reaching the door as raised voices penetrated to the street beyond. He recognized both Tabby and Ison, yelling to beat the band, and didn't hesitate to push his way inside.

"—don't understand, she's not the only one who can help. I can, too, you just gotta give me a chance."

The sheriff stood behind his desk, his hands up in a placating fashion. "That's fine, Miss Tabitha, and I believe you, but you still need to go somewhere and sober up. I understand you're upset, but you can't do anyone any good, the state you're in."

Williams' gut churned as he looked at the young woman, hoping like hell Ison was wrong, that she was just worked up and not inebriated. But the sweet smell of bourbon overpowered the small room, and Tabby swayed on her feet, a bottle in her hand. He frowned at it—it didn't look like the usual ones the sisters delivered to town. What the hell had she got hold of?

"Miss Tabby," Williams said in a low voice. "Can I take you somewhere to get a bite to eat?"

Ison looked up and breathed out heavily, his shoulders dropping. "That's a fine idea, Mr. Williams. I'd appreciate that. Then after you've had a chance to get in a better frame of mind, I'd like to hear what you have to say, ma'am."

Tabby ignored Williams and took two stumbling steps closer to the sheriff. "You don't understand. I have to drink to help you— that's how it works. That's half of why we make the stuff."

Ison frowned and cocked his head. "I'm not sure I understand. I don't believe I've seen Miz Ersham drunk a day in my life."

Tabby glared, snorted. "You've barely seen her at all, have you? Because she's afraid. She stays up on that mountain, sends us to do her work so she doesn't have to get her hands dirty. But she lied to you today, Sheriff. She said she couldn't help, couldn't tell you anything about those missing people. But she *can*, she just won't."

Williams' shoulders tightened and dread filled him. If yesterday's funeral had primed the gunpowder, Tabby held the spark to it. He stepped closer and put a hand on her shoulder. "You heard the sheriff, Miss Tabitha, let's go. You'll feel better for some food, then we can talk it over."

Ison raised a hand. "Hold on a minute. I want to hear this." He transferred his gaze back to Tabby. "She lied to me? Does that mean y'all know where those people are? Is that why she wouldn't let me search the mountain?"

"Search the mountain?" Williams said. "What the hell for? You can't seriously think Jude—*any* of them had anything to do with this."

Ison flicked a grim look his way, then returned his attention to Tabby. "I didn't when I went to see her this morning. But if Jude's got nothing to hide, why'd she say no to the search?"

Williams glared. "I'm sure she had her reasons."

Tabby shook off Williams' grip. "Sure she did. Laziness. Cowardice."

"Tabby! You don't know what you're saying." And she sure as hell didn't follow Ison's train of thought. The girl was digging a deep hole she couldn't even see.

The sheriff put a hand up once more. "I want to hear what she's got to say. You're telling me you know where the missing folks are? And what happened to the Helstroms, and that lawyer?"

Tabby nodded. "I mean, I don't know yet, not exactly. But I can find out. I can do what she does, I just have to be in the same state of mind. And that's why I brought this." She raised the bottle and tipped it to her lips, taking another swallow and grimacing at the burn.

"Miss Tabby—" began Williams again, but Ison stepped in once more, ignoring the other man.

"Why would Jude lie to me? If it's that easy, why wouldn't she just help? Did she have something to do with these deaths?"

Tabby shook her head. "She lied because she's scared."

Williams stepped close and took hold of her shoulder again, his face set in stone. "That's enough."

Tabby turned on him, a snarl twisting her lips. "She ain't my mom, and you ain't my dad. You think you know her just cuz you moon over her all the time, but you don't. None of you live with her. I do, and I say she's scared."

"Of what?" asked Ison, his gaze almost painfully intense.

"Of people coming to the mountain. Seeing what it really is, what we do there. What *she* does there."

Cold anger took hold of Williams. "Keep your fool mouth shut, girl. Don't you see what you're doing?"

Ison stepped from behind the desk and put a hand on Tabby's arm, guiding her to the back hallway, out of sight. "I'll take it from here, Mr. Williams. You go on back to your store—I'll make sure Miss Tabitha's taken care of."

Williams stood helpless and stared after them for long seconds, trying to listen, until Ison's deputy, Brian Chellgren, stepped from the shadows. "You heard the sheriff. We've got it from here."

Williams had nothing to do but turn and head back to the street. When he opened the door, he nearly knocked over a gaggle of Arnett's citizens standing just outside. One look at their faces told him they'd heard every damn word. He shoved through their midst, back to his store, ignoring the covered walkway to stride through the rain and mud. He had to get to Jude, before someone else did.

CHAPTER NINE

"**M**AGGIE!" Jude stopped to listen, held her breath, but heard nothing over the rain. She fought the certainty that there wasn't anything to hear, that the spirit she sought had left the Backbone altogether, intent on revenge. If that were so, there was little she could do, and if there was one thing Jude couldn't stomach, it was helplessness.

"Maggie, please. I think I know what's got you worked up now—is it that man? The one who tried to buy the mine? Did he find another way in? If that's the case, I can help. Just give me a chance, please. You don't want to hurt anyone else."

Only silence answered her, and she felt the difference in the mountain's energy. It was inert, dead, unresponsive in a way she'd never felt. Even when the cave-in happened, the magic stayed put. She hadn't even known it could leave, and she tried not to think about what would happen if it never came back. Or what it might do, once free of the anchor that had held it all these years.

"Maggie," she said softly, her breath coming hard. She leaned against a large oak tree at her back, took a halfhearted swig from the bottle in her hand. Grimaced as the drink hit her empty stomach. God only knew what she'd done to her gut in all these years. It had gotten to where the sight or smell of bourbon turned her stomach—funny how as soon as something became a job, a responsibility, all the enjoyment got sucked right out of it. Still she clutched the bottle tight—she was down to the last dregs of this one, and beyond that only one bottle remained. There'd been two, but Jude could guess what happened to the other one. Tabby. Grabbing it and heading out with the sisters' only car, not knowing how much worse she made things with her theft. It was hard not to take it personal, but Jude knew the young woman had no idea what she'd set in motion, or how worthless her interference was.

"Doesn't matter. Can't stop what's been started," she said under her breath. She straightened her shoulders, closed her eyes and thought. If she couldn't rely on magic to guide her anymore, she'd just have to count on herself. She had a brain in her head still, even if everyone thought it had been pickled over the last few decades.

The problem had to be tied up in Dan Boots. She hadn't known until Ison's visit that the man was back in Arnett, but if he was, she knew his purpose would be tied up in the land. In the Backbone, specifically. He'd grown up in Arnett, but left as soon as he could, headed into the wide world to make a name for himself. Jude didn't grudge anyone their dreams, but she couldn't abide them stepping on other folks to get what they wanted. That was what he'd done, every time he breezed back into town. Filling young women's heads with promises of luxuries they'd never seen, impressing everyone with his cosmopolitan air. He'd tried to buy the abandoned mine from her the last time he came around, and got a little ugly when she wouldn't entertain his offer, or blink at the money he promised. He didn't understand why she'd bought it in the first place, assumed it had to do with profit. But Jude didn't give a shit about his money. She'd brought the mine under her protection in order to preserve the balance, to keep the mountain's anger at bay. She'd been truthful with the sheriff when she told him Boots hadn't been seen on the mountain, but that only meant he'd decided to go around her.

With Tabby taking the only car, Jude couldn't leave to find the man, at least not with enough speed to do any good. Best to start close to home, where she knew the land. She pushed off the oak tree and headed in the direction of home. She wished home was her destination, but instead she veered toward the mine, sweat slicking her palms, making the bottle slide in ways the rain hadn't. Maybe the underground would be as dead and cold as the last time she'd been inside. Maybe she'd made a bugbear out of nothing for all these years. Didn't matter—she had to try. She'd pledged her life and fealty to the magic, and the debt would come due one way or another.

CHAPTER TEN

WILLIAMS HEARD THE echo of his dead wife's name the moment he turned his truck's engine off. His stomach dipped and he closed his eyes. *Not now,* he thought. She'd only come to him at night, never in the light of day, and only at his home. *Their* home, the one they'd so briefly shared.

"Maggie," came the cry again, a woman's voice, a haunting quality to it as though it came from a place too far to reach. He braced himself for the smell of woodsmoke, for the wave of fear that crashed through him every time he saw her shadowed face, her burning eyes. Braced for the guilt he felt each time, that he wasn't grateful to see her again. Not like that.

But nothing happened. No smoke, no eerie approach or gaze of flame. He opened his eyes warily, scanning his surroundings as best he could in the storm, but nothing moved.

"Maggie, please."

He narrowed his gaze and opened his car door. That was Jude's voice, though it echoed oddly—that hadn't been a trick of perception. But why would she be calling for a woman twenty years dead? Especially a woman she hadn't much cared for when she was alive.

Williams closed the door softly, tried to make his footsteps quiet in the mud though he wasn't sure why. He'd come up here to find Jude, talk some sense into her. He'd known her most of their lives, so why was he suddenly uneasy?

He shook it off, put it down to the unreality of the past weeks. Nothing felt right—not the weather, or the people, or the town itself. And worse than all of it was this mountain.

He'd lived in the shadow of the Devil's Backbone all his life. It was a comforting backdrop, both a sentinel and a protector from the world beyond Arnett. Once Jude moved up here for good, the

Backbone became a repository for his hurt, but looking up at it each day, knowing the way she loved the place, he'd chosen to love it, too.

But today that comfort was gone. He felt like an intruder, and he supposed he was. He cast a glance over his shoulder at the shadow of the peak, framing the two-story house the sisters had called home as long as anyone could remember. He didn't see any of them now, but with the rain he supposed that made sense. They'd seek shelter same as anyone else.

Was that what Jude had done? Taken cover in one of the caverns that dotted the mountainside? Maybe that one back beyond the house where she'd spent so much time when she was younger? Back when he'd truly known her, as she was, and not just a head full of memories. It took him a minute to get oriented to where it was, but when he saw it, he headed straight for it.

"Jude?" he called when he got close. "You in there, Jude?"

"Stop." Her voice rang out behind him, loud enough she might have been five feet away.

He turned but couldn't see her until she spoke again and he caught sight of her at the mouth of the mine.

His stomach clenched at the sense memory of falling rock, the shaking beneath his feet, the rumbling carrying through his body, a warning of death coming fast. His chest tightened, his throat feeling like it was closing. It wasn't real, the sensations twenty years in the past, but seeing the mine brought it back. He fought to breathe, to talk himself down. Pushed away thoughts of Maggie dying there in the dark, coming to look for him, not knowing he'd already made it out. The rumble of approaching catastrophe he'd felt all those years ago bore a disconcerting similarity to the quakes and disturbances he'd noticed the last few weeks in Arnett. The cave—had the earth shifted within? Could it be trouble? He headed swiftly back down to Jude. He wanted her out of the reach of the mine's dark mouth, shoving down an image of a wall of rock knocking her flat, taking away another woman he loved.

"Jude? What the hell are you doing in there? Get away from it. It's not safe," he called when he got close enough.

She put both hands up, took a step back. "Stop there, Williams. No farther."

He frowned and stopped ten feet away. "I won't come any closer if you get out of there. Come on, you're giving me palpitations." He tried to make it a joke, but his fear was too big to get his arms around, an unwieldy weight that threatened to overwhelm them both. He held a hand out. "Please. For me, if no other reason."

She sighed and cast a glance behind her, then came toward him. "What the hell are you doing here, anyway?"

He breathed easier with every step she took, let his shoulders drop. Strode to meet her, his hands itching to grab her and shake some sense into her, but he kept them at his sides. "Never mind that, what the hell were you doing in there? I thought I heard you calling for Maggie."

He didn't like the look in her eye, the way her lids slid low and her gaze drifted back toward the mine.

"I wasn't," she said, her tone cold and hard.

He frowned, peered over her shoulder. "I heard you, clear as day. You said her name at least twice. Why?" His eyes widened, thinking of the tumultuous earth. "Did you . . . find her?" he whispered. Was that why his long-dead wife had visited him? Was her spirit finally free to haunt him, remind him of his failings?

Jude's mouth thinned and she moved to block his vision. "No, I didn't. And you won't either, so stop thinking it."

Anger licked at his exhaustion, bit away at the edges of it and sharpened his vision. Williams set his jaw, his own voice turning cold and hard. "Tell me why you were calling for her. Tell me what that has to do with that cursed damn mine."

Jude lifted her chin. "It's not your business, what goes on up here."

His brows snapped together. "You've made it my business. Now get out of my way."

He didn't need to add the rider—she had no real chance of stopping him, not with so much open space. He moved around her and stepped inside, his earlier fear burned away in his need to know. That lasted as long as it took for the smell to register in his mind, for his body to process the insanity of coming back here to the place that cost him so much. He froze just inside, his hands opening and closing into fists.

A hand touched his arm lightly and he jerked away, his heart rate skyrocketing, his breath coming fast. It was dark as hell in there, but he recognized Jude in the dim lighting from the world outside. A place that felt far away now. A dream he'd woken up from, now he was back in the mine. Maybe he'd never really left.

"Come on," she said softly. "You shouldn't be in here."

She was right, and relief filled his heart at the idea of walking out with her, of never looking at or thinking about this place for at least another twenty years. He didn't know what came over him, beyond a sudden but fading certainty that Jude was keeping something vital from him. Before he could take a step back, another smell filled his nostrils and stopped him cold.

Rot. Wet and musty, but there nonetheless—the unmistakable odor of decomposing flesh. An image of Maggie's face flashed in his mind, her pretty jawline sagging as her flesh rotted away, her bony fingers frozen in the act of clawing her way free. It couldn't be her—it had been too long for the smell to be any of the poor souls who'd been entombed here, when the rest of the miners, Williams included, made it out into the sunlight.

"What is that?" he asked, stepping farther into the dark. "What's dead in here?"

She sighed but made no effort to stop him. "Watch your step. You don't want to put your foot through something like that."

The uneasy feeling created a high-pitched ringing in his ears, a sound effect to signal the end of one reality, the entry into another. "Through what?" he asked, his own voice sounding muffled and far off in his head. "I can't see a damn thing."

"You sure you want to?" Jude asked.

Williams thought again of Maggie, of what time and insects would have done to her. He swallowed bile and nodded before he remembered she wouldn't be able to see him. "Yes. Give me a light."

She hesitated, unmoving and silent in the dark with him, then she shuffled to his side and he heard the click of a lighter, smelled a brief flash of ignition fluid. A small flame sprung to life next to her face, its well-loved planes turned to dark hollows by the fitful flicker. For a moment he saw Maggie again, the twin fires of her eyes, and took a step back. His boot connected with something solid but he caught himself before stumbling any farther.

"Show me," he said hoarsely.

She lifted the lighter and brandished it against the cloying blackness beyond, and Williams followed her gaze down, to the shapes that lay by his foot. He sucked in a breath and took the lighter from her, barely noticing the heat of the metal against his fingertips. With a shaking hand he held the flame out as far as it would go, then he counted the sodden bundles that lay beyond.

"That's five," he said to her, numbness creeping over his body, slowing his mind. When she didn't answer, he turned to her. "Five bodies," he repeated. He hadn't gotten a good enough look to identify all of them, but the wide-eyed and tortured countenance of Dan Boots was burned in his retina.

Still she said nothing, only watching him as the lighter's flame grew dimmer.

"Jude. What'd you do with the other two?"

CHAPTER ELEVEN

"IT'S NOT WHAT you think," Jude said, without hope Williams would listen to her.

"You don't know what I think," he said softly, his voice shaking as bad as his hands.

She didn't smile, but she wanted to. "I bet I have a pretty fair guess. You think I had something to do with these folks dying? Why else would their bodies be up here on my land, in the mine I own?"

"I didn't say that."

"You didn't have to." Jude blew out a breath, exhaustion overtaking the adrenaline that had flooded her body when she made her discovery, and again when she heard Williams' voice. She'd have spared him this if she could, but there was relief in having it in the open, not adding hiding corpses to her staggering responsibilities. "Hell, I'd think it myself. But I didn't kill them. I didn't kill anyone."

"Okay," he said, the two syllables stretched well past their limits. Again she had to fight a smile—none of this was funny, it was too dark for that. So why did she feel like giggling until she collapsed?

"Why don't we come out of here? Come up to the porch, get dry and have something hot to drink."

"Jude," he said. "Tell me what's going on."

She sighed. "I'm not entirely sure."

"Oh, don't give me that bullshit," he said, giving reign to his anger. "You know everything about this mountain, so don't tell me you don't know what's happening." He gestured to the dead behind him. "Where'd they come from, if you didn't put 'em there? And why didn't you tell Ison when he came up here asking questions this morning?"

Her gaze narrowed. "How'd you know about that?"

Williams shook his head slowly. "I came from town. Tabby's down there raising hell—she wouldn't come with me."

Jude squeezed her eyes shut. "That girl."

"She wants to help, which is more than I can say for you. She might be going about it wrong . . . but then again, she might not. Did she see these people?" he asked, still refusing to look at the corpses.

She gave a hollow laugh. "I suppose it's possible. I didn't know about 'em till just before you came. That's why I didn't say anything to the sheriff—I didn't know anything to tell."

He watched her face in the near dark, swallowing the bile that rose with the stench of rot. "That doesn't explain why you wouldn't let him search. You gotta admit, that looks pretty bad."

She wiped a hand across her dry lips, turned her back and walked to the mouth of the mine again. She didn't step outside, instead leaning against the support posts Williams had passed every morning for ten years, the ones that now served as a grave marker for his dead wife.

"I'll tell you what I told him. I didn't authorize a search because it's not fucking safe here. Not just the mine—the whole Backbone. I didn't want to add to the body count, which is why I told him I'd search myself."

He hesitated, then moved closer, sucking in the clean air carried on the rain. "So that's what you were doing? That's why you found those folks?"

She nodded. "Found 'em just like that, all lined up. I don't need you or the sheriff to tell me that's not natural."

"Someone put them there."

She sighed. "Looks that way."

"Who? The same person who killed them?"

She lifted a shoulder. "How do you think they died?"

He cast a glance back to the darkness but all he could see were lonely outlines against the pitch. "I don't know."

"I do. Same way as the lawyer, and the poor Helstroms."

Williams frowned. "They drowned?"

She kept her gaze on the mountain beyond. "Drowned, but not in water."

"Then in what?"

A hysterical laugh escaped her. "The Devil took 'em."

His brows shot together. "You think that's funny?"

"Not even a little. And I mean it—it was the Backbone. They suffocated on land. Earth. The mountain itself."

He sighed. "You're not making sense."

She turned to him at last, lifted one hand briefly. "Their mouths, throats, noses. Hell, even their eyes—all filled with mud. Looked just like Branden Gross when we found him. And I didn't see the Helstroms, but from what Pepper told me, they went the same way."

Williams shook his head against the image of the Helstrom girl's corpse sliding from her coffin, the way mud seeped from the corners of her mouth. "How the hell does that happen? Especially to so many people?"

"The mechanics of it? I'm not sure. If I had to guess, it has to do with this rain—long as it's gone on, we're lucky we haven't had a mudslide take out all of Arnett."

"Is that what happened, then? You think a mudslide killed all these folks, then someone brought them here? Natural causes, that what you're telling me?" Skepticism warred with a need to believe her. It sounded ridiculous, but better than believing the woman in front of him was a murderer.

She turned again and leaned heavily against the support posts once more. For the first time he noticed the empty bottle at her feet, the same kind Tabby had. Was she drunk? She didn't seem it, but then she'd had years to build one hell of a tolerance. "Natural in a certain sense, yes. This place, this mountain, the valley below—the magic here has always been rooted in nature."

"Magic," he said flatly, disappointment cresting. He was a fool for thinking he'd finally get a straight answer out of Jude. "So a magic mudslide."

She laughed. "Sounds funny when you say it like that."

"Sounds funny no matter how you say it."

"I suppose. But funny or not, it's what happened. The Backbone took them, all of them. I suspect the ones you haven't found yet, it's because they were swallowed deeper in the earth. You may never find 'em."

His anger rose again, but exhaustion was close behind. "You can't expect me to believe that shit. And if I don't buy it, you know damn well Ison won't."

She laughed again and there was a tinge of mania on the end of it. "Ison is the least of my worries right now. I'm trying to stop this before it gets even worse."

"Stop what, the mountain?"

She turned on him, nostrils flaring. "Yes. And before you go yucking it up with your sheriff buddy about the crazy old witch who's finally gone round the bend, tell me something." Her gaze held his. "You felt any disturbances down there? Felt the ground moving? Felt things changing, getting precarious, maybe?"

Williams stared at her. He didn't want to believe those things were connected.

She smiled. "Yeah, that's what I thought. And it *is* precarious—make no mistake about that. We haven't seen the worst of this, and if I can do what I aim to, we never will."

He put a hand to his mouth, stared out into the rain. "We need to evacuate the town," he said slowly. "Get everybody out."

She cocked her head. "Maybe. Maybe you'd be able to do it, save everyone in time. But maybe not—people are stubborn, especially people around here."

He sighed. "Then what the hell's your plan? Keep praying to this mountain of yours, the sentient one that's killing off our neighbors and lining them up for you?"

"The time for praying's over. She's too angry for that—far too angry. Too much has been taken from her, and she won't rest until she gets what she wants."

Williams felt cold. She seemed so lucid, conviction strong behind her words. He could almost believe her, but for the sheer insanity of what she was saying. He'd seen a bit of magic in his time, back when Jude was his. He didn't dismiss the whole concept of it, but in his belief system it was small potatoes. The ability to harness healing properties of the mountain's offerings, maybe a little divination. He couldn't fit the image of a sentient, moving mountain into his world view.

He looked down at her, mouth pressed in a thin line as suspicion rose in his mind. "You said 'her'."

She nodded, her eyes still locked on his.

"Who do you mean?"

When she didn't answer, he took two quick steps to close the distance between them, grabbed her by the shoulders. "Tell me.

Why were you calling Maggie's name? Does she have something to do with all this?"

There was no fear in her eyes, only pity. "She chose to. Twenty years ago now—it should have been me, but she went first."

The world seemed to spin around him, his face going from hot to cold. "Tell me straight, and no more of your mountain magic bullshit," he said, giving her shoulders a shake without meaning to.

She didn't react, except for the small smile that didn't reach her eyes. "I'm afraid I can't do that. Maggie *is* the mountain now, and she's the magic. It's what she chose."

CHAPTER TWELVE

EFORE HE COULD ANSWER, refute her words with the rage that bubbled within him, the ground rumbled beneath his feet. Deep down, a low and resonant hum that traveled all the way up his legs to his belly. He braced himself, fear once more taking the place of anger. He looked down at Jude in panic.

She moved his hands from her shoulders. "I don't think she likes that very much," she said.

"What the fuck does that mean?" He stumbled to one side as the ground kept shaking, increasing in intensity with every passing second. He looked wildly into the mine behind them, saw the way the silent dead moved in place, giving the illusion of life, as though they would rise any moment. A cave-in. It was happening again, and somehow he was here, back where death came so close to claiming him. Maybe it did, that long ago day, and was coming now to collect the debt.

Jude took his hand in hers, pulled him nearly off his feet. "Move it, now. We don't want to be in here."

He followed numbly, stumbling in the slight depression at the entrance to the mine. A place beaten down by the passage of miner's steps for generations. He was breathless though they hadn't traveled far. They stopped twenty or so feet from the entrance of the defunct mine, and when they looked back, he saw rock crumbling from the roof, the wooden posts bending and splintering against the weight from above. He watched, unable to move as the earth at last reclaimed what was hers. Just before the roof collapsed and cut off his view, he saw the outline of a woman standing in the back of it, two fiery eyes fixed on him.

"Maggie," he said hoarsely, but made no move toward the apparition, gone now behind tons of rock and dirt.

Jude, panting beside him, looked up at that. "You've seen her?"

He was slow in looking at her, his mind spinning through molasses. "Yes. Every night now, for weeks."

She closed her eyes and put a hand on her chest. "Then we've less time than I thought." She opened her eyes again, straightened her shoulders. "You need to go. Back down to town, fast as you can, and see how far you get in evacuating the place. Don't bother convincing the folks who don't want to believe—concentrate on saving who you can."

He shook his head, frowning, his brain slowly catching up. "You can't just send me away again, expecting me to follow orders. I need to know. Why's she here? What happened to her? And what did you mean when you said she chose it?"

"Jude? What the hell, are you okay?"

Williams glanced up and saw Pepper running hell for leather down from the house. He turned back to Jude.

"Please. I need to know."

Pepper reached them, spattered in mud, breathing hard. "Were you in there? In the damn mine?"

Jude took the younger woman's arm. "I don't have time to talk this out like I ought to. I should have done this a long time ago, but I guess you never think . . . " She sighed heavily.

Williams stepped between the women. "Don't do this to me. Don't shut me out, pretend you don't hear me and head off on some mission. *Tell me.*"

She patted his hand. "I am. I will." She looked at Pepper. "You come, too. Are the other sisters okay?"

Pepper nodded, frowning. "Everyone's up at the house—didn't hardly move a hair up there, but we heard it coming from the mine. Scared me to death when I looked out and saw you." She looked down, cleared her throat. "I thought I'd lost you."

Jude smiled faintly. "I'm sorry, Pep. You don't deserve any of this." She looked up at Williams. "Neither do you, but I don't have much time. Come with me, both of you. You need to see something."

CHAPTER THIRTEEN

PEPPER STOOD BEHIND Jude and Williams, a few paces away. She felt like an interloper during their time together, which she felt growing shorter with each breath. Jude had insisted, though, and Pepper wasn't about to deny her sister.

Williams' anger faded as soon as they crossed the cavern's threshold. Pepper wondered if he'd been here before, in the hazy days of the mountain's past that Jude never wanted to talk about. He stood at the water's edge, staring down into infinity, his hands shaking in the cold.

This was only Pepper's fourth time coming here, and her sense of awe was as strong as ever. It was like stepping into another world, one where the rules of reality as she knew it held no sway. In the echoing confines, the stalactite-studded, soaring ceiling to the place, anything seemed possible. It wasn't always a comforting thought. If dreams could be conjured, so too could nightmares. *This* was where the real magic was, and Pepper understood Jude's desire to keep it out of the hands of those who would use it carelessly.

No one was allowed here without Jude's express invitation, and even Tabby respected that particular boundary. Pepper was the only sister still on the mountain who'd been here, and she wasn't sure what to make of that. She knew Jude had only come here a handful of times with Angie before she passed. The eldest and senior sister at the time, Jude had learned everything she knew from Angie. It was an uneasy thought and Pepper shoved it away. Angie died too early, that was what Jude always said. That didn't have to mean Jude was in any danger.

"What is this place?" whispered Williams, his eyes on the impossibly still water.

Jude stood by his side, her hand in his. "This is her heart. Her resting place, most of the time."

He turned to her with effort. "M-Maggie's?" He stuttered over his dead wife's name.

Pepper watched Jude for a reaction, but there was none.

Jude seesawed her free hand. "In a sense, yes. She gave herself to the mountain, so for now, the two are one and the same. But it's not just Maggie. There's always been a vessel, as far back as our oral history goes."

The temperature in the cavern was icy, but it was more than the ambient air that made Pepper wrap her arms around herself. This couldn't be what it sounded like. They were witches, but only in the most innocuous sense of the word. A coven of women living and working together, communing with nature. Carefully keeping the balance of give and take. They didn't do sacrifices. Did they?

"What do you mean, *gave* herself? She died in the cave-in. That wasn't intentional." He laughed bitterly. "Unless you consider it a choice to die when she came in after me."

Jude kept hold of the man's hand, her own body steady and still. "Maggie didn't die in the cave-in, Les. She's not in the mine at all."

Goosebumps rose on Pepper's arms and she held herself tighter.

"What the hell are you talking about? Of course she did. She didn't know I was out already, thought I needed help. She came in to get me, and she died because of it. I know the guilt I carry, and I don't need lies to alleviate it."

He tried to pull away from her, but Jude held fast to his hand. "She died *because* of the cave-in, that's true. But it wasn't an accident. She came here, found me trying my damnedest to stop it. She understood, and she *believed*." Jude's laugh cracked in the middle. "I wanted to hate her, but she was just so damned *good*. She deserved you, far more than I did."

"Jude. Tell me."

She nodded, dropped his hand at last. "Time was short. We didn't have as long as we thought—the mine, it shortened the cycle, near as we could tell. It was robbing the mountain, taking from her without asking, without showing the proper respect. Without an eye to the balance of the place. A balance the women in this coven have always kept." She took a deep breath. "This place has been called the Devil's Backbone as long as anyone can remember. Gives it a connotation, like the land itself is bitter. Dangerous. But it's not—it simply is. It's up to us, what we do with it. Make no mistake though, this mountain will rise up to protect itself, like any living creature."

"Living creature." Williams' tone was flat.

"Yes. It's my job—*our* job to care for her." She blew out a breath. "Angie was young, too young to die. She hadn't taught me half what she needed to, hadn't had a chance to prepare me the way she'd been prepared." She cast a rueful glance at Pepper. "And I've gone and made the same damn mistake."

Williams shook his head. "I don't understand, what the hell does Angie have to do with anything?"

"She was supposed to be next. She understood that, and even when she realized how soon it would be, she didn't shirk her duty. Didn't try to talk her way out of it. She believed in this place, and she knew what she had to do."

Pepper crept closer, her eyes on Jude's reflection in the dark water so she didn't have to look at her sister's face. "What did she have to do?" she whispered.

Jude looked over at her. "She had to take her place. Become the vessel for the mountain's magic. But it's not as simple as just dying. You can't give yourself like that, it doesn't work. There's ritual to it, ceremony." She smiled faintly. "All the stuff Tabby thinks is such a waste of time."

"Ceremony?" Williams repeated. "Are you telling me Angie sacrificed herself to some death cult god up here, and that's why she died?"

His eyes were on Jude, so he missed the faint ripple in the deep, dark water. Pepper watched it distort Jude's reflection, warp it into something old. Something angry.

"There's no death cult here," said Jude softly. "And no god or goddess. This is a hell of a lot more tangible."

Williams stepped away from her, closer to the water's edge. "No death cult? But you're telling me Angie sacrificed herself to . . . what, the mountain?"

Jude kept her hands folded in front of her, her voice low. "It's not common, and certainly not often. It's only ever one woman, and it's always her choice. Most sisters live and die and never so much as spill blood for this place." She pulled the sodden sleeves of her shirt down as she spoke, but Pepper had seen her scars, many times. It was something they never spoke of. "And for the last few generations, the vessels were able to grow old, to give themselves to the mountain only once their time on earth was up."

"But because of the mine, Angie had to . . . " Pepper couldn't finish, couldn't follow the thought to its logical conclusion. She wouldn't so much as look at the inevitability of Jude's fate.

Jude nodded. "I assume so. The mine was active long before that, but not worked the way it was toward the end." She gave Pepper a sad smile. "I was pretty torn up about it. I didn't want to lose her—she was my friend. My sister, and in a lot of ways, a mother to me."

"Like you are to me," whispered Pepper, fighting the too-ready tears that burned her eyes.

Jude gave a short laugh. "I'm not half the woman Angie was. Maybe because I didn't get the chance to learn what she had to tell me. The rituals, the ceremonies—there's power in them being passed down from person to person. A long, unbroken line leading back to the very first witch to give herself to the mountain."

"I don't understand," said Williams. "If Angie killed herself for this place, then where does Maggie come into it? What does she have to do with any of this? She wasn't like you. She wasn't a witch."

Somehow it wasn't an epithet on his tongue, despite his anger and heartache. He was a good man, thought Pepper. A good man with rotten luck in romance.

Jude sighed. "Angie didn't get the chance. She never made it here. She was almost ready, but the creek was swollen, like it is now. It spilled over the banks and a couple of the sisters were stranded. Angie ran to help—she'd give anything of herself, but no way in hell would she let anyone else get hurt."

"She got to 'em, didn't she?" asked Pepper in a low voice. "I remember hearing that story. They both lived because of her."

"They did," said Jude, tonelessly. "Angie didn't. The water took her. I was right there next to her, had a hand on her skirt. I wasn't strong enough." She looked down at her empty hand, the fingers curled against phantom cloth. "In the space of a breath she was gone. The current was stronger than any of us knew." She blew out a breath, lips trembling. "Her face," she whispered. "I saw her face underwater, just for a second or two. She got trapped under deadfall, couldn't move or push it off. She knew she was drowning, and she was so scared." Jude's voice broke and she lowered her head. "I was right the hell there, and I couldn't help."

Williams stepped closer again, put a hesitant hand on Jude's shoulder. Pepper was glad—she couldn't have moved if her life depended on it. Frozen in place, horror burning in every joint. She couldn't help but picture Jude like that, trapped, drowning, with no hope of rescue. And no matter what people thought, drowning wasn't a peaceful way to go. Not by a long shot.

"I'm sorry," said Williams. "I didn't know you were with her."

Jude nodded, didn't look up. "Not something I wanted to spread around. That I was right there, and I let her die."

"You were young, Jude, barely in your twenties. It's not your fault," said Williams.

Jude spoke over him without seeming to have heard. "Anyway, with all the deaths that day, her name was just one of many. No one had time to help me look for her, and the mountain never did give her back." She looked over her shoulder at the silent pool of water. "She never took her place—I don't know where her body lies."

Pepper winced at Jude's unspoken implication. Angie's death, the death of a witch, would barely be a footnote against the town's losses.

"I still don't understand. If the mountain took Angie, why did Maggie have to . . . why did she . . . " Williams cleared his throat and fell silent.

Jude lifted a shoulder, moved to sit at the water's edge, her knees drawn up, arms resting on top. She looked so damn tired, every step a struggle. Pepper swallowed back her own guilt—she should have been helping, instead of letting her sister carry the burden alone. She'd thought she was protecting herself, protecting everyone around her, by not putting the bottle to her lips. But her weakness, her fear, meant Jude carried everything alone.

Jude sighed and brushed flyaway hairs from her face. "It didn't work. At least it didn't seem to. With Angie gone, if the ritual worked the cave-in would have stopped. Everything would have gone calm again, and I'd have been able to feel . . . " She shrugged. "Something. But I didn't. Nothing changed, and the mountain was still angry. So I knew it had to be me."

"You?" asked Williams, standing above her, frowning.

"Yeah. With Angie gone, I was next in line. I'd seen her work the ritual, knew what to do, but I was scared. Of dying, but also of being so afraid it wouldn't work."

"It has to be a willing woman," said Pepper softly.

Jude glanced up and met Pepper's eyes, then looked away. "Yes. And I could make myself die—at least I believed I could. But I couldn't kill the fear. I couldn't make myself *want* it in the way I assumed you needed to. I figured that was why Angie didn't sate her. She'd been afraid, fought to live."

Pepper wondered if anyone could truly face death without fear. She doubted she could, certainly not in circumstances of premeditation.

"And Maggie found you," said Williams, keeping his distance.

Jude didn't look up. "Yes. Maggie found me. She went to the mine first, looking for you, but she couldn't get close. It was chaos, so many miners trying to get out, rescuers trying to get in. She'd heard it, down there in town, and knew what happened. So she came looking for me, found me here."

"And you told her how she could help, is that it?"

"No," she said sharply. "I had no intention of her taking my place. I'd worked myself into a fit of indecision—I kept psyching myself up to do it, then worrying because I was afraid, and backing off so I could calm down. When she showed up, it was a reprieve for me—a brief one, anyway. I still intended to do it, but maybe a part of me hoped she'd talk me out of it. And at least I wouldn't die alone. I swear that's all it was."

"But that's not how it turned out."

Jude kept her eyes on the water. "That's right. She believed me, without hesitation."

"She always had," said Williams roughly. "She admired you. Sometimes I got the feeling she'd rather be up on this mountain learning with you than down there with me."

Jude's shoulders tightened. "Well anyway, she saw the problem immediately. Saw what a mess I was, hands shaking, breathing hard. And she sort of smiled at me, said something about me not having anyone to die for. And I didn't understand what she meant, thought she meant to say anyone to live for, and then, before I knew what she planned to do, she took the knife from the side of the pool and she did it. She slit her wrists, and threw herself into the water. She gave herself to the mountain without hesitation."

"She killed herself," said Williams hoarsely.

"Yes." Jude's voice was low and tired, and Pepper again felt out of place, an unwanted witness to what should have been a private moment. "For me."

Williams gave a harsh laugh. "No, for me. That's why. She came looking for you because she figured you had the best chance of stopping things. And when she saw what had to happen, she gave herself up so I could live."

Pepper closed her eyes against the pain in his voice, fought the rise of her own sense memories, embedded in her body by guilt. The loss of her family, the ache in her arms where her children used to rest. The heavy weight of failure. Christ, but she wanted a drink.

"I don't understand," said Williams. "You said there was a ceremony . . . a ritual. What kind of ritual?"

Jude bit her lips. "It's . . . a callback, of sorts. To the first witch whose bones were laid here. An offering of her suffering."

"Suffering?" Williams' voice broke. "She suffered?"

Jude shook her head. "No, I told you. She grabbed the knife, cut herself and went into the water. She didn't perform any of the rites."

He frowned. "So why did it work?"

Jude shrugged. "I've asked myself that, and the answer is, I don't know. Maybe there are circumstances that transcend the need. Or maybe they're only in place to calm the vessel enough to die, and Maggie didn't need that."

The silence in the cavern drew out, the tension in Pepper's body drawing ever tighter. It wasn't up to her to break it, but if no one else did soon she'd let loose the scream that built within her.

"Where's her body?" asked Williams. "Where'd you put her? Is she in the mine with all those others?"

Pepper opened her eyes and frowned. "What others?" she asked.

Jude acted like she hadn't heard her. She shook her head, eyes on Williams. "No. She's not in there."

"Then where?"

"I'd have given her back to you, if I could, Les."

Williams' tone was hard. "Where?"

Jude dropped her gaze, gestured to the surface of the dark pool with one shaking hand. "She's still here. This is where she's always been, where she'll always be. With all the women who came before her."

Pepper's eyes widened and her breath caught in her chest. She and Williams stepped close to the edge at the same time, standing a few feet apart but somehow she didn't see his reflection next to hers. She stared into the endless black depths even as she told herself there couldn't be anything left. Yet as she squinted, something rose to the surface. A pale, indecipherable blur at first, then gradually it resolved into a face. Stark white, smooth-skinned, with dark eyes. Young. Eternally young, and Pepper felt the tug of familiarity even if she couldn't place the features.

The woman's face was upturned, appearing beside Pepper's reflection on the still surface of the water. Pepper stared, forgetting to breathe, frozen by the woman. She reached a hand out slowly, leaned close over the water's edge.

"Maggie?" whispered Williams hoarsely beside her, and Pepper blinked, dropped her hand. She didn't know what he saw, whether it was the same face, and a glance at Jude showed her gaze still downward between her knees. Pepper frowned and looked back at her own reflection; her eyes drawn to the deep, dark eyes of the woman from the water.

As Pepper stared, the eyes grew larger, deepened, sunk into the pale face. The woman's jaw fell open, sagged to one side, the flesh tightening around her skull until Pepper realized all at once that was all she was looking at: a stripped skull, mouth open, the dark and endless eyes traded for pits where eyes had once been.

Pepper cursed and stumbled back a step. Dimly she heard Williams' rough cry, saw him falter, as well. Pepper scuttled to the water's edge to see once more, and her mouth fell open. What had once appeared as an onyx, glassy surface now revealed a boneyard below. Skulls, femurs, ribs, disarticulated fingers and toes, all resting at the bottom. A pool of the dead, and when Pepper glanced at the empty bottle Jude had left by the water's edge, bile rose in her throat. The special sort, the batch no one else was allowed to partake of. Made from the clear, cold water of the cavern's pool. Made from the flesh of the dead.

CHAPTER FOURTEEN

"**D**ON'T DO ANYTHING before I get back," Williams had said before leaving them there in the cavern. "I know where this whole story's leading. Give me a chance to fix this, okay?" His voice softened. "Don't do to Pepper what Angie did to you."

Jude had nodded, reached across for his hand and squeezed it. Williams tried not to feel uneasy about that nod, the unspoken promise. It came too fast, without argument, but he'd felt the same urgency she did. Time sliding away from them, worries nipping at his heels. So instead of staying where his heart wanted to be, he'd thrown himself in the truck and headed down the mountain as fast as conditions allowed.

The road back to Arnett was sodden, nearly washed out in places, and wherever he caught sight of the winding creek peeking through the underbrush, it was swollen, dark brown with swirling white caps on top. He couldn't remember ever seeing the water this high.

"I can fix this," he said under his breath, at least twenty times during the solitary drive. Every time the mud gave way and the truck slid close to a drop off. Every time the tires got stuck and he had to get out and push, his clothes a mess of water and muck.

Every time he thought of Jude fading into the darkness, joining Maggie in burning shadows.

"I can fix this."

His words lost force with each repetition, doubts creeping in the closer he got to Arnett. What if he was too late? What if something had already happened to Tabby? Would Jude ever forgive him for walking away from the girl before? Would he forgive himself? He fought a cresting wave of fear, not just for the sisters, but for the whole town. His home, since the day he was born. He felt the weight of wasted years, of time spent frozen in limbo, pining for a second chance.

"Shit!" He stomped the brakes, fought the truck's crazy fishtail. He'd almost seen it too late—a rushing stream had broken loose from the creek proper, flowing across the road and cutting him off from town. He sat breathing hard, wondering what the hell to do. His truck couldn't ford the water—even if it wasn't as deep as it looked, he could see from here the current was too strong.

He narrowed his eyes, squinted through the windshield. Arnett was just visible on the horizon, the fitful flicker of torches already lit to fend off the early nightfall.

Except it wasn't nighttime—not yet. And no one in their right mind would bother setting torches in this weather—they'd fizzle right out. He leaned closer, studying the way the lights were concentrated, a sense of unease growing in his gut. He'd have to walk the rest of the way, and something told him he ought to do it fast. He set his jaw and threw his door open to the wind and driving rain. The handle was torn from his fingers and the door swung wide, soaking the truck's interior. It didn't matter, there was no time. He left the truck and wiped water from his eyes, looking for a place to cross the stream. He had to head back the way he'd come, twenty or thirty yards away where the water was narrow enough, pushing through wet trees to get there. He almost didn't make it, twice slipping on unseen rocks and dunking himself, and once getting his foot stuck under a fallen tree limb. Once he was across, he took off for Arnett at a run.

When he got close enough, his stomach sunk. His eyes hadn't deceived him—the flickering torches he'd seen from afar were concentrated in one spot, protected by the overhang of the second story above. Held high by shaking hands and illuminating angry faces. All of them gathered just outside the last place Williams wanted to see them: the jail.

CHAPTER FIFTEEN

TABBY BLINKED BLEARY eyes against the sight that awaited her, should she be fool enough to step foot outside the sheriff's door. The chest-tightening terror that should accompany it was blunted by the bourbon she'd drunk, else she'd barely have been able to stand. What looked to be the entire town stood out there, torches in hand. At least one citizen gripped a coil of rope, and Tabby knew that didn't bode well for her, even the state she was in.

"Hell's bells," she whispered, lifting the nearly empty bottle to her lips.

Ison pushed her hand down before it got there. "That's about enough of that, Miss Tabby."

She glared and turned on him, straightening out her swaying body on the second try. "Bullshit, Sheriff. I done told you, this is how it works. The whiskey's part of it."

He sighed and put his hands on his hips. "So you say. And I took your word for it, but I haven't seen any sign that it's helping a damn thing, and you're gonna want your wits about you."

Tabby twisted her lips. "You gonna throw me to that mob?"

Ison frowned. "Mob?"

Deputy Chellgren stood close to the window on the far side of the cell, where he was less visible peering out. "Been getting bigger. Gotta be at least half the damn town out there now, and they don't look too happy."

Ison frowned, pushing Tabby behind him as he went to look. "Well, fuck," he whispered. He drew back too late to avoid being seen, and a rumble of anger rose from the walkway beyond the door.

"Sheriff," called a shrill voice that raised the hairs on the back of his neck. "We've come for the witch."

Ison glanced at Chellgren. "Is that Beth Helstrom?"

The man nodded. "She don't look like she's slept or eaten. Got a look in her eye I don't much like."

Ison crept to Brian's window and looked again. From the changed angle it took him a minute to find her face, and when he did, he sucked in a breath. Chellgren was right—it wasn't just the fitful burn of torchlight or the shadows cast by the endless rain. Beth Helstrom had the fire of zeal in her eyes, the reddened spark of righteous anger. Ison wasn't sure when the mood had changed in Arnett, but the widow had found a target for her pain and ire, and she wasn't alone.

"Sheriff," came the voice again, high and hard. "We know the witch is in there. Bring her out and we won't have a problem."

Ison narrowed his eyes and looked beyond Beth, gauging the crowd behind her. The sisters were well-known in Arnett, and for the most part well-liked. People knew which side their bread was buttered on, and setting aside the steady supply of liquor currently denied the rest of the country, it was a rare resident who hadn't had cause to use one of their cures. He had himself, more than once. His mother too, and likely his grandmother and every generation on back. That was part of why he hadn't pushed harder with Jude that morning on the mountain. In spite of her cagey demeanor, he believed her to be a good woman at heart. Had the winds changed that quickly, or was it simply folks getting caught up in Beth's grief and their own fear? He couldn't tell. A few of the ones closer to the front had that same light in their eyes, a cruel curve to their lips to match the widow's own. But many of his neighbors looked hesitant, or downright scared. He might have a chance to defuse this, at least long enough to get Tabby back up the mountain. If she'd agree to go.

He glanced over his shoulder to where the young woman stood, slumped against the far wall, away from the window. Her lids were heavy over reddened eyes, her mouth half open, two seconds from snoring. He wished now he'd let Les Williams take her when he'd had the chance. He was an idiot for believing she could help. It had made a certain kind of sense, that the liquor had something to do with it—most of the other cures were infused as well, so why not other forms of . . . not magic, exactly, but whatever Jude and the other sisters did up there. But Tabby had only gotten drunker and more resentful. She had an ax to grind, as became obvious over the course of the afternoon. Ison didn't blame her for wanting acceptance, a normal life, but right now he'd be lucky to get her out of there unharmed.

"Go and check the back door," he muttered to his deputy. "Make damn sure it's locked, and stay back there. I want to know if anyone tries to get in that way."

Brian nodded, pushed away from the wall. He turned at the entrance to the back hall and frowned at his boss. "This gonna get violent? I mean, these are . . . they're just people. Folks we've known our whole lives."

Ison pressed his lips together. "They've known the sisters their whole lives, too. Sometimes that doesn't save you."

Brian looked pale, swallowing hard, but he did as he was told.

Ison straightened, smoothed his uniform shirt. He was letting the same wave of fear carry him, making enemies of neighbors, dire situations out of what should be easily contained. He took a deep breath, but stumbled and cut off a scream when Tabby grabbed his arm. She'd been so quiet he'd almost forgotten she was there, but now she held tight to him, swaying but holding his gaze.

"You gonna throw me to 'em?" she asked again, her jaw set, fingers curling around the neck of that damn bottle.

He pulled away from her. "I'm not throwing anyone anywhere. We're gonna sort this out. Stay outta sight, hear me?"

For a beat or two it seemed she wasn't going to obey, but then she lowered her eyes and shuffled back behind his desk, sliding to the floor.

Ison breathed out, put a hand on the butt of his gun then thought better of it. He needed to tone things down, not stir them up.

He eased open the front door and stepped out, closing it quickly behind him. "Evening, folks. Sure are a lot of you out in this rain." He looked around the semi-circle of shadowed faces, making eye contact wherever he could. He was relieved to see gazes drop, a couple of hesitant smiles in return.

"We're not here to talk about the weather," said the widow, pulling herself straighter. One dirt-covered hand clutched a torch, the other fondled the rough cross at her neck. "We're here for the witch. Bring her to us and you can go on about your business."

Ison lifted his hands, palms out. "Beth, I have every sympathy for what you're going through. What you've lost . . . it's staggering, and no one expects you to be okay. But what happened to your family is not Tabby's fault. It's not anyone's fault, and taking it out on her or anyone else isn't gonna bring them back."

"Maybe not," she said, her upper lip curling. "But it'll stop anyone else getting hurt. How many people have to go missing before you'll do something, Ison? How many people have to die?"

His response died on his lips, his mouth at half cock, breath frozen in his chest. A shadow wavered at the edge of the crowd, deeper and darker than the others, full night set against gray dusk. It could have been anything, anyone. Just another figure behind the others, out of his direct sight line, cast in relief by flickering torches. But it wasn't. The shadow was too still, too *present*. Now he'd seen it he couldn't tear his attention from it, until its eyes lit with fire. It was wrong, that flame, reflecting a suffering he felt deep in his bones. He choked on a breath, stepped back, a move which caused the mob to surge forward. Ison felt the intense heat of flame near his face and hoped it was only a torch he felt. Anything would be preferable to those burning eyes.

Before he could speak the ground trembled beneath his feet. He staggered against a wave of vertigo, his whole body off kilter. He grabbed for the door behind him, tried to steady himself, waiting for the tremor to pass. Each time it had happened, the last few weeks, it filled him with dread, made the whole town hold its breath. This time it didn't stop.

The world tilted. Wooden planks rose beneath his feet, knocking him sideways before buckling and breaking. There should have been ground beneath, but instead the earth yawned open. Ison teetered on the side of it, his gaze locked on a pit to nowhere, barely noticing when people on the other side of the chasm tumbled in, screaming. He pushed himself back as hard as he could, over-corrected to fall back on his ass. It hurt, several thick splintered chunks piercing his flesh, but it was a damned sight better than pitching forward.

His relief was short-lived. The ground continued to rumble, to move beneath him. A feeling like water trickling beneath his legs, or of a thousand tiny insects running over his flesh then falling away. The edge of the hole in the earth crumbled, expanded. *Breathed.*

It rose up to reach for him, grasping, the hungry ground opening wide. The dirt dropped from beneath his palms where he tried to scramble away, and he pitched backward, arms and shoulders dangling in space. He fought and hoped, believing he would either free himself, or a hand would reach for his at the last second, pulling him to safety.

No hand appeared, and the gash in the ground widened, sucking him in.

The last thing he saw as he tumbled into endless nothing were two fire bright eyes watching from above.

CHAPTER SIXTEEN

ARNETT TREMBLED ON the precipice of its destruction. Williams could see that even as he ran—the ground hadn't ceased trembling, and as he watched, whole buildings tilted impossibly before disappearing from sight, right into the ground with no trace they'd ever been there.

Screams rent the hazy air, cries to God and to mothers either long gone or unable to help. Some even beseeched the mountain and Williams gritted his teeth. They had no idea it was the mountain come to collect her debt.

He couldn't think too hard about the ache in his chest he felt each time he felt the ground giving way. It stirred memories of the day Maggie died, the day he *should* have died. The way death had swept toward him underground with no way out of its path. He'd done his best over the intervening decades to forget, not to let it live in his nightmares, but he'd never quite outrun it. And now he was running toward it.

When he reached the town limits he pulled up, frozen. The scene was chaos—yawning holes opened in the earth, people teetering on the edges, some hanging on by ragged nails, slipping ever closer. Screams and a deep, rising reverberation that made his back and teeth ache. The groan and crack of wooden frames and planks, the crackle of fire from dropped or thrown torches swelled the cacophony. And over it all the ceaseless rain, dripping into his eyes, turning everything into an unstable, sodden mess. It wasn't that there was no one he could help, as he'd feared: there were too many to help, and he froze with indecision. He needed to get to Tabby, stop whatever Beth Helstrom had planned for her—Jude would expect it of him. But he couldn't simply walk past people suffering, crying out for help.

He knelt at the edge of the pit closest to him, recoiling at first from unexpected heat rising from within and the stench of sulfur. A young woman held onto a root with bleeding hands, her feet dangling and kicking, unable to gain purchase on the muddy walls beside her. Williams bent and grasped her under her arms, his hands too slick from the rain to effectively hold her hands. He pulled her to safety and all but threw her to the side, pushing himself back fast to avoid the still widening hole.

The woman sat sobbing, fire reflected in her gaze in a way that made him go cold. "Get out," he said, leaning in so she could hear him. "Out of town, as far as you can. Take anyone else you can find."

"Where?" she asked, her teeth chattering from shock and the sudden change of temperature now she was free of the burning earth. "Where is safe?"

Williams looked over his shoulder, up at the ever-present shadow. He had no reason to believe the mountain was any safer than anywhere else, but it was all he had. Torment seemed to have no limits down here in the valley—Jude mentioned the McPhersons going missing, and they were well beyond the outskirts of Arnett, past where anyone fleeing on foot could get.

He armed rain from his eyes and pointed up. "Get to higher ground, but watch yourself. Nowhere is sacred." He felt the deeper truth of his words—nowhere was sacred because they'd violated it, over and over.

She nodded and pushed to her feet, took off running. He was glad to see her stop and take a young boy by the arm, pull him in her wake. Williams stood and scanned the gathering darkness, looking for that grouping of torches, for the sheriff's office. But nothing was where it should be. There were great gaps where buildings were only hours ago, and other places where real estate had been turned on its side, redeposited. He couldn't tell which direction was which, and so he set out on the most likely path, stopping to help those he could as he went.

All the while he felt her at his nape. Maggie, or whatever she'd become, following close, keeping to the shadows. It made his flesh creep. He didn't want to look, didn't want to see those eyes of fire anymore. What did it mean, those flames looking back at him? Maggie hadn't died by fire, if he could believe Jude. He fought the urge to turn and face the threat. It wouldn't help anything. Wouldn't change anything. What followed him had its own agenda, one of retribution and death. How many lives would it take to regain the balance between nature and man? If the death of a single woman every twenty or fifty years was enough to appease the mountain, why now was it still so angry? But he knew the answer. The mountain would not value any life that was taken and not given freely. He couldn't think about that too hard, couldn't face the likelihood of what was happening back in that cavern. He couldn't look back—not at Maggie, and not at Jude.

"Let me go, you fuckin' nutters! Whole town's burning down and you think you need to add to it?"

Williams stopped, recognizing Tabby's voice. She sounded angry rather than scared, filled with the fury that came naturally to her, and he allowed himself to hope she was okay. But when he climbed over a waist-high pile of debris and she came into view, his breath caught in his chest.

It was a sight that belonged to another place, another time. Centuries ago, and across an ocean, for Williams knew no witch had been burned on American soil, only hanged. But there, next to what had once been the sheriff's office and jail, rose a pole two stories high. With effort he recognized it as the flagpole, though no flag waved from it now. Instead, the base of it bristled with chunks of wood, much of which appeared to have been taken from the town's buildings as it suffered its death throes. Tied above the bonfire waiting to happen was Tabby, her hands behind her back, blood flowing freely from her nose and mouth.

And at the ground below her, clutching a torch that sputtered in the rain, stood the widow Helstrom.

CHAPTER SEVENTEEN

PEPPER WATCHED WITH numb fascination as Jude laid out the instruments of her own destruction. She felt sick in some far-off place, unreachable to her now behind the wall of disassociation. Ill with the chafing need to *do* something, to stop this. It was insane, archaic. Brutal and surely unnecessary. Jude shouldn't need to die for the mountain and its magic, and even if she did, she didn't need to die hard. But the implements she laid out with chilling calm promised a very hard death indeed.

"Jude," croaked Pepper finally, shuffling closer on her knees, wincing but not shying away from the sting and ache of stones and grit through the fabric of her jeans. "Jude, there's another way. There has to be another way."

Jude looked up and smiled, a warm smile that made Pepper's chest ache. Jude tested the edge of a gleaming knife with what appeared to be a bone handle. Pepper shuddered, knowing it was almost certainly human. How could she have been so blind to what this place was?

The long knife opened a paper-thin cut on Jude's thumb and she laid it atop a flat stone next to flint and steel, a small wooden bowl, a straight razor, and an old, fraying rope.

"Jude," Pepper tried again, but Jude spoke as though she hadn't heard.

"It's nuts, isn't it? To think how many bones lay at the bottom of that pool. How many women's bodies have fed it."

Pepper cleared her throat. "Nuts is one word for it. And here you are, getting ready to add to the tally."

Jude lifted one shoulder. "A drop in the bucket."

Pepper scooted close enough to take the other woman's shoulders. "Not to me. Not to every sister on this mountain. And not to Williams."

Jude sighed and patted Pepper's hand, not trying to pull away from her white knuckled grip. "I do feel bad about that. That man has terrible luck. He ought to have married again, a long time ago."

Pepper let her go and sat back on her heels. "He would've, if you'd said yes."

Jude shook her head. "My place was here." She looked around, the strain around her eyes easing as she took it in. "Now it always will be."

Pepper gave a hysterical laugh that choked off abruptly. "Guess at least we'll always know where to find you."

Jude looked at her, a frown darkening her features. "Not "we." You, and only you, do you understand me? It's important."

"Why? Why is any of this the way it is? Do you even know, or are you blindly following some stupid, made-up fable meant to keep you in line? How is that any better than any other man-made religion?"

Jude smiled again. "There you have it. Man made. By men. But this mountain, the magic that lives here, courses through its veins with more strength than any mineral—it wasn't created by men, and it didn't come with a set of rules."

Pepper stared wildly at the altar of torture Jude had created. "If there aren't any rules, then what the hell is all this?"

Jude looked down at her lap. "I guess it's more akin to making bourbon. The way we do it, the ingredients we use, the construction of the still, even the barrels we store it in—you wouldn't call those rules, would you? It's a recipe, based on generations of trial and error. It's what works."

Pepper looked away, her whole body trembling with need for a drink. If ever there was a time to hit the bottle, surely this was it. Then Jude stood and all other thoughts fell away.

"No, don't—you can't leave me yet. You haven't told me anything. What about when it's my turn? How will I know?"

Jude bent to kiss her cheek. "I'll tell you now." She straightened, then turned her back and began to undress. "No one knows how old the magic here is." She'd slipped into her storyteller voice, and Pepper could almost believe they were sitting around a campfire, letting Jude weave tales of the old days.

"No one knows how old the mountain even is, or which came first. Doesn't much matter, I guess—it was here before us, and it'll be here when we're gone. But the history we do know . . . that starts with a young Scottish woman named Elizabeth."

Pepper's hands shook, her mouth dry. Every word Jude spoke, every move she made brought her closer to death, and Pepper couldn't think how to stop it. "Elizabeth?" she said breathlessly. "Who the hell is that?"

"We don't know her surname. Don't know much about her at all, really. Not her life, anyway. But we know plenty about her death."

Pepper looked again at the knife, the razor. The things that would hurt her friend, take her away. "Was she a witch?"

Jude shrugged, then bent to slide her pants off. "Who knows? At that time it didn't take much to find yourself at the end of a rope, or feet first to a fire. The end result was the same. Elizabeth was executed overseas. She was cut, burned, and ultimately strangled."

"And what the hell does that have to do with us, here? You said she was from Scotland, that she died over there."

Jude straightened, fully nude now. She folded her clothes as she spoke.

"Yes, that's right. But her sisters had no intention of leaving her there. They were furious and heartsick about what happened to her. The pain, the unfairness. The indignity." She laid aside the clothes and knelt again by the alter, seeming not to notice the bite of the rocks against her unprotected flesh. "So they took her and they fled, all the way across the ocean. I don't know if they sought out the Backbone, or if this is just where they ended up."

"Took her? You said she died."

"She did. They took her bones, the flesh still binding them together. They brought her to this place, and they buried her where she could be at peace. No one knows if there was magic here before that—I suspect there was. This is a big range, and there've been stories for so long. But this offering, the body of a woman who suffered yet still was given back to the earth—it changed things. Strengthened them. The sisters decided to stay, to live out their days where they could keep Elizabeth close."

Pepper looked down between her knees, numb. "So that's our creation myth, huh?"

Jude laughed. "If you like. I happen to believe it. If you'd seen what I have in the time I've been on this mountain—"

"Yeah, well I didn't, did I?" Pepper interrupted. "No one has, because you won't let anyone help you. You've worn yourself nearly to death trying to fix this by yourself, and now things are as bad as they can be."

Jude frowned but didn't look at her, her gaze on the water. "Yes, you're right. I've made a lot of mistakes. I know that, but it's too late. This is all that's left, and if I can do it right . . . " She trailed off, still staring at the dark surface.

Pepper hoped for a brief and breathless moment that Jude would change her mind. Would back away from this precipice and find another way. Then she reached for the bone handled knife, grabbed the long braid at her shoulder and sliced through it, close enough to her scalp to make her bleed.

Pepper gasped, a visceral pain at the sudden loss of what wasn't even hers. Jude laid the braid aside, next to the length of old rope. She traded the knife for the razor, turned the pages of a book at her side, and began to carve the flesh of her thigh.

Pepper screamed and reached for her, made to take the blade from her, but found she somehow couldn't. Her arms were heavy, her body responding only sluggishly to her commands.

"What I need you to know, to remember," hissed Jude through gritted teeth as her flesh split beneath the razor, the edges of her skin spreading wide, spilling blood in rivers. "Is that there is always a choice. Your choice. You don't have to choose the same path, and even if you do, you don't have to die for it. I never planned to. And who knows, maybe I'd have left this place if Maggie hadn't died. Maybe it was guilt that kept me here, but it doesn't much matter now."

"Jude," Pepper moaned as the other woman's body became a map of blood and suffering. A reflection of what had been inflicted on those who came before. Did it help anything? Repeating that hurt, keeping it alive? Jude stopped every so often to let blood flow into the wooden bowl, squeezing her sliced flesh to get the most from it. Pepper shuddered and looked away until she heard the click of metal on stone.

Finished with the razor, Jude set it aside, great gobs of flesh stuck there in the blood. She struck the flint and fire bloomed. Something was at work here, keeping Pepper in place, feeding a flame that needed no fuel. Pepper watched as Jude held her hand over it, close enough that the smell of burning flesh filled the cavern. Jude's eyes were wet, her teeth bared, but still she took the pain. And in them Pepper saw that flame reflected, the same fire every woman burned as a witch faced in their final moments. The fire of the stake.

"You don't have to drink, either. It's part of it, at least I've always understood it to be. But maybe that's one of those rules you were talking about before. I know what the drink cost you, and how hard it's been to find your way back." She raised her gaze to Pepper's, her face reminding Pep too much of the face in the water. Had it been Elizabeth? Angie? Any of the other women who'd died through the centuries? Did they all become the same, in the end?

With a gasp, Jude pulled her hand away, the flesh of it blackened, splitting to show deep red between her fingers. Painfully she took the rope and eased it over her head, her burned hand almost useless. Pepper looked wildly around the cavern—there was nowhere to tie the noose, no way for Jude to hang herself as she seemed intent on doing.

Jude smiled and met Pepper's eyes, seeming to read her mind. "It's that ritual I was telling you about. I can't replicate Elizabeth's suffering, not really. These things are a stand-in for that." She touched her good hand to the rope burn that stood out on her flesh. "I've done what I could to alleviate her pain, but this requires more."

Relief spread through Pepper's body. Ritual. A stand-in. Surely that meant Jude didn't have to die—not for real.

Jude knelt before her and took Pepper's face between her hands. Heat from the burned one singed Pepper's skin and the stench of cooked meat filled her nostrils, ruined flesh crumbling against her cheek. "Whatever choices you make, Pepper, I need you to do one thing for me. Don't let them take me from here, do you understand? Here's where I have to stay."

Pepper could only whimper as Jude stood, walked to the edge of the water. She looked over her shoulder one last time, gave Pepper a smile and a wink. "Remember. This is my body and my blood, given freely. And not for anyone but myself."

She raised her unscathed hand swiftly to her throat and slid the knife across it in one sweeping movement. Blood surged to the surface, her eyes rolled back in her head, and she fell forward into the dark water without a splash or so much as a ripple.

Beneath Pepper's knees, the earth trembled.

CHAPTER EIGHTEEN

"**Y**OU HAVE TO stop this," called Williams to the widow, afraid to move any closer. As soon as he'd tried, Beth had held the torch to Tabby's unprotected foot and her howls kept him in place after that. He'd seen the flame reflected in the girl's eyes, and for a frozen moment was convinced Maggie had somehow taken her over.

But that wasn't it, was it? The similarity was only surface-deep, binding the women in a sisterhood of those who'd suffered at the hands of those who believed they had the right to judge. Jude said Maggie hadn't suffered, that she hadn't felt the lick of that fire, but Williams wondered what his wife had seen and felt as her body descended to the depths of that dark lake.

"I *am* stopping this," Beth said, her back straight, the light of zeal in her eyes. She bore little resemblance to the broken woman he'd seen at the funeral—she'd found a new sense of purpose. "I'm putting a stop to *everything*. The sins of the witches have put us all in danger, and if no one else will save us, I will."

She turned her gaze on Tabby again, her teeth bared, the fire making shadows on her face, turning her monstrous. She really believed she was doing God's work, Williams thought, his body going cold in the ceaseless rain. This wouldn't be like talking down a rowdy drunk, or a matter of helping her through her grief to the other side. Beth Helstrom was on a mission and would not be turned from her purpose.

Without dropping her gaze, she lowered the torch to Tabby's other foot, holding it closer than the last time. Tabby screamed and her skin began to smoke, the flesh reddening and cracking in the space of seconds.

Williams stood frozen, the horror of the situation shutting down his brain. He had to stop this—setting aside his promise to

Jude, he couldn't stand by and watch a young woman burned for the gratification of a vengeful God.

A few moans and the sound of retching came from the crowd behind the waiting bonfire. Williams saw they'd stepped back almost as a whole, distancing themselves from what was about to happen. Hope lifted his heart—Beth might be unreachable, but it wasn't as though all of Arnett had been taken over by religious fervor. The fact that the town had never been raided by the U.S. Marshals was proof enough that no one had snitched on Jude and her sisters. He couldn't let fear turn his neighbors to strangers.

"Folks," he called above the sounds of rain, fire, and screams of the damned. "This isn't us. This isn't Arnett. We've survived a lot worse than a little rain, because we stood together. That's what country folk do—I've always been proud of that." He couldn't tell if he was getting through, but no one made any moves to set flame to the kindling. "We can't sentence a young woman to death. She's not responsible for the tragedies that have befallen us, but even if she was, this isn't how it works. You want Ison to look into it, then you ask, but you don't carry out executions."

"Ison's dead," called a male voice from the shadows. "Gone the way of half the town, straight into hell. You telling us that doesn't have biblical connotations?"

The knowledge that Ison was gone sunk Williams' stomach. Aside from the grief of losing another friend, Ison was a reasonable man who had the respect of Arnett. Williams had garnered a lot of goodwill during his life, but he was no replacement for the sheriff.

"Fuck your bible," cried Tabby in a voice cracked from screaming. Beth had removed the flame from her flesh for now, but the sight of her burnt and mangled foot made bile rise in Williams' throat. She'd never walk on it again, and the stupidity of it all was almost overwhelming. He had to tamp down his own fury, his disgust at torture in the name of God. There would be time for that later—for now he had to keep calm. If Tabby wanted to set her own torch to Beth Helstrom on down the road, he'd light the damn thing for her.

"Blasphemy!" screeched the widow, flinging herself forward until Williams managed to get between her and the girl. "Get out of my way, Les Williams, or I will cut you down, too."

Tabby wasn't done. "Cram it up your ass when you're done, lady. You live by your rules and I'll live by mine—you ain't got the right to hurt people like this."

"Tabby, honey, please, let me get you out of this," Williams said over his shoulder, desperation threatening to take over.

"*Hurt* people?" said Beth. "You've hurt more people than I can count, you and the rest of the Devil's brides. You've broken up families, destroyed lives. My family is dead because of you."

Tabby panted; her teeth gritted against the pain in her foot. "Your family's dead because your husband was a no good fuckin' *drunk*."

"How *dare* you?" screamed the widow, leaning past Williams to press fire to Tabby's calf. Williams pushed her back, hard, the hair on his arms crisping and curling away as they passed too close to the torch, still burning somehow in the pouring rain. It wasn't natural, and Williams' sense of unease grew.

"Beth, please," he said, trying to keep hold of her arms. "Don't do this."

She brandished the torch in his face and his eyes stung, drying instantly in the heat, his skin tightening. He had no choice but to let her go, but pushed as he did in the hopes of increasing the distance between them.

"People are dying because of *you*," snarled the widow. "This rain ain't natural, and all of you know it. Things have been happening, unnatural things."

Tabby howled with manic laughter. "You think rain is *unnatural*? If brains was gunpowder, you wouldn't have enough to blow your damn nose."

"The rain is from God," called another voice from the crowd, though Williams couldn't tell who the speaker was. He stood, breathing hard, waiting to see what direction this might sway the crowd.

"That's right," said Beth, her mouth puckered tight. "Sent from God to cleanse the world of sin, as he did in the time of Noah."

Murmurs spread through those gathered and Williams tensed.

"We have no ark," she continued, playing to the crowd now. "No way to save ourselves except to rid the world of those who've cursed us for far too long. The earth is swallowing us whole—what more proof do you need?"

"Proof," said Tabby, giving vent to another hysterical laugh. "You call that proof? You're a loon, lady. Now get me the fuck down before I make this a whole lot worse."

Beth laughed. "You're in no position to threaten me—the Lord protects his faithful."

Tabby, panting between clenched teeth, lowered her head as much as her bindings allowed. "And the Devil protects his brides."

There were several gasps and Williams closed his eyes, feeling the tide turn against them. "Wait, please," he said, holding his hands up again, moving to keep his body between Tabby and the mob. "She's not being serious, that's not how it works. She's in pain, terrified. She doesn't know what she's saying."

"Fuck you, Williams, I ain't afraid of shit. Now *let me down.*"

Everything went still in the wake of her words. He realized the ground had ceased shifting, the otherworldly growl of buildings rising, breaking apart, falling into the abyss, had stopped. There were no screams, only the rain and the flicker of firelight. Yet the atmosphere felt heavy, oppressive. He was getting air, but it felt like concrete in his chest. His ears popped and he struggled against a compulsion to drop to his knees in the mud.

"What's happening?" someone asked in a high voice.

"It's the work of Satan," called Beth, unmoved from her path of righteous cruelty. "We've lived in the shadow of the Devil's Backbone our whole lives—is anyone truly surprised to find these *women* have given him a toehold?"

Williams would have laughed if he'd had the strength. The name of the mountain range was just that—a name. There had always been stories about the place, but that didn't make it evil. He realized as he struggled to stay upright that everything Jude had said about balance made perfect sense. It fit with the feel of his home, with the observable effects of the sisters on the natural world.

He felt something brush his nose, patter his head and shoulders. Slow, drifting movement in his peripheral vision drew his attention, and something white dotted the ground beneath him. Something settled softly in his hair, and he reached up to see what had fallen upon him.

He frowned at the little thing pinched lightly between his fingers. He squinted, brought it close to his face. It wasn't fully white, he saw—there were black marks all through it. Words, he realized as his vision focused.

Shreds of paper continued to fall on the town like snow, muffling all sound. Others reached up in wonder, catching a piece, frowning as they stared down at what they held.

Many of the words were truncated or torn in half. Out of

context he could make no sense of them. He bent to gather more pieces, to see if they fit together in any kind of meaningful pattern. A few others did the same. Williams had no luck, but a minute later he heard someone say: "Mineral rights?" in a puzzled tone.

Before he could confirm the words, the ground shuddered once more. He bent his knees, braced to stand against the crazy tilt of the earth, but nothing happened. Another thud, followed slowly by a third, and Williams went still. It sounded like footsteps, of something heavy, approaching in dragging slow motion.

Someone screamed and he whipped his head around, saw a nightmare on legs approaching them from the direction of the mountain. It was a man, yet only in the loosest sense of the word. His steps did not match up with the booming impact—instead his ankles were bent as though they were boneless, his feet trailing behind him. His mouth hung open, black and squirming mud oozing from both sides, a purple tongue swinging beneath its chin. His head was bent unnaturally far to the left, and more mud leaked from his ear. Something thick with many legs dangled from the lobe before dropping onto the man's shoulder and disappearing beneath his sodden collar.

When the figure stopped at the edge of the firelight, Williams gasped. He recognized that slack and empty visage—it was Dan Boots, the boy who'd left Arnett to make his fortune, then returned a man in an attempt to scrape it from his hometown. Who, last Williams saw him, was lying dead in Jude's mine alongside four other corpses.

"Mineral rights," he said, the pieces clicking together. Boots had blasted out of town in a miff when Jude denied him what he wanted, but Williams had heard one or two people mention seeing him recently.

"*Blasphemer...*" croaked a wet and glottal voice from the dead man's throat, though his sagging mouth did not move. "*You have desecrated that which does not belong to you.*"

Mineral rights, Williams thought again. He looked up, held his hand out flat to catch more drifting flakes of damnation. These were contracts, deeds, shredded small, but the words within could not be taken back so easily. He groaned, feeling hope leach from his heart. He'd had some unacknowledged idea that he could save Jude, prove to her she didn't have to sacrifice anything, that the mountain could be appeased without her blood. With the mine closed off, protected by Jude, the land should have been allowed to heal, the mountain left in peace to lick her wounds and keep her secrets.

But Boots being here, that proved how wrong he'd been. Boots had found another way to pierce the veins that ran beneath the Devil's Backbone—he'd conned half of Arnett into selling off the mineral rights to their land, if the volume of drifting paper were any indication.

"What have you done?" Williams said in a low voice, addressing the question to no one and everyone. He didn't expect an answer, but a shaking voice came from the dark, and he recognized Rick Larkin.

"It did belong to me," he said, his shaking hands at his sides, slips of sodden paper clutched between his fingers. "It's . . . it was my land, and my rights. I had every right to sell it. I didn't know what he meant to do . . . " His voice broke and he lowered his head.

Wind gusted through the town, snuffing each fire as one. The torch Beth held, somehow unaffected by the torrents from heaven, went low, then died out in silence. No light penetrated the darkness of the night. No sound came from the heavy silence that blanketed Williams, and a primordial fear of the dark overwhelmed him. For in the darkness, he was alone. They all were.

"Tabby?" he called, but his words carried no sound, and there was no response. Had he gone deaf?

Panic gripped him in the absence of sensory input, and he felt himself losing control inch by inch. He wanted to run, to pound through the darkness until he found someone, anyone to share it with. Then a blast of heat flared behind him, scorching his back, and he turned to face what dwelt in the dark.

Two flaming eyes stared at him from perfect night, illuminating the proud tilt of his dead wife's chin. Fire that danced as it licked at the feet of doomed women, creeping up splintered stakes to split their flesh and boil their brains.

"Maggie," he breathed, hope dying hard.

CHAPTER NINETEEN

THE DEAD WOMAN gave no sign she'd heard her name on his lips. Instead she watched him from inky blackness and his gaze traveled down, catching glimpses now and then of a graceful shoulder, an arm, the swell of her hip. She stood naked and all he could do was tremble before her. She wasn't his Maggie. She belonged to the mountain now.

"Shed no tears for me," came a low, hissing voice. One moment it sounded like running water, the next like a serpent threatening to strike. "I chose this fate willingly."

Grief flooded Williams' heart and he dropped his head. "Because of me."

"Because it needed to be done."

"Balance," he said hollowly.

"Yes."

The silence stretched between them, and still Williams could not make out any other sounds or sight anyone beyond the tiny circle of fiery light from her eyes.

"I made my choice. I'm giving you the chance to make yours."

Williams looked up and met her eyes. "What choice?"

"You know what will happen next."

His breathing went shallow. "Is there no chance to save them?"

The eyes didn't move. "Not for those who have damned the rest of you."

"And everyone else?"

"That depends on you. They have no right to life, no virtue that sets them above any other living thing on this earth. If you choose to save them, you may. It makes no difference to the mountain."

He frowned, shook his head in an attempt to clear the pressure between his ears. "I don't understand. I thought you *were* the mountain now."

"I am the vessel. The Backbone will have its way, whatever you choose." His cheeks stung when those fiery eyes moved closer to his. "It will be bad. And you cannot save her—she is already gone. I feel her—she is one with us."

He wanted to ask who she meant, but he knew. There was no reason to utter Jude's name between them. Grief threatened to overwhelm him, pushing from behind his eyes, creeping over his heart. He pushed it back. "I don't . . . if she's gone, if she gave herself willingly, then why hasn't all this stopped? Why is it going to be bad?"

Maggie turned away and he saw only one flame in profile. "Balance is not restored so easily, once things have gone so far. They have taken it from us, and we must take it back. Blood for blood."

She was gone on the last syllable, and the rest of the world faded back in for Williams. The freezing rain and acrid smoke slapped into him, awakening him from his stupor, and he stared at a scene that remained frozen. He looked around the tableau—Tabby with her head thrown back, arched in pain or defiance. Beth Helstrom with her teeth bared once more, her hatred focused on the bound girl, the torch still clutched in one hand. The shadowed faces of the crowd, all focused on the walking horror that had once been Dan Boots. Was this his choice? Was this his chance to turn his back on everything about to happen, to save himself and his sanity? He was sorely tempted. People like Beth Helstrom and Rick Larkin didn't deserve the sacrifices made by women for generations. Leave them all to Maggie's mercy—that was fair.

It was also irrelevant. Williams didn't want to become judge, jury, and executioner. That made him no better than them, so he straightened his shoulders and breathed. He wasn't going anywhere.

CHAPTER TWENTY

THE SILENT TABLEAU surged to life, Beth Helstrom screaming and setting her torch to the wood at Tabby's feet.

"No!" cried Williams, lunging for the girl, but he didn't need to. The fire, so content to burn at the end of Helstrom's torch, would not catch to the sodden timber surrounding Tabby.

"What?" panted Beth, turning the torch to look at the end of it. As she did, the fire rose, bursting forth and licking her face. She howled and dropped the torch, covering her face with both arms.

Tabby laughed high and shrill above her. "Did karma just bite you in the ass, bitch?"

Rick Larkin stepped forward, whether to help the widow or take to his heels, Williams would never know. The ground beneath his feet opened all at once, a neat circle of nothing just big enough to swallow the man. He screamed as he . . . struggled for purchase on footing that no longer existed, shrieked when he dropped from sight, then gave a clotted gargling as the dirt reformed around him, covering his mouth and nose. The top of Larkin's head was visible, and a single hand protruded. The man's fingers opened and closed, clawed at the suffocating earth, but he could not free himself, and what remained of Arnett watched as he struggled, sucking in dirt and worms in place of air. It took a long time for him to die, and Williams remained riveted until Larkin's fingers gave a final twitch, and he went still.

"That's what you get!" cried Tabby. "That's what you *get* you fuckers!"

Her words brought Williams back to himself and he turned, went to her side. "Come on, let's get you down from there," he said in an urgent undertone, hoping like hell the crowd was too frozen to pay attention.

Tabby barely noticed, ignoring his movements beneath her,

making no move to help herself. "Who you think's in charge here, huh? You think Jude would let you do *shit* to me?"

The sound of her name filled Williams with another wave of grief, this one climbing higher, spilling over the wall of his defenses, but again he pushed it back. "None of this is guaranteed, Tabby. Now help me out—put your arms around my neck."

"No you don't," screeched Beth, pushing to her feet. Her eyes had gone a milky white, the flesh of her face around the sockets bright red and splitting in places. She groped around on the sodden ground and Williams groaned. Even maimed as she was, without the benefit of sight, still she stuck to her purpose of causing pain.

A hand closed around Beth's shoulder from behind, and Williams nearly jumped out of his skin. Boots' corpse had moved behind the woman, gotten close enough to touch without any of them seeing. The air felt heavy again, in a way Williams was beginning to associate with the natural magic of this place.

Beth froze in place with that dead hand on her shoulder, her mouth wide, eyes staring at nothing. She made a guttural choking noise, one hand going to her throat, but still her chest did not rise. Even Tabby went silent, all of them watching as Beth's face seemed to shrink in on itself, blackened veins rising slowly beneath her pale skin, then increasing in speed and reach. Her blinded eyes grew smaller, shriveling in their sockets until they dropped from her face like raisins. Her fingers clawed at nothing, the flesh of her hands pulling taut against the pressure of something that had wormed beneath her skin, into the hidden, vital parts of her. Whatever controlled Boots was sucking her dry, Willams realized. Harvesting her lifeblood, the very air she breathed. There was no telling himself she didn't suffer—she writhed and fought and tried to scream, twisting in the dead man's hold. Then, shuddering, her body reduced to standing bones with desiccated flesh clinging to their dried surface, she swayed in place, and Boots let her go.

She has to be dead, thought Williams. There is nothing left of her to suffer—she must be dead. It was surely a fluke of physics that she still stood upright, and fixed her gaping sockets upon him, before letting out a final breath and dropping to the ground. Bones that had only minutes before supported the structure of a living, breathing woman, jittered in the mud, still moving with the force of Boots' assault.

Tabby went silent after that, letting him pull her down from the stake she'd been meant to die on. Her mouth hung open as he held her in his arms, her gaze glued to the dead woman. "Holy fuck," she whispered.

Boots' corpse dropped to the ground beside Beth Helstrom's shuddering skeleton, and the spell of gruesome silence over the townspeople fell away.

"It *is* the work of the Devil," shrieked a man from somewhere in the back.

"Bullshit," boomed a woman's voice, low and powerful. Williams recognized Georgie, the owner of Arnett's only liquor store. "You all just watched what happened when Beth tried to pass off her own choices as God's work. It ain't, any more than the rest of this is the Devil's."

"Look at this town," called the first man. "People are dying."

Georgie had come to Williams' side, putting a hand on Tabby's shoulder. "Then I say we damn well help 'em."

"Get her away from here," she murmured in his ear before turning away. "We've seen enough punishment tonight."

Williams nodded and fought through the mud to get enough distance from whatever else might happen. Tabby sagged against him, her head dropping to his shoulder. He stopped once he'd reached the edge of Arnett once more, nearly at the base of the mountain, leaning against a handy oak tree and breathing hard. He looked up in the darkness, made out the shadow of the Devil's Backbone far above. Jude was now a part of it, beyond his reach for good.

When he lifted his face to the sky, he found the rain had stopped.

CHAPTER TWENTY-ONE

AT THE SOUND of crunching footsteps, Williams tore his gaze from the opening to the cavern where both the women he'd loved gave their lives. He couldn't see inside, not from this distance, but he felt drawn to it. It seemed from time to time he could make out movement within, the flicker of shadows. The burn of twin flames. He took a breath and turned his back on it to face Pepper.

"How is she today?" he asked.

Pepper nodded, her face set in a frown. She looked so different these days. Older, maybe. Wiser . . . "who was he to say? All he knew was she'd stepped into her new role with determination. "The skin's healing well with Jude's salve. We'll need more before too long, but I know how to make it. I'll show Tabby, if she's willing to learn."

"Good. I think that's a fine plan." He sighed. "What about . . . "

"Walking on it? No. Most of the flesh was gone, stripped to the bone. I had to take off what was left, to stop infection setting in. She'll have to be content with one foot. We'll help her figure out how to get around."

Williams nodded. He liked the sound of "we"—Pepper had learned from her predecessors' mistakes and would not be shouldering the burden of balance on her own.

"How is it down there?" Pepper asked after a minute. "We've made up another case of cures for you to take."

Williams lifted a shoulder. "Coming along slowly. We're rebuilding, but it was an almost total loss." He forced a sickly laugh. "At least there's fewer people needing a roof over their head."

Pepper didn't answer, and he felt a rush of shame at his callousness. But he hadn't been able to stop his anger. His fury at the actions of people who had cost Jude her life. He knew what she would have said—they couldn't have known. People have reasons for the things they do, and it wasn't up to them to judge. Williams judged anyway.

He cleared his throat. "Thanking you kindly for the bottles. They'll be put to good use."

They stood in silence for a minute or so before he broke it. "You been in there?" he asked, jerking his head in the direction of the cavern.

Pepper nodded. "I had to . . . clean things up. And we were out of Jude's special sort."

Nausea rose in Williams' gut, made saliva gather under his tongue. "So you're sticking by that tradition?" he asked, trying to keep the revulsion from his voice.

Pepper chuckled. "Is it so different from communion? This is my body . . . "

"I don't think that was ever meant to be literal," Williams said.

She lifted a shoulder. "Maybe not. And maybe we'll end that tradition—I don't know, until I've had a chance to look into all this. Figure out what's real and what's made up."

"And will you drink?" he asked.

She lifted her chin, her gaze following his to the cavern. "Maybe. I haven't decided that, either."

"Remember—" he began but she cut him off.

"I know. It's up to me." She laughed. "Not always much of a choice, when you know the alternatives."

Williams sighed. "I suppose."

"Do you want to go in?" she asked softly. "Pay your respects? It ain't off limits."

Williams looked at her, frowning. In a way he did—he wanted to step to the edge of that still, black water again. Stare into it until a face rose from the depths, desperately seeking any sign of Jude's face in the cold eyes that stared back.

He shook his head and turned his back. "I don't reckon it'll help anything. She's not there anymore. Not really."

Pepper didn't stop him when he dragged himself back to his truck, never once looking back. She didn't say another word or bother to correct his misapprehension. Jude was there, and always would be, now. Not just in the cavern, but all over the Backbone and down within it. At peace, Pepper hoped, but knew she had no control over that, either. All she could do was her best—make her own way using the little that she'd learned at Jude's feet. Do her best to keep her sisters safe and protect the valley below. For the mountain, while sated for now, would always keep the score, and she knew it would one day rise again.

She hoped when that day dawned she'd be a willing sacrifice. But for now, she turned and faced the day, and whatever the future brought.

THE GATHERER

RED LAGOE

CHAPTER ONE

MARTIN FORSYTH

MORNING FOG SETTLED in Gray Hollow and rarely left. It squeezed between the choking peaks of the surrounding mountains, clung to old barns and buildings, seeped through warped wood and rusted, abandoned farm equipment. It slithered across weeping hemlock and towering oaks, carpets of moss and fern, leaving a coat of dew that rarely dried up. Martin Forsyth wiped the cool condensing fog from his lips with his sleeve and shoveled the last of the manure from the Andersons' barn stall. He'd been doing Andersons' barn chores for pocket cash since he graduated high school last summer.

Dawn broke down in the valley town of Blackmoor. But here, up in the holler, tucked between the westernmost ridge of the Virginian mountains, sunlight wouldn't pierce the dense forest and hit Martin's face for another half hour at least . . . and that was if the fog ever lifted. He couldn't sleep last night. Nightmares about his brother kept him from any shut-eye, and the clouds—as usual—kept him from stargazing. There was nothing else to do but work, so he got up before first light and walked next door to the Andersons.

This was when the holler was most quiet—during this blurred vision of reality when the crickets and creatures of the night had gone to rest, but the morning birds hadn't woken. Martin pushed the wheelbarrow of horse manure out of the barn to the back of the Anderson property, which pushed up against the edge of the dark forest. A weather-aged, splintered post-and-rail fence failed to keep the ferns and feathered moss from spilling onto the Andersons' land. The summer hadn't yielded much of any green this year on this side of the fence. Stillwater, the Andersons' old prized Appaloosa, chewed what grass was left in their pasture by the barn. The old horse didn't have much life in him, like everything else in this Godforsaken place. He dumped the wheelbarrow onto a growing mountain of shit, under which he imagined his hopes and dreams were buried.

Martin removed his gloves and strained to look deep into the holler, where the lowland tapered to a V and where the dark forest liked to lure in wayward travelers.

They hadn't had many hikers in this area of the forest for a good while, but yesterday Martin saw a man hiking the perimeter of the fence along their properties. He was a lone traveler and wore his hair long. His bell-bottom pants were hardly the attire needed for the trek into the darkest part of the mountains. Yesterday, when the bell-bottomed hippie's body shrunk in the distance among the growing forest, Martin had shouted warnings from the fence line.

"There's nothing that way!"

The hiker had given a friendly wave but continued toward the overgrown trailhead. Martin had pressed his hands on the top fence rail and yelled louder, "Hey! Turn right at the fork! There's a cool waterfall!" It was a lie. Taking a right at the fork would lead him down the opposite side of Bald Mountain and into the town of Blackmoor. But it was better than letting the man venture into oblivion should he veer left at the fork instead.

He supposed he knew how it looked from the hippie's point of view. Mom stood deadpan at the coop in muck boots and a robe, chicken in her arms. Mom hated that forest more than anyone. Martin couldn't blame her. Like everyone else in the holler, Mom believed the forest was inherently evil; small-town minds believed the biggest nonsense.

Where the holler squeezed into a V was the forbidden part of the forest that Martin and his brother were warned as kids never to venture. It was known all over Gray Hollow, and even in the town of Blackmoor, that those who trekked farther rarely returned—at least not in their right mind. Occasionally, Martin and his brother Gary would dare each other to cross the fence and cozy up to the cusp of evil that lurked beyond. He'd tempted fate once as a teenager, hiking all the way to the Devil's Bathtub and back, and nothing ever came of it. Martin was old enough and smart enough to know the holler's folklore couldn't possibly be real, yet he never ventured into the woods again, since that day as a curious teenager.

He didn't know what happened to that hippie who hiked into the woods yesterday. He liked to believe that there was really nothing terrible hiding in there at all—that the whole town had lost their minds with a wild old fairy tale. The hiker was probably fine, Martin told himself. The people who'd hiked into the woods simply hiked out the other side. Maybe to some side of the mountain range that Martin had never seen, where the grass was greener because the sun actually shone there. Maybe beyond the ridge of the Devil's Backbone, there were nicer houses with roofs that weren't covered with tarps, and windows that weren't patched with fifty-year old rotting boards . . . Where the mountain didn't devour.

Today, through the asphyxiating, dense fog, Martin made out the subtle movement of something between the trees in the distance. It moved quickly, disappearing behind full summer foliage and thick trunks, but Martin trained his eyes to narrow in, wondering if he'd catch a flash of those blue bell-bottom pants that the long-haired hiker had worn the day before.

But the clothes were the dark gray color of a fire pit's ash after it had rained. There was a suggestion of antlers, however the distance and dense forest proved impossible to focus on a definitive form. As Martin narrowed his eyes to home in on the animal, he couldn't see a hind end. It was upright, *man*-like. For a moment it appeared cloaked in a hood, but there were spiked protrusions jutting out from its back. Antler-like spikes ran the ridge of its spine. It was swift and deliberate with its movement through the woods.

The fog obscured it as it slunk through the forest, edging closer and closer to the back end of Martin's property, only a few hundred yards away.

Martin dropped the wheelbarrow handles and started along the fence, moving in for a closer look. He tried to keep track of the dark figure in the woods, to make sense of it as something other than some mountain superstition, but he couldn't keep his eyes locked on it and it vanished within the fog. Martin's pace quickened, on course for his home, where his mother was still sleeping.

The tall grass and brush between their properties made it difficult to walk from one yard to the next, so Martin cut back to the side driveway and ran down the packed dirt path that led from the Anderson place to his house.

This wasn't the first time Martin had seen this beast. Some lost memory from when he was too young to clearly remember, of little more than a hooded figure standing over him. Unnaturally occurring antlers grew from its body at all angles, it hovered, backlit against the moonlight. But the memory was so distant, Martin wasn't even sure if it was real. People in the holler said there was a creature that came to steal children and travelers, as well as the elderly and the weak. The folks of Gray Hollow had whispered about what they called "The Gatherer" for as long as Martin could remember.

Most of his life, he believed he'd imagined it all those years ago—some manifestation of the stories he'd been told became a false memory. But now, here it was, heading out of the forest and straight into the holler.

He picked up his pace and sprinted across his yard, past the dilapidated utility shed, stumbling over discarded two-by-fours and scrap wood that the earth hadn't finished devouring. Martin stopped at the edge of the chicken coop, where the fowl were stirring with excitement inside. His heart pounded so hard he thought he might puke.

Get a grip. He took a steadying breath, eyes wide, fog condensing into droplets on his lids. He wiped it away and blinked for clarity. There was no sign of the creature.

Martin was a scientist at heart. If he wasn't stuck in this hellhole, he would've been in college. He rationalized that it could've been his imagination getting away from him. He'd been under a lot of stress with his brother off in Vietnam, with taking care of his mother, and half the barn chores in the holler. To give into the fear of some imaginary mountain creature would be ludicrous. Martin shook his head and groaned at himself.

Through the fog-choked trees he watched keenly for any sign of movement, but there was nothing. Not a crunch of last season's fallen leaves, nor the snap of a twig. Between the muddy, gray mist was nothing more than spindly, young, dying trees.

The chickens continued their fuss, wings flapping, clucking and screaming inside the coop. Something had them roused. Martin turned the knob, slowly at first, then flung it open so it slammed against the outside wall.

Inside, Mom turned around, seed flying from her hands. She gasped and clutched her heart. "Dear goodness! You scared me!" She stood in her cotton-candy pink, terrycloth bathrobe that Gary had bought for her before he was sent away to the war. Her ashy hair was oily and fell over her shoulders into a gnarled tangle of split ends. After Dad went missing, Mom said she didn't have anyone to be pretty for anymore. People in town said Mom let herself go, but Mom liked to say that she set herself free.

He wanted to warn Mom about what he'd seen, but she'd had enough to worry about lately. No sense in giving her a fright over what could've simply been his imagination.

"You're up early," Martin said, entering the coop. The scent of hay and shit assaulted him.

"So are you." Mom reached for her egg basket, but there weren't many eggs to pluck from the coop.

"Couldn't sleep, so I got a start on the day over at the Andersons'."

The bags under her eyes were gray and pronounced, as if the weight of eternity sat within them. She reached into the nesting boxes and began collecting eggs. A board creaked beneath her and bowed to her step. She adjusted her footing.

"I'll grab a plank and replace that today," Martin said.

"No, you won't." Mom waved a hand, knitting her eyebrows together. "This is *my* coop. It's *my* responsibility, and I will take care of it."

"Mom—"

"I won't hear it!" She pointed a finger. "You have your chores, and I have mine. The coop is my project, even before your dad, so let it be."

Martin surrendered.

"You want to be helpful?" Mom asked. "Then I suggest you go check in on Ellie-Mae."

"I'm sure she's fine . . . "

"No respectable young lady should have to handle the hardships of running a home all by herself."

A smile crept to his lips with the thought. "I think you underestimate Ellie-Mae. She can handle—"

"But she shouldn't *have* to handle it." Mom set her egg basket on the floor and reached for Martin's face. "Ellie-Mae was very lucky to have Gary, but let's face it . . . " A glassy sheen coated her eyes. She blinked it away. "We haven't heard from Gary in months. Not a single letter." Mom fought the tremble in her voice with a deep breath. "Please, just go check in on her again and make sure she doesn't need help."

CHAPTER TWO

MARTIN

MARTIN AGREED WITHOUT a word. He left his mom to her coop, and after wrapping up the Andersons' barn chores, he drove the pickup to Ellie-Mae Matheson's. She lived less than a quarter mile down the drive, closer to town, but still within Gray Hollow. There were only three families left up here: the Andersons, the Mathesons, and the Forsyths. There used to be at least fifteen families living in the holler, but with each passing year, more people left, though it seemed none ever said goodbye. Martin believed they were fed up with being cut off from town. The school buses stopped serving the area. Plows found the steep road too difficult to reach. Only dilapidated structures that used to be homes now sat in overgrown lots. Fortunately, the few remaining families still had electricity and phone service from a single row of telephone poles running up the mountainside. It wouldn't be long before the holler was nothing more than a ghost town, devoured by the forest and forgotten by the world.

All the houses in the holler once boasted bright colors, which faded to a dull gray with time. Ellie-Mae's was no different. Once pale yellow, her home was now the color of the morning fog which had finally lifted for the day. The only splash of color was a yellow ribbon tied to the old pine tree at the corner of the house.

Martin shifted the rusty '57 Chevrolet pickup into park and stepped onto the gravel driveway. Ellie-Mae swung an axe and split a log in two on one swing. She raised her axe instead of her hand to wave hello, placed another small log onto the stump, and swung again. The crack echoed off the house.

"Hi, Martin," she said as he approached, but her typical upbeat bubbly voice had been drowned by melancholy. Sweat dripped from her hairline, down her neck.

Martin lifted his chin to return the greeting, mesmerized by the bead of sweat as it rolled over her collarbone and disappeared beneath the collar of the cropped short-sleeved shirt that hugged her body. Her bony knees were adorable beneath the cuff of her green polyester short pants, which were filthy with dirt and bits of bark.

"Mom told me to check on you," Martin said.

Ellie-Mae set down her axe and put her hands on her hips. "I appreciate the gesture, but I can manage."

"That's what I told her."

Her smile didn't boast the familiar luminosity that Martin was used to. Something in her had dulled.

"It's been kinda hot for the woodstove, don't you think?" Martin said, nodding to the pile of chopped wood.

Ellie-Mae shrugged. "Gotta get a head start on the winter." She held the axe in her right hand and used her left to place another log on the block. "It's just me here, and I can only do so much each day, so I gotta start now."

"Can I help?"

"Don't you think you're spreading yourself a little thin?" Ellie-Mae left the narrow log standing upright and leaned on the axe handle.

Martin shook his head. "What do you mean?"

"I mean you take care of you and your mom, and the Andersons, and you got the farmer's market, all on top of college applications and stuff."

Martin felt the dull stab of regret at his core.

"Ain't you still going to college?" she asked.

"There's too much to take care of here."

Ellie-Mae took another swing and split the narrow log in two. "Folks like us ain't never gonna leave this town, huh?"

"What do you mean?" He knew exactly what she meant, but for some reason it didn't feel right to admit it.

"We're too nice, Martin. I wanna leave, but now Mama is sick and I can't. Otherwise, I think I'd be gone. Outta here, you know? What's your excuse?"

Martin jammed his hands into his pockets, avoiding the question.

Ellie-Mae rolled her eyes. "Don't tell me you ain't going to college because Gary ain't home yet?"

"I can't leave Mom to handle it all on her own, can I?"

"Us women can handle more than you boys think we can."

"Yeah, but my mom isn't like you."

A confident smirk softened her expression. "No. I s'pose not . . . " She set down her axe and wiped her hands on her shorts. "Come inside. I'll give ya something to do so you can tell your mama you helped little ol' helpless me." She placed the back of her hand on her forehead and pretended to faint like a damsel in an old movie.

Her house was damp inside, thick with the odor of mildew from seasons' worth of a leaking roof. The noise from her washing machine was so loud Ellie-Mae had to raise her voice to speak over the ruckus.

"I thought you wanted to be one of them spacemen. How you gonna do that if you don't go to college?" Ellie-Mae kicked the base of her yellow-beige Maytag, forcing it back into balance. The volume reduced, as did Ellie-Mae's. "You can't live in the holler forever, waiting for your brother to come home."

"Neither can you . . . "

Her eyes moved to the window, where the yellow ribbon was framed in view. Ellie-Mae chewed a thumbnail. "Have you heard anything?"

Martin shook his head. The last letter he received was in January. "You?"

Ellie-Mae hung her head, giving a subtle shake. She twisted a piece of bailer's twine on her left ring finger. The promise Gary had tied to her finger the day before he'd left for Nam. "Do you think Gary is . . . "

"No."

"I mean, the news . . . "

"No." Martin kept his answer short and sharp, hoping to cut her off from asking the question he didn't want to hear.

"I watch for his name every night."

"Me too," Martin said. "His name isn't on the news, so it means he's okay." Martin reached for her arm and attempted a display of empathy by petting her gently. For as tough as Ellie-Mae appeared, she was as soft as goose down.

Martin pulled his hand away. "How's your Mama?"

Ellie-Mae nodded toward a closed door. Rebecca, her mother, had gone for a walk into the forest a month ago and had been sick ever since. She'd been acting like someone completely different, sometimes raving like a lunatic, but Ellie-Mae had been nursing her back to health at home.

According to Ellie-Mae and the doctors, something in her brain got scrambled while she was out there. Rumor had it that Rebecca had gone to the waterhole and bedded with the Devil Himself. Martin, of course, scoffed at this rumor for reasons beyond the nonsense. Rebecca—after years of warning the town and all of God's creation—decided to wander into the forest against her own advice. It didn't make sense to Martin. But Ellie-Mae said she came back angrier, meaner, and desperate to go back for more. Devilry, according to everyone else, but Martin knew there was a scientific explanation for everything.

"She keeps to herself in there. She won't eat . . . can't get her to have much of anything other than bourbon."

"Is she going to be okay?"

"She stopped trying to escape," Ellie-Mae said. "At least during the day. At night though, I gotta guard the door. She tries to wander out. Got the window boarded up from the outside, now."

"And you think she wants to go—"

"To the Devil's Bathtub. She's obsessed with it. I don't know why she ever went there to begin with."

Martin sighed. "All this stuff about the mountain, the Devil's Bathtub, and the Gatherer are just stories to scare us."

"Something happened to my mama out there."

"Maybe she ate some bad mushrooms or something."

"Bad mushrooms?"

"Yeah. I know a guy from school who ate some mushrooms and wasn't right because of it."

"This ain't some bad trip," she scowled. "She been like this for weeks."

"Well, it ain't the Devil neither!"

"You don't know everything, Martin Forsyth."

"I know that—"

"Are you here to help me or not?" Ellie-Mae's lips tightened into a straight line, nostrils flared.

Martin threw his hands up in surrender. There was no arguing with her right now. "Yeah. What do you need?"

"I want to have a shower, but I can't do that anymore without leaving Mama unattended. Will you watch her for me?"

"You want me to babysit Rebecca?"

"If you're here to help, this is what I need. Or should I tell your mama that you're too good for that? That your big, smarty-pants brain is too superior for such a—"

"That's not what I said!"

"Groovy." The corner of her lip twitched into a smile. "I'll be only a quick spell." Ellie-Mae spun around and disappeared into the hall bathroom.

The beige-yellow Maytag rhythmically pounded against the kitchen wall, and Martin remembered the day the Mathesons had gotten it six years ago. That was before Ellie-Mae's dad abandoned them. Ellie-Mae and Martin were still just kids back then. Seemed like everyone in the holler had come to see the space-aged washing machine. It was yellow, like their house before it faded. Ellie-Mae's favorite color—the color of sunshine, she'd said. Martin loved that about her back then. She was his sunlight when the real one always failed. But her shine was diminishing, fading to gray like everything else in this damned holler.

The hiss of the hall shower carried to Martin's ears, and he couldn't help but picture Ellie-Mae beneath the falling water, head tilted back with her eyes closed. He pictured a curtain of water draping her face, flowing along her neck and collarbone, washing away the sweat of her labor.

A pulsing whimper, weak and desperate, drew his thoughts away from the shower and to Rebecca's bedroom door.

Martin approached, pressed his ear to the door, and listened to the sound of a woman crying. "Mrs. Matheson?"

There was no response, so Martin knocked twice and turned the knob.

Her voice cut to silence and the dark room seemed to consume all light as he peeked inside.

"Mrs. Matheson? Are you okay?" He pushed the door open fully.

In a dingy white nightgown, Ellie-Mae's mother stood barefoot with her back to Martin. Bony fingers pressed against the window, through which there was no view other than the backside of the imprisoning, weathered boards nailed outside. A dresser with no picture frames or doilies. No lamps or flowers in vases. The room had been stripped of everything, including light.

Rebecca turned her head enough that he could see the side of her pale face. She lowered her hands and shuffled back toward her bed. The clank of metal on the floor drew his eyes to her feet, where a chain tethered her by her ankle to the bed.

"Oh my God," Martin whispered.

"Oh my God," Rebecca repeated. "God ain't in Gray Hollow, Mr. Forsyth."

Martin edged closer to the bed.

She smiled, exposing blackened teeth, then sat down, patting the mattress in a request for him to join her.

He refused, keeping back a few feet from the deteriorating woman. He'd just seen her a few weeks ago at church. Chestnut hair shone like lacquer. Cheeks rosier than the petals outside the church doors. "Can you be a dear and unchain me, Martin?" Her breath expelled a plume of rot.

"Why are you chained up?" Martin felt his brow furrow; he couldn't hold back his expression of confusion and anger.

"My daughter worries too much."

"I'd say so." He inspected the cuff around her ankle; inflamed and bruised flesh had torn open and scabbed. "Oh my God . . . "

"Oh my God . . . " she repeated with a chuckle. "God ain't in Gray Hollow, Mr. Forsyth."

"Yeah . . . you said that." Martin rubbed the stubble on his chin.

"Ellie-Mae don't want me to go back."

"Go back where?"

She lowered her voice to a whisper and leaned forward. "To the water."

"Are you talking about . . . the Devil's Bathtub?"

She nodded, pressing her hands between her knees, rocking forward and back. "It wants me to come back so it can show me more."

Martin backed closer to the door, then leaned out of the bedroom and scanned the kitchen. When he poked his head back into the bedroom, Rebecca was on her feet, stretching the chain to its farthest length in the middle of the room, only a few feet from him. Sallow skin hung from her frame, eyes sunken as deep as ghost ships.

Startled, he nearly gasped but kept his composure. "Do you know where Ellie-Mae keeps the key?"

Rebecca's lips stretched into a smile again. In the black room, it was difficult to see if her eyes smiled, as well. They were orbs of dark gray, no more than the sheen of the kitchen light reflecting off their darkness. "The water showed me everything I wanted to know," she said, " . . . and it wants me back. It wants me back like her daddy never did."

"Let me talk to Ellie-Mae—"

"Fuck that little cunt!" Rebecca lunged, but her chain stopped her hands inches from Martin's neck.

Martin backed out of the room, and Ellie-Mae crashed into him.

"What are you doing?" Ellie-Mae dragged him away by his shirt and closed the door.

The rhythmic clanging of her chain tugging at the bedframe echoed through the wall.

"What the hell is going on, Ellie-Mae?" Martin asked.

"I didn't say you could go in there!" Ellie-Mae tightened a ratty bath towel around her naked body. Soaking wet hair hung over her shoulders, dripping onto the floor.

"You got your mom tied up!"

"You heard her! When have you ever heard my mom say a curse word? She ain't right in the head."

"So you chained her to the bed?"

"Well, what else am I supposed to do?"

"Get her some help!"

"There is no help for her. Even the preacher says she's been touched by evil." Tears flooded Ellie-Mae's eyes, but she steeled her face and fought them from falling. "I'm the only one who's *trying* to help her."

"Well, whatever you're doing isn't working. She needs a doctor or something."

"A doctor can't fix what she's got."

"Have you even tried?"

Ellie-Mae's nostrils flared, teeth gritting like a snarling dog. "Of course, I tried! Preacher Sam brought Doc Sanders from Blackmoor. Mama didn't like them . . . she was out of her mind. I never seen her act like that. They ran outta here so fast, and I ain't heard back in over a week."

"You can't keep her chained up until they get back to you, neither."

"She'll go back to the Bathtub if I let her go."

"So let her!" Martin paced, a storm raging within. "It can't be as bad as what you're putting her through."

Ellie-Mae's reluctant tears spilled. "You get outta my house, Martin Forsyth."

"Ellie—"

"You don't get to come in here all high and mighty when you don't know the half of it."

"Ell—"

"Please . . ." She wiped the tears from her cheeks. "We're all just trying to get by and we're all hurting, you know. You're not the only one who misses Gary."

"This has nothing to do with my brother." Martin headed toward the front door.

"It has more to do with your brother than you'll admit."

"What's that supposed to mean?"

"You're hotter than a cornered possum 'cause you burned your draft card, and now *you're* stuck in this damned place, doomed to die here just like the rest of us."

He flung open the screen door and it smashed against the side of the house. Martin whipped around and pointed a finger at her. "At least Gary got to die in Vietnam instead of on this mountain full of crazy people!"

Ellie-Mae's shoulders dropped. All emotion, fire, and fury were extinguished with his one cold sentence. It was the first time he'd admitted out loud that he believed his brother was never coming home.

She chewed her bottom lip. "I hope you don't mean that."

CHAPTER THREE

ELLIE-MAE MATHESON

MAMA HAD STOPPED tugging on her chain about ten minutes earlier—once her sedative kicked in. Just in time for a visit from Victoria Forsyth, who'd invited herself over after her son, Martin, had left.

"The blackberry bushes aren't producing fruit this year," Victoria said, sipping from a cup of lemonade.

"Ain't nothin' producing fruit, Mrs. Forsyth. Even the saplings are shriveling. The holler is dying. I'm afraid, soon, we'll all have to leave this place, don't you think?"

Mrs. Forsyth cocked an eyebrow and set down her lemonade. Her hair was tangled, graying all over. Back when her mama and Victoria Forsyth were church friends, the two women could've stopped traffic with their snug sweaters and poodle skirts. But the mountain was taking its toll on them, just like it had with the blackberries and other produce lately.

"It's just a cycle," Mrs. Forsyth said. "Sometimes it feels like the mountain takes too much. But without us here to sow the land, to harvest, and to give back, then . . . well, I don't know what would happen. But I know we're here for a reason, and we need to stay put and ride it out."

Ellie-Mae sank into the wooden chair, tipping onto its back legs. If she weren't sitting around pining for Gary, she'd be packing up her things and leaving, even if she had to drag her crazy mama away from this place kicking and screaming.

"Sit up, dear." Victoria pursed her lips. "I need to ask you something."

Ellie-Mae brought all four legs of the chair to the floor and sat up straight.

"Martin told me that you've chained Rebecca to the bed. Is that true?"

Ellie-Mae chewed her lip, wondering if she should lie, but she never felt right inside when she told lies, so she held up her chin and owned her decision. "Yes, ma'am. That's true."

There was a stare-down. Victoria waited for an explanation and Ellie-Mae tried like hell not to give it, but Mrs. Forsyth won the silent battle.

"Mama went to the Bathtub," Ellie-Mae caved. "And now she's real sick. If I unchain her, she'll go back."

Victoria's hand went to her mouth and the other hand to her heart, clutching the fabric of her shirt. "My goodness, I never thought she'd actually do it!"

"Did you know?"

"Of course not! Dear, she was having a hard time after your dad left. She said she wanted to *know* where he was . . . I didn't think she'd go so far as to ask . . . " Victoria trailed off.

" . . . as to ask the Devil Himself where my pa went?"

With eyes as round and big as the Church collection plate, Victoria nodded.

"Well, she done it. She got into the water and she says she saw Pa with another woman."

Victoria's eyelids fluttered closed. "Such a shame. Rebecca had a moment of weakness . . . Much like Adam and Eve in the Garden of Eden."

Ellie-Mae chewed at a sliver of dead skin that hung from the edge of her lip.

Mrs. Forsyth must've noted the confused look on her face because she went on explaining. "Remember the Tree of Knowledge? God forbid anyone from eating its fruit, but what happened?"

"Yeah, but it's just a water hole, Mrs. Forsyth. In Virginia. And it's not Biblical times."

"All times are Biblical times, and we must all pay for our sins."

"Mama isn't a sinner—"

"We're all sinners in the eyes of God." Victoria leaned in, face softening. "Rebecca was my dearest friend." Tears welled and she blinked them away. "She was desperate to know where her husband was, and she had a moment of weakness. I suppose it could happen to any of us."

"Even you, Mrs. Forsyth?"

"I'm certainly no saint," Victoria smirked. "But I try to live up to the highest standards I can . . . " She fell silent for a moment, mind lost in thought, staring toward some distant space in the corner of the kitchen. After a moment, her attention came back. "You know what I'd want to know if I could know *anything*?"

The question felt like a dirty secret. She whispered it as if God might not be able to hear through the leaky roof above them.

"I'd want to know if Gary is okay." Victoria's chin trembled, bouncing up and down like an acrobat. Tears spilled in a sudden flood, inciting Ellie-Mae to cry along with her.

"Me too," she said.

"Sometimes I think the people who go to the Devil's Bathtub are just lost souls who simply don't have the fortitude of mind to stand up to evil."

Ellie-Mae wiped her tears on her own shoulder. "Mama had fortitude—"

Victoria waved her hand, "Oh . . . I know, dear. I'm sorry. I'm just rambling. It's best we all just stay away from that place, don't you think?"

"That's the problem. Mama wants to go back. She's obsessed."

"You mustn't let her do that, Ellie-Mae."

"That's why I had to put a chain on her. I didn't wanna, you know? I tried to tell Martin that, but he got upset—"

"Martin is too stubborn to believe anything he can't understand."

"That big brain of his sure is a pain in the neck." Ellie-Mae laughed a little, but stifled it, ready to change the subject. "Martin really is meant to do great things in life, don't you think? I mean, with people going to the Moon and all . . . I bet he could do that."

Victoria sipped her lemonade and composed herself. "Martin's head is always up in the clouds instead of down here on earth. I think he forgets that his place is here."

Ellie-Mae retracted, teeth sawing through the piece of dead flesh on her lip, tearing it away. A dab of blood bloomed to the surface and she soaked it up with her tongue.

"I'm not here to talk about Martin's space-dreams or his cowardly choices avoiding the war."

Nervously, she interjected. "I don't think burning the draft card was cowardly . . . a lot of people were taking a stand against—"

Mrs. Forsyth stood. "It was cowardly! The sooner he realizes that, the sooner he'll become a man, rather than a boy with silly dreams."

Victoria's words severed the conversation. She owned the speaking floor and Ellie-Mae was there to listen. "I'm here to help your mother, but to do that, I need you to trust me, and trust in God." Victoria took Ellie-Mae's hands.

She noticed that, despite the shower, there were still bits of filth caked under her short fingernails.

"Do you trust in God, Ellie-Mae?" Mrs. Forsyth asked.

"Yes, ma'am."

"Good. Let us pray and set your mama free."

CHAPTER FOUR

ELLIE-MAE

AFTER MRS. FORSYTH LEFT, Ellie-Mae sat on the floor with her back against Mama's door. Even though Mama was heavily sedated, Ellie-Mae didn't leave her guard position for more than a minute at a time, keeping an eye on the only way in and out of the house—the front door. She wrapped up some chores while the news played on the TV. Mostly static, all they got was one channel, and that was if the rabbit ears had some aluminum foil extensions reaching up to the ceiling. A news clip played of President Nixon waving to a crowd. Someone yammered on about how with the new amendment, finally, our soldiers were "old enough to fight, old enough to vote." She didn't trust anything that man, Nixon, had to say after he lied about the war coming to an end, and couldn't stomach watching the news lately anyway. She turned the knob and the black and white screen shut off.

What she'd give to know if Gary was all right . . . to really know where he was right now.

With that thought came the will of the Devil Himself. He slithered into her mind like a serpent, whispering that it was all right. That she had the right to know where the love of her life was. The idea flicked its pronged tongue between her ears, enticing her to find out. What if she were to hike down to the bathtub and just take a look? She'd seen it once before when she was a kid. Gary, Martin, and she all sneaked down as teenagers, daring each other to see what would happen, but none of them had the guts to get in.

They knew, even as kids, that it was wrong.

But she wasn't a kid no more. She was a grown woman who deserved some answers, and no matter how much she prayed to God, He wasn't dishing them out.

Daylight faded to twilight and the moon rose above the trees.

It was near-full tonight, and for once, the clouds were nowhere to be seen. Ellie-Mae checked on her mama, who slept peacefully unchained on her bed. "Right where I left you," she whispered and covered her with a freshly dried bedsheet from the line.

Ellie-Mae reclined on the couch with a cold beer but only took a few sips before her exhaustion took over.

She woke with an ache in her upper back near her shoulder blade. Swinging that axe overworked her muscles more than they were used to. Ellie-Mae felt like she owed it to women nowadays to be stronger than the previous generation—like she had to prove she could do anything a man could do and she could do it all on her own with no help. But if she were being honest, she was tired of the struggle, and more than anything she wished Gary would come home and marry her so she could get out of this Godforsaken holler.

The yellow table lamp glowed hot, burning dust that had settled on the bulb. The silence was broken only by the hands of the clock, ticking like tiny shotgun blasts. It was after midnight.

As she came to her senses, the sounds of crickets spilled into the house on a layer of sticky humidity. The front door was wide open, but she remembered it was shut before she fell asleep. She jolted upright and ran to Mama's room.

Her bedroom was empty.

Ellie-Mae called for her mama and checked the bathroom without any hope of finding her in the house. She shoved her feet into a pair of muck boots, snagging a flashlight from the top of the fridge before running outside. She wore a pair of terrycloth short-shorts and a tank top. Black muck boots high-stepped through tall weeds until she reached the far end of the holler. She couldn't take the truck, or it'd wake the neighbors. Not that she had many of those left—just the Forsyths until the Andersons came back from their vacation. The last thing she needed was Mrs. Forsyth getting involved or Martin casting his holier-than-thou judgment.

Ellie-Mae didn't need help looking for her mama anyway because she knew exactly where she'd find her.

THE GATHERER

The moon was damn near directly overhead, a giant silver angel guiding her to her mama. She climbed over the post-and-rail fence behind the Forsyth's place. Martin's bedroom light was still on, and she wondered what he did all night long. He was probably reading those science books, or sometimes she liked to picture him thumbing through encyclopedias, especially after that one time when she caught him reading the dictionary when they were kids. He used to sit outside with a little Tasco telescope and look up at the heavens so hard it was like he was searching for God Himself. But Martin never found Him, and he hadn't brought the telescope out in a long time. Gray Hollow was known to obscure the starry skies with a thick bank of cloud cover, so it was a surprise that she didn't see Martin standing out in the field tonight looking up at these skies. If she didn't have to go chasing down her mother, she'd knock on Martin's window and let him know that the clouds parted and the moon was out. But then he'd try to stop her.

She kept the flashlight off until she was across the overgrown field of dead grass and dried-up saplings that never had a chance to grow any taller than her shoulder before their lives shriveled away. Once the triangular field tapered to a point, that's when things were the scariest. Stepping beyond the threshold into the dark forest felt like she'd allowed evil to sink its talons into her. But Ellie-Mae couldn't be afraid. She was here in the forest for good, selfless reasons; she was confident that she had the fortitude of mind to resist any temptation thrown her way.

The dead saplings gave way to taller, more mature oaks, elms, and evergreens. She turned on her light, making her presence known to the forest. She moved slowly, cautious at first, as if The Gatherer might be waiting in a shadow for some wayfarer to stumble along. But if Ellie-Mae was going to reach her mama in time, she'd have to hurry and stop fearing things that may or may not lurk in the dark.

Ancient trees towered overhead. Ivy climbed their broad trunks, leeching nutrients from them. Every column was like an entity watching her, waiting for her to misstep and fall to the forest floor where the mountain would eat her.

At the landmark moss-laded boulder, she turned to the left and followed the trail—a trail rarely hiked, but somehow the mountain never swallowed it up. As if it wanted to be discovered and followed.

A few years back, someone had been putting up flyers down in Blackmoor, with trail maps leading to "the best swimming hole this side of the Mississippi." The whole holler was in an uproar, pissed that someone—one of them Anderson teenagers, no doubt—would try to lure people straight into evil.

Her feet and instinct found the way, even when the trail wasn't clear. She cut across a winding stream, tripped on massive roots, and scrambled over fallen logs, but she was guided by something other than memory. If she closed her eyes, that hook in her chest would tug and reel her forward, all the way to where she needed to be.

It was a couple of miles, at least—she and the boys never clocked it to estimate how far. Nobody had. Ellie-Mae kept as swift a pace as she could, trudging ankle-deep through warm creek water multiple times to stay on the path. With all her heart, she wanted to call out to her mama to come back, but she knew better than to draw any more attention to herself.

Sweat beaded between her breasts, soaking through her tank top. Water and mud sloshed and squished between toes in her muck boots. She reckoned she might end up with foot rot if she didn't empty them out soon and rinse her feet clean.

Here in the deep of the forest, there were no crickets chirping. No night owls or cicadas. No mosquitoes swarming for a feast or clouds of no-see-ums to swat at. Nothing dared move down this path tonight or make a sound in this part of the woods, other than Ellie-Mae. The wildlife had been driven away.

Ellie-Mae never gave much thought to the old story about The Gatherer. They'd said that The Gatherer was an ancient servant that lured people into Hell. The Gatherer collected souls, lured them with the magic of the Devil's Bathtub, and guided them to damnation. She imagined it was a tale that the grown-ups conjured to keep the kids from going into the forest—as if entering the Devil's lair wasn't scary enough. But now that she was here, and the glow of a faint blue light was ahead, she believed anything was possible.

She flicked off the light and moved to the edge of the trail, pressing against an old tree to stay out of the light up ahead. Bark crumbled and fell to her feet. She held tight to the edge of the path and eased sideways toward the glow until she realized its source was simply the moonlight in a clearing ahead. Against the gray-blue luminescence, a small silhouette moved across the path.

"Mama!" she whispered as loudly as she could, rushing down the path. Fallen twigs snapped underfoot.

The open expanse of light didn't grow bigger as she drew near. The path to her mama felt like it grew longer and longer with every step. Mama's silhouette moved out of view, and another took her place. This silhouette stopped Ellie-Mae in her tracks. She cowered, hoping she couldn't be seen within the shadows by whatever was up ahead. It moved like a hunter, stalking across the end of the path, hunched back with long spindly spikes running along its spine. Antler-like things perched on its head, but it appeared to be cloaked in fabric, or perhaps a long, thick coat of hair that dragged behind it.

It stalled for a moment in the light, turning in her direction. Ellie's pulse throbbed between her ears, wondering if it could see her, but it moved on.

Mama . . .

Roots ground against her knees while she was down on all fours, hiding in shadow. Her fingers froze around her flashlight, sweat making it slippery in her hand. She wanted to turn around and run—let Mama suffer whatever was coming her way, but she couldn't.

Dear Lord, please give me strength . . .

Trembling, stomach flipping, Ellie-Mae got back to her feet and ran down the path toward the clearing. Rubber legs absorbed the impact of each footfall, going numb with fear as she approached. When the trees opened up, moonlight spilled across a water hole. Flat wet rock glistened around it. Ferns and moss lounged around its edges like families at a public pool, where everything glowed like silver and nickel. Beyond the large water hole, over slabs of slate, she climbed and stood high on a platform between the large water hole and a smaller bathtub-shaped one on the other side.

It was difficult to see the actual shape of the tub beyond the black water—which she knew to be turquoise during the day. It nestled up against a wall of mossy rock. There was no sign of Mama or the beastly thing she'd seen moments earlier. Careful of her footing, she edged closer to the Bathtub, wondering if her mama was within. As she leaned over, she was startled by her own reflection in the water.

A rustling in the woods just beyond the Bathtub made her jerk away from the water.

The thick brush adjacent to the rock wall parted.

"Mama?"

The rustling stopped with the sound of her voice. Ellie-Mae scrambled over wet rocks, around slick moss-covered logs to the dense patch of forest that was so black, she couldn't see beyond her outstretched hand. But there, where the weeds, gnarled branches, and hemlock had parted, was a path. One that parted out of nowhere, seemingly just for her.

"Mama?" she whispered into the black hole of the forest.

Ellie-Mae shone her flashlight into the opening that was no wider or taller than her refrigerator, but it was as deep as eternity. The ground was lined with stepping stones, like shiny black glass. She swallowed the lump in her throat. "It's Ellie-Mae. Are you in there?"

Shuffling footsteps could be heard deep inside. Branches and twigs snapped. The forest broke and bent in the path of whatever was coming toward her. From the blackness beyond her flashlight's beam, a dark, ashy figure—large, horned, and hooded—charged toward her. Ellie-Mae screamed, scrambling backward and falling on her tailbone.

Sparks shot up her spine and into her shoulder, but she twisted around and got to her feet. The slick rock was tricky to navigate in her panicked state. Her boots slipped on wet slate and lost purchase on moss-covered logs. But she scrambled away from the creature until all that stood between her and it was the Devil's Bathtub. She waited, chest heaving in anticipation of the thing she'd expected to come barreling out of the secret pathway, but moments passed, minutes, and it never came. Her flashlight had fallen to the edge of the water. She crouched, eyes riveted on the black hole in the forest.

Unsure how much time had passed, she stayed frozen in place until her legs cramped beneath her. The warm stagnant summer air suffocated, dampness clinging to her skin and mixing with the sweat seeping from her pores. Ellie-Mae cautiously rose to her feet, standing over the massive bathtub in the earth. As she regained control of her panicked breaths, her reflection glared back at her. Her face broke with gentle ripples in the water as her heart quaked within.

She'd lost her mama to the mountain and The Gatherer, and she knew with all her soul that she'd never get her back. That was how it worked in the holler.

She waited by the water, body numb, unsure which parts of her face were tears and which bore dew or sweat. But if she waited any longer, she might get swept up by The Gatherer and taken all the way to the ridge of the Devil's Backbone, from which nobody had ever returned. It was too late for Mama. The sickening thought sent bile up her throat. Elli-Mae wanted to be brave and charge into the dark wooded corridor, face The Gatherer, and get her mama back. But fear paralyzed her. All she wanted to do in this moment was run away. With that thought, she wondered what she would do now. This was her opportunity to finally get out of the holler. She could go get Martin and they could leave together . . .

A twinge of guilt prickled her insides. Giving up on her mama should not have been an option, but as she stood staring at her reflection in The Devil's Bathtub, it was the only option that felt reasonable.

The dark fingers of selfishness crawled through her head, urging her to let her mama go. But if she escaped this place, then what? What if Gary were to come home from war looking for his fiancé?

The rippling water ceased and her reflection stilled.

It'd be a lot easier to make the next decision if she *knew* what happened to her mama . . . and if she knew whether or not Gary was alive.

Maybe Ellie-Mae had the strength to lie in the Devil's Bathtub, to absorb the knowledge she needed, and then refuse the Devil her mind. God would certainly be on her side for this. God would have to understand her motives were pure.

She prayed silently, eyes locked on the moon overhead. There were no words in this prayer. Only an abstract cloud of thoughts and emotions and pure intentions sent out across the universe to the Almighty, and she knew He'd hear it. He'd understand.

Ellie-Mae took a deep breath. "I have the fortitude of mind." She removed her muck boots and placed them neatly to the side. Her foot hovered over the edge of the water, tempted to absorb its knowledge. Ellie-Mae slipped a big toe into the ice-cold water. She closed her eyes and a flash of green replaced the night. Then, without a moment's hesitation, she took a leap of faith fully into the Devil's icy embrace.

CHAPTER FIVE

MARTIN

MARTIN HAD FALLEN ASLEEP with the black spots of a water-damaged ceiling between himself and the night sky. He'd stayed up reading old magazines—his favorite was the moon-landing issue of LIFE. Since he was a kid, he'd dreamed about going up there. Deep within the core of his being, he knew it was his destiny. And if someday he got a chance to climb into one of those space shuttles that NASA was planning, he'd go far beyond the moon. Beyond the grips of this rock, he'd explore the universe and learn everything there was to know about where they came from.

When he woke predawn, he could hear the soft rumble of Mom's snoring through her bedroom door. It was later than she normally slept, so he got dressed and took care of her chickens. While leaning over to grab one of the only eggs in the coop, his foot nearly broke through the creaky board in the floor.

"Damn it, Mom," he mumbled under his breath, irritated his mother wouldn't allow him to fix her coop. For as much as she prided herself on taking care of things, she sure did let it all fall apart.

Sometimes he wondered why he bothered staying here in the holler. Or why anyone stayed, for that matter. Though, he couldn't recall anyone ever leaving. No moving trucks ever came or went out of the holler. No goodbyes. It was like everyone just faded away, forgotten to time. The same was bound to happen to him if he didn't get out.

Martin headed to the Andersons' to bring Stillwater to pasture, but when he got to the barn, the door was open and his stall was empty. He traced last night's chores in his mind and remembered closing everything up. Stillwater could barely walk without buckling, let alone break out of a stall.

Martin grabbed the keys to the Chevy and drove around the holler, searching for him. After driving the loop and checking the dead berry fields behind the old Harris place, he set down the hill for the town of Blackmoor. The horses tended to travel down the mountain toward the lush fields when they escaped. Even the damn horses knew the holler was no good for them.

The steep, winding narrow road had to be driven with a foot on the brake nearly all the way down. Halfway down the hill, the fog cleared, and sunlight kissed the tips of green grass. Trees were full of leaves, rustling in a summer breeze. Soon, folks would be setting up for the farmer's market with bins of fruits, veggies, and fresh-cut bacon strips, and the town would be alive and pulsing. Telephone poles downtown were littered with yard sale signs and lost dog notices.

He drove the perimeter of town, but there was no sign of Stillwater. He'd have to give up, as he'd already lost nearly half an hour of his time for morning chores. The horses always turn up within a day. In this small community, someone was sure to find and wrangle the old horse by the day's end.

On his way out of town, back toward the holler, one telephone pole sign caught his eye. Something about "Off the Beaten Path Hiking". Martin pulled over and inspected the paper taped to the pole. Stenciled letters read:

Best swimming this side of the Mississippi.

A crude, hand-drawn map directed how to get to the holler, and where to park to pick up the trailhead. Mom's church group used to rip these signs down. But hikers, like the guy in blue bell-bottoms, always managed to find them.

"Martin Forsyth?" Preacher Sam stood behind him with his arms crossed.

Martin nodded hello to the stocky man dressed in slacks and a button-down shirt.

"What have you got there, boy?" He leaned toward the flyer and ripped it from the pole. His brow furrowed, eyes furious with judgment.

"That's not mine, sir." Martin put his hands up. "I'm just looking for Stillwater. He broke out of the Andersons'—"

"Then who put this here?"

"I don't know, sir." Martin shrugged and moved toward his truck.

Preacher Sam followed Martin's movement with narrowed eyes. "Whoever is hanging these maps will have to answer to God."

"Like I said . . . it ain't me."

Sam Giovani never cared much for Martin—always looking for something to pin on him. With a glare cast down his nose, Preacher Sam arched his eyebrows to Kingdom Come. "I'll let your mama know I saw you down here."

"Okay, sir." Martin wanted to cuss him out, but he was taught to respect his elders, so he tightened his lips and got into his truck without another word.

On his way back through the holler, Martin swung by Ellie-Mae's.

It was mid-morning when he arrived at her house. She sat slumped on her porch in short shorts and a tiny tank top that hung from her shoulders like a loose pair of undergarments on a clothesline. One swift breeze and he might see everything underneath. The tank and shorts were stained, legs coated in dried mud, and her black muck boots were caked, as well. Her hair was ragged and wind-swept, and she didn't bother to look up when he pulled onto her gravel driveway.

"Ellie-Mae," Martin said as he climbed out of the truck and closed the rusted door.

Finally, a smile graced her lips and her eyes lifted to greet him.

"You okay?" Gravel crunched underfoot as he neared the wooden planks laid flat across packed dirt, which acted as a porch.

Ellie-Mae stood, tank top hanging loose from her breasts, exposing her pale white belly—a stark contrast to her tan arms. Martin's averted vision noted the outline of her nipples through the thin fabric. He turned around. "Jesus, Ellie-Mae, do you need to go get dressed or something?"

"No. I'm fine. Why?"

Martin faced her but forced his eyes to steer clear of her body. "Stillwater got out of his stall."

"How'd he do that?"

"I don't know. You seen him?"

She shook her head, eyes wandering off into the trees. "Andersons are gonna be pissed."

"No shit." He headed back toward his truck, placed a hand on the door handle, and turned around to see Ellie-Mae standing only inches away. Her arms hung loose at her sides and her body swayed gently like dead branches in the wind. Her face was sullen, the sparkle in her eyes diminished.

"Where you going?" she asked.

She stood so close it was easier to avoid looking at her breasts, but now he was a mere footstep from pressing against them.

"Are you okay?" he asked. "You're acting weird."

"I'm fine."

Martin climbed in the truck, and Ellie-Mae held on to the door, leaning in.

"If you see Stillwater, snag him and bring him back, will ya?"

Ellie-Mae gnawed at her bottom lip.

"What's going on with you?"

She didn't reply as she held on to the side of his truck.

"Is your mama okay?" He was stupid not to ask already, but he was so hung up on finding Stillwater that it didn't occur to him.

"She's doing great," she answered in a snap.

Her mama hadn't been anything close to great in weeks. He looked back to the house. "My mom told me you unchained her yesterday."

"Yep."

"How's she doing?"

"Fine."

"She didn't try to run away?"

Ellie-Mae turned her head slowly. Her eyes were lost to the forest behind her house. She mumbled something incoherent to him.

"What?"

Attention returning, she repeated herself. "It ain't running away when you're already free."

Martin's hand stalled over the ignition. "What the hell are you talking about?"

Her gaze drifted dreamily back to the woods.

"Damn it, Ellie-Mae. What's going on with you?"

"You and Mrs. Forsyth told me to unchain her. I told you . . . " Her chin lowered as she glared through her eyebrows. "I fucking told you!" she screamed.

Martin jolted to attention and got out of the truck, avoiding Ellie-Mae, who seemed too eager to get close to him. He stomped toward the house and swung open the screen door. "Mrs. Matheson?"

Ellie-Mae lingered outside, arms dangling by her sides.

"Mrs. Matheson?" He checked the bedrooms and the bathroom, then flung open the porch door and met with Ellie-Mae outside. "Where'd she go?"

"I *told* you." Now there was a serenity to her tone that made her voice as soft and sure as the summer breeze. Again, her gaze drifted away, through the trees, through the boulders and rocks and forest, to a place farther away than Martin could imagine.

He tried to get a look in her eyes, but they were distant—as if she were looking through time and space itself. A peaceful smile came to her lips. "She found what she was looking for . . . and so did I."

"Ellie-Mae . . . "

She faced him, eyes glistening wet. "It was so beautiful." She hugged her body, breasts squeezing together and showcasing her cleavage.

"What are you talking about?"

She closed her eyes, holding her chin up with a smile. "The Devil's Bathtub showed me something wonderful." Arms stretched to the sky, her tank top rode up farther, exposing more skin. Martin averted his gaze.

"What did it show you?"

She tugged at his wrist. "You should come with me and see."

Martin didn't pull his wrist away from her grip. Her fingers excited his flesh, but he tried to stifle the feeling pumping through his veins. He placed an open palm on her shoulder blade and tried to guide her toward the house. "Come on . . . let's get you cleaned up and we can talk about it."

She leaned into his body, warm and inviting. "I don't want to talk about it. I want you to come with me and *see*."

"I'm not gonna do that."

"Why not?"

"There's obviously something out in that forest that makes people sick . . . "

"You think I'm sick?" She nuzzled her face into the crook between his shoulder and his neck. Hot breath grazed his skin.

"I don't know. I hope not." Martin pulled himself away before acting on the passion rising below his belt.

She crossed her arms and chewed on her lower lip, and then she mumbled something about Gary, but he couldn't make out what she'd said.

Martin sighed. "That's right. *Gary.* Look, Ellie-Mae, I know you've got a lot on your plate. And loneliness—"

"Gary died." Her words severed whatever he was about to say. They sliced cold and sharp, silencing him.

Tears brimmed at the ledge of her lower lids. "I saw it. I saw it happen. There was blood and . . . " She snaked closer, tanned arms slithered around his waist for a hug. She nuzzled into him, burrowing into his soul. "I'm sorry, Martin."

CHAPTER SIX

MARTIN

MARTIN COULDN'T STAND being around Ellie-Mae after what she'd said about Gary. He didn't know what the hell was wrong with her, but he couldn't deal with it now. He stormed away in a fury, charging into his house with fists clenched. Mom had already left, borrowing the Andersons' car to go into Blackmoor to sell eggs, so he had the house to himself to simmer down.

He removed his work boots and stepped inside the shrine of his brother's bedroom. The place was frozen in time from his high school days. A baseball bat and glove lay in the corner collecting dust. Gary was a star player for the Blackmoor team back in school. While Gary was out with his jock friends in Blackmoor, playing sports, and being the All-American kid, Martin stayed home, watching Captain Kirk and Spock on another epic space adventure, so long as the reception wasn't too bad. Gary was Martin's Captain Kirk in a lot of ways, and Martin deemed himself Gary's Spock.

That was until Uncle Sam took him away. He was the tall, handsome fellow who everyone loved and respected. The war-hero revered in church. The son their mother loved the most. She didn't have to say it for Martin to know.

The door had been left open since Gary left a year ago, but Mom always got upset when Martin went in there, as if he would mess up her precious baby's room. The war was supposed to have been coming to an end, but days and months went by and he never returned. And then the letters stopped coming. Ellie-Mae may have been crazy to think she had a real vision out there at the Bathtub, but what she'd said was probably true. Gary wasn't ever coming home.

Tears dribbled down Martin's cheeks but he sopped them up with his sleeve. Outside, clouds loomed, oppressing the holler in a gray shroud. From Gary's bedroom, he spotted movement in the triangular field leading to the forest. He stood startled, expecting to see The Gatherer—or whatever he'd seen yesterday morning. But it was Ellie-Mae. Still wearing the loose-fitting shorts and tank that weren't much more than underwear. She stood a couple hundred yards away where the field tapered to the trailhead. She was ghostly against the dark gray, staring in his direction as if she knew he was watching from the tiny dark room.

Martin jammed his feet into his work boots and went outside, hands shoved deep in his denim pockets. "What are you doing?" he shouted, but Ellie-Mae didn't reply. She turned her back and disappeared behind the columns of dense trees.

"Ellie-Mae!" Martin remained calm and walked from his back porch to the fence line, then craned his neck in every direction to see if she was playing games with him, hiding behind a tree. He squinted, trying to catch a glimpse of stark white against the forest backdrop, but she was gone.

Martin ducked between the rails of the fence and hurried across the field of brambles and dead weeds. The unbearable weight of being responsible for everything pressed down on him like the holler clouds. More than anything, he wanted to turn around, grab the truck keys, and drive straight out of Gray Hollow, never looking back. But as mad as he was at Ellie-Mae, he couldn't abandon her.

He was friends with Ellie-Mae long before she ever caught Gary's eye. But when Ellie-Mae started looking at Gary the same way, Martin was too scared to say anything. He was terrified to admit that he loved the girl and never told her. So, he did what he thought was the noble thing—he let her go. But it wasn't noble at all. It was cowardly.

Martin Forsyth . . . town chicken.

An unsettling warning sat in his sternum as he approached the trailhead into the forest. A push to stay away, but also a curious pull to give into his desires and follow Ellie-Mae to the water hole.

Years' worth of local stories to scare the kids was why he still feared the forest. A simple matter of conditioning—something Martin was smart enough and strong enough to overcome as he stood at the cusp of the forest, heart pumping between his ears. He pushed through the fear and followed Ellie-Mae inside.

He hadn't stepped foot this far since that day back when he,

Gary, and Ellie-Mae all braved the trip to the Bathtub. It felt wrong back then, and the same feeling sat in his gut as he trekked the bare dirt path that remained untouched by forest growth.

Martin made it to the boulder at the fork, where Ellie-Mae stood with her back to him, frozen as he approached.

"You okay?"

Her body swayed side to side facing the boulder.

"I'm glad you came," she said.

"What are you doing?"

She turned quickly and seemed to snap back from the spell she was under. "I'm looking for my mama." Ellie-Mae took one of Martin's hands in hers. "Thank you. I'm sorry I've been acting strange. I . . . I . . . "

"You're under a lot of stress, Ellie-Mae."

"Yes . . . " Her voice was soft, lacking emotion. Lacking hope.

"Did you call the law about your mama going missing?"

Ellie-Mae started down the trail. "You and I both know the fine folk of Blackmoor don't care about us holler folk."

He blindly followed Ellie-Mae down the trail, led by a desire to do something helpful, but more so by the desire to explore the forbidden area of the forest once again. To get a peek at what made everyone lose their minds. An exploration in the name of science. Curiosity at the helm.

He'd nearly forgotten about the multiple creek crossings leading to the Bathtub, wading through ankle-deep water of the winding creek over and over. Mud caked to the hems of his jeans. It was just like when Martin and Ellie-Mae were younger, exploring the woods—thick as thieves—back before Gary began to join them. Usually, it was the other side of Bald Mountain they'd explored, the part of the forest they were permitted to play in, but it felt just the same here today.

After a long and strenuous hike, they reached the larger water hole in the clearing. Martin stopped to admire the emerald green water, the cloudy sky breaking for a moment to allow sunbeams to play on the surface. Scents of petrichor and moss-ridden slate played in his nostrils. Ferns crowded the edges of the water. When Martin turned to smile at Ellie-Mae, she'd already climbed over the great slabs of rock and vanished from sight on the other side.

"Ellie-Mae?" Martin traversed the slick rock carefully. "Wait up!"

He navigated the shelf of rock and stood on top, overlooking a bright turquoise pool reflecting the sun. The oval pool sat like a blue-green gem amidst the lush forest floor. A rock wall lined one side of the Bathtub. It was much bigger than an actual bathtub but shaped exactly like a deep clawfoot dug into the earth. Beneath the surface of the water, Ellie-Mae lay suspended, palms up, eyes closed. Her back arched and her body undulated in a gentle wave, but the surface of the water remained still like a sheet of ice.

He shouted to her as her hair splayed like a crown. She was a peaceful, sleeping princess whom he wasn't supposed to disturb.

As he knelt by the water and leaned over to investigate, Ellie-Mae's eyes opened. Submerged only a few inches, not a single air bubble escaped from her nose or mouth. However, it looked as if she was somehow breathing, emerged in a deep slumber.

Her arms lunged from the water and grabbed hold of Martin's elbows, but he braced himself and pulled back so as not to topple into the icy pool. Martin counter-gripped her arms, his fingers latched onto wet, cold skin . . . and a flash of darkness cloaked the world. A lightning strike of inky black flashed before him. He shook his head and the dark greens and turquoise of the water hole came back into view for only a second. Ellie-Mae's body rose from the water hole with ease and he fell back to the rocks, keeping hold of her arms. Her soaking wet body fell onto his, and the darkness flashed again.

Pinpoints of light emerged with his adjusting eyes. There were no sounds, no feelings but the vacuum of nothingness between stars. Had he died? Was this his heaven, floating among the stars? After his eyes came into focus, his body's nerves woke to the soft lapping of space-time against his flesh. As if every cell of his visceral body was awake and craving the touch of the cosmos, craving to know where all the elements of its being came from.

An icy grip clenched his chest and pressure built within. The flash faded to light and Ellie-Mae was on top of him writhing in ecstasy.

Her eyes locked on his, wild and hungry. She didn't wait a second, didn't roll off of him, didn't bat her eyelashes dreamily. She lunged in for a kiss. As the freezing water of the Devil's Bathtub dripped from her lips into Martin's mouth, his body awoke again in a new time and place. Flashes of Ellie-Mae's naked flesh blacked out to nebulae from the beginning of the universe. His body floated among the stars while Ellie-Mae pinned him down, slithering her wet, frigid body onto his. They'd become entangled; Ellie-Mae sat on top of him, droplets of icy water falling to Martin's bare stomach. He watched as the water absorbed into his flesh like sentient things seeking a way in.

Her silhouette against the cloud-patched sky turned to an inky shadow against the backdrop of space. It was as if the universe itself was fucking him.

He ventured farther and deeper into the vastness of the unknown, starlight became sparse, and flashes of something else replaced the light. Something *wrong* and unnatural. Something inherently evil—something undefinable. Martin felt scraping against his flesh, and his body stretched beyond possibility. Flayed skin and blood splattered in the sky. As he screamed, he came, thrusting into Ellie-Mae, and the flash of darkness flicked off like someone had flipped a light switch.

Ellie-Mae's head was thrown back, hips rocking and grinding against his. Starshine faded from Martin's eyes, and he scrambled out from under her. "What the fuck was that?" He checked his body for injury but seemed to be fully intact.

Ellie-Mae rolled onto her side, wriggling and laughing. "Did you see it?" Her giggle turned into a cackle. "Did you see Gary?"

He shook his head, watching Ellie-Mae writhe like a crazy person, rolling in mud and rubbing her hands along her naked body. "I saw Gary. He's here!" She slid her shorts up around her waist and clumsily jammed her feet into her muck boots.

Martin wanted to ask what she was talking about, but he couldn't find the words. He couldn't manage to open his mouth and speak a single sentence about what he'd seen.

Ellie-Mae charged up to Martin and kissed him, passionately moaning like she could fall into his heart and stay there forever. "Shhh . . . ." She pressed a finger to her lips. "Don't tell Gary what we did."

A rustle in the nearby brush pulled their attention away. Ellie-Mae's eyes jerked to the opposite side of the pool, where a narrow opening in the wall of weeds and hemlock parted by themselves.

Something strangely familiar called to Martin from within that passageway.

"It wants you," Ellie-Mae whispered.

Martin felt in the marrow of his bones that she was right.

Glassy black stepping stones formed a narrow path into the darkness—to the heart of the mountain.

"Can you feel it?" Ellie-Mae slid her hand into his and entwined their fingers. She closed in, lips damn near devouring his ear.

He felt the water inside of him. It was the trickling stream that a lost soul should follow to find their way home. It was guiding him, but he needed more information first to trust it.

Her breath lingered on his skin. "Let's go get Gary before we go." Ellie-Mae scurried away, disappearing on the other side of the rocks, running toward the trail back home.

Martin tried to suppress the overwhelming desire to submerge himself in the water, but his curiosity about Gary, and what Ellie-Mae had seen in her hallucination, eclipsed his need to dive in. The water would have to wait.

"Ellie-Mae!" He pried himself away but felt its icy hooks in his flesh, tugging for him to stay.

He caught up with her on the trail, breathless and sweating. "What do you mean 'Let's go get Gary?'" He grabbed her elbow.

Her eyes wandered aimlessly. They had dulled to a nickel gray. "He'll be home soon." Her smile twisted. "I saw it. He's in Blackmoor on his way back to the holler."

"But you said . . . " He pulled her in closer and whispered, "You said Gary died. You said the Bathtub showed you."

She yanked away, devoid of all emotion, eyes avoiding his gaze.

Ellie Mae shrugged. "I lied."

CHAPTER SEVEN

GARY

GARY FORSYTH CAUGHT the afternoon bus to Blackmoor, but when he stepped onto the cracked pavement with his duffle over his shoulder, it didn't feel like he was coming home. The war was supposed to be behind him, but he carried it within. It was in the weight of the things on his back, in the blood crusted under his fingernails—which had washed away only visually. War would never be behind him, but always staring him in the face.

The town of Blackmoor bustled on what he would've considered a beautiful summer day back before he was drafted. A gentle mountain breeze swept through the valley, ruffling his shaggy hair. It should've been a sensation he enjoyed, but he wasn't sure if joy was something he'd ever be able to feel again.

He stood at the T-section of the main road leading into town, and the narrow winding road that led up the mountain to the holler. The steep incline of dense conifers loomed before him, daring him to come home. If he were a cowardly man, he'd turn around and run—never look back. He'd considered bypassing Blackmoor altogether, staying on the bus and continuing west. The only surviving friend of his platoon, Private Enrique Delgado, lived out in Arizona. The two of them had been through so much together, that he already felt lost and alone without his comrade. He could've turned around, hitched out of this town, and let his mama, Martin, and poor Ellie-Mae live out their lives believing he was dead. It'd be better for everyone that way.

But Gary was supposed to be a man of honor—or that's what everyone believed. They wouldn't think it anymore if they'd known about the things he'd done under the orders of Uncle Sam.

The mountain called him home, but he wasn't the same man anymore. He didn't belong here.

Run.

A rusted white car rolled toward him from town. It wasn't too late to get out of town. Gary threw a thumb out, gut twisted in painful knots.

Run.

Everything about being here felt wrong. His outstretched arm waved his thumb and the car slowed. A blinker flicked on, but they weren't stopping. The car was making the turn into the holler. The Andersons, he thought, but in the driver's seat, was his mother. Victoria glanced at him with suspicious eyes and turned onto Holler Hill Road without stopping. A few seconds passed and the brake lights glowed hot red—right when his mother must've recognized who he was—and the car came to a sudden stop.

Gary dropped his hitching thumb and his arm fell to his side. All hope of escape drained from him.

"Gary?" She stepped from the vehicle with a shock-stricken face.

He should've said something. *Hi Mother* or *I missed you.* Or he should've felt the need to run toward her loving embrace, but he couldn't. All he could do was amble forward, all emotions ravaged and decaying within. The sounds of explosions echoed between each beat of his heart, and the faces of dead soldiers and civilians haunted the backs of his eyelids.

"Gary!" his mother screamed as she wrapped her arms around her boy. Her first-born—she'd always placed too much importance on him. Her tears soaked through his shirt. Tears that he imagined held all the worries of the past year. Tears he caused when he stopped caring about life enough to write home.

He wanted to say something like *It's okay Mama*, but he couldn't. That would be a lie. Nothing would ever be okay again. He let her hold him as long as she needed, and despite wanting to pull away and to never see her again, he held strong for her.

When she finally loosened her grip and let him go, he uttered nothing more than an, "I'm here."

He sat in the passenger seat as his mother wiped the tears from her face. She put the car into gear and climbed the steep hill. The mountain wanted him to return. He could see it in Victoria's pleased grin. He could smell it in the moist summer air as they eased into the cloud cover.

One more soul to devour—the one that got away.

It didn't feel like going home. It was more akin to heading back into the jungle knowing that no matter what precautions were taken, half the platoon would die from enemy landmines. He made it through war and came back in one piece. Most people would thank God for that. But somehow Gary didn't feel like God gave a damn about his life. No. If God cared, he'd spare him the agony of returning to Gray Hollow. Gary survived Vietnam, not because a god spared him, but rather because the mountain had called him home to die here instead.

When the car made it to the crest of the holler and leveled out, it felt like there'd be no way back out again. They crept down the broken pavement of the single-lane road and drew closer to Ellie-Mae's driveway.

There, she stood at the end of the gravel drive waiting for him. She was lifelessly weak, wavering like she might blow away with a swift wind. A dirty tank top and short shorts sagged from her gaunt frame. Her muck boots were coated in layers of dried mud. Frizzy hair was wild like it hadn't seen a brush in weeks. She held out a hand and summoned him with a come-hither finger.

"Did you tell her I was coming home?"

"Darling, *I* didn't even know you were coming."

He wasn't ready to face her. He wasn't prepared to talk about the things he'd been through, and knowing the sweet nature of Ellie-Mae, she'd want him to open his heart. But his heart had already been hollowed and scraped. There was nothing left of him to share.

Gary opened the door as Ellie-Mae staggered toward him like a rabid drunk, wild-eyed, with a toothy, forced grin. She leaped at him, throwing her arms around his neck and legs around his waist. Gary supported her weight, returning the embrace. She smelled of sweat and mud, the sour stench of summer labor—she reeked of the mountain. He gently pried her body from his and set her down on her own two feet.

"I knew you were coming." Her lower lip was cracked and scabbed over, hanging from a loose jaw, like she was too tired to close her mouth.

Now that he could get a look at her face, there was something off about her. Her smile wasn't warm and welcoming, but maniacal. Her eyes weren't full of sunshine, but rather bloodshot and unnaturally alert, irises as gray as the sky.

"Are you on something?" Gary asked.

"Are you on something?" she mocked, head swaying side to side like she was jiving to music in her mind. "Yes! I'm on a mountain!" A cackle followed, and Ellie-Mae charged in for a kiss.

Gary let her press her cold dry lips against his, but there was no love within that kiss—there was only eagerness, and maybe lust. This was not the same Ellie-Mae he'd left over a year ago. The same piece of bailer's twine was on her finger, but the girl he'd known before was not in front of him.

Gary pulled away, holding her by her shoulders, gently steadying her snakelike body. "How'd you know I was coming home?"

Ellie-Mae's lips stretched into a sinuous grin. The scab broke open and fresh blood flooded to the surface. "I saw you."

⁕

Mother exited the car, slamming the door. "Ellie-Mae, go get cleaned up and put some clothes on. You're indecent."

"*I'm* indecent?" A bout of crazed laughter bubbled forth and the dab of blood dribbled down her lip and onto her chin. "Mrs. Forsyth, *you're* the indecent one. I saw *everything*."

Victoria stepped back, hand pressed against her heart. "What on earth are you on about, young lady?"

Gary's eyes bounced between the two of them. "Mother, why don't you head home? I'll make sure Ellie-Mae has some coffee and gets cleaned up."

"I am not leaving you alone with this harlot!"

"Mother! My fiancé ain't a harlot. She's just . . . "

"I've seen things . . . I *know* things."

Mother made a cross over her heart. "Lord help her, she's gone to the Devil's Tub."

Ellie-Mae took Gary's hand into her soft palm. "I wanna show you something. Will you come with me?"

Victoria jumped between them. "No! Not my Gary! You ain't taking him!"

"Gary?" Martin's voice interjected, silencing everyone as he came out of the woods.

CHAPTER EIGHT

GARY

VICTORIA MANAGED TO get Ellie-Mae inside, to get her cleaned up in the bathroom while Gary and Martin stood in the kitchen. Martin's mouth hung agape. He hadn't spoken a word—neither of them had. But after what felt like an eternal standoff, Martin broke the uncomfortable tension and held out a hand to shake. "Welcome home."

Gary shook his brother's hand. His touch sent an intense surge of emotion through his body. Before it overtook him, he yanked Martin closer for a hug. Gary squeezed his little brother like a lifeboat he could never let go of. If he held tight enough, and long enough, he could stave off the emotional deluge that flooded his empty heart. Martin was the only thing that felt like home. His baby brother—not so much a baby anymore—made him feel human again, at least for a moment.

"We thought you were . . . " Martin trailed off and pulled back from Gary.

"I thought I was too," Gary whispered.

Neither of them knew what to say that wouldn't be some emotional purge of a conversation, so they sat across from each other at Ellie-Mae's kitchen table, wordless until Gary finally broke the silence. "Where's Rebecca? Down at the market?"

Martin shook his head. "Long story."

Gary appreciated not hearing whatever that long story was. "Hey . . . " He couldn't find the right way to say it, so he just blurted it out . . . "Thank you."

"For what?"

"For watching over Ellie-Mae while I was gone."

Martin's eyes wandered away, keeping something from Gary that he didn't want him to know. Gary had a guess—he could feel the sexual tension between Ellie-Mae and Martin the moment he'd stepped onto the driveway. A jealous part of him wanted to put his little brother in his place, throw a punch, and kick him while he was down. The raging, angry monster within thought of doing far worse, but Gary tried to leave that guy in Vietnam.

For now, Gary would let it go. If he were being honest with himself, he stopped loving Ellie-Mae in that way over half a year ago. It's hard to have room for love when your life is so full of death.

Martin shrugged. "Yeah, whatever. She pretty much took care of herself." There was something else strange about Martin. Something other than his feelings for Ellie-Mae. A distant and dreamy quality lingered in his eyes, like Martin couldn't wait to be done with the formalities of welcoming home his brother so he could get on with his life. Get back to following his dreams. It was about time the kid got on with his great enterprises.

⁂

Ellie-Mae entered the kitchen smelling of castor soap. Filthy muck boots were replaced by a pair of house slippers, and she wore an old church outfit—a blue, knee-length dress that had been through the Maytag so many times it faded to a dingy gray.

"Now here's our young lady," Victoria said, displaying her like a prize on the *Price Is Right* before seating herself at the kitchen table.

Ellie-Mae stood wavering, head loose on her neck like it was too heavy to hold up. She stared at the screen door. "Thank you for cleaning me up, Mrs. Forsyth. I'm feeling much better now and would like to go for a walk."

"A walk? Why that sounds like a lovely idea." Mrs. Forsyth reached across the table to take Gary's hand. "But my Gary just returned, and I'd like to spend more time with him. Maybe Martin can escort you on a walk?"

Gary leaned back, easing his hand away from his mother's.

Martin's brow furrowed. "Mom . . . that's not a good idea."

"And why not?"

"Because Ellie is obviously sick . . . " His eyes met with Gary's, waiting for his response. "She ain't herself right now."

Gary cradled his head in his palms, closing his eyes and trying to block out the arguing that ensued. Their voices blended into screaming and he couldn't decipher what it was all about. It was chaos, gunfire, and explosive mines. They bickered about stupid things that didn't make any sense—not out in the real world.

When Gary looked up and his ears tuned back into the reality before him, Martin and his mother were pushing their chairs from the table to stand.

"Ellie-Mae! Where you going?" Martin said.

Gary followed them outside.

"I'd like to take a walk now." She staggered closer to Gary in a sloppy motion, like she'd been soaking in her mama's bourbon. Delicate fingers hooked through his belt loops and drew him near. The scent of castor soap, already worn thin, pierced through by an aroma of petrichor that seemed to plume out of her pores.

"I wanna show you things, Gary Forsyth," she whispered.

"I've seen enough, Ellie-Mae."

"You haven't seen *this*."

"No!" Victoria wedged an arm between them, pushing Ellie-Mae back so hard she stumbled into the wood pile. "Ellie-Mae Matheson, if you wanna run off and bathe with the Devil, you don't bring my boys into it!"

Martin was at Ellie-Mae's side, protecting her.

"Sorry, Mrs. Forsyth. It's too late." Her lips twitched, lifting above her teeth like an alien smile. "Isn't that right, Martin?"

Run. It was all Gary could think of in this place. It was how he and Enrique survived the war. *Run.* Some things couldn't be fought.

"What is she talking about, Martin?" Victoria asked.

Martin shrugged. "How'm I supposed to know. She's the crazy one!"

"Crazy?" Ellie-Mae's hand slid sensually along the handle of the woodcutting axe leaning against the stack of logs. "Was I crazy when you made love to me today?"

Victoria gasped.

Gary's head fogged over. A storm cloud choked out all of his thoughts. It should've ripped his heart out, but all he felt was the subtle twinge of disappointment. This wasn't his family anymore. His family was flown home in boxes, courtesy of the U.S. government. Those who remained were scattered about the country, broken and dead inside just like him. Gary didn't bother looking them in the eyes. He simply walked to a truck parked in the driveway and slipped into the driver's seat.

Run.

"You can't leave, Gary!" Ellie-Mae said. She followed with a loose grip on the handle, dragging the axe in the gravel behind her.

Gary started the ignition. "I'm sorry . . . " he said.

Ellie-Mae's frail body stiffened. Her head dropped, and when she lifted her eyes, they were no longer dull gray but clouded white. Lips, blue and stained with blood, trembled as they curled back to expose snarling teeth. Those soft delicate fingers—one wrapped in a promise with bailer's twine—gripped the handle of the axe, and her muscles tightened. Ellie-Mae raised the weapon overhead and charged toward the truck.

Gary threw it into reverse and pealed out. Gravel sprayed like bullets into his fiancé as the axe came down on the hood of the truck. It ripped through the metal. She yanked on the axe handle, but it had wedged in place. The truck lurched backward, and Ellie-Mae shrieked—a guttural howl poured out of her, arms thrown back and head to the sky, she charged again empty handed.

Martin launched after her, wrapping his arms around her body. They spilled to the ground and wrestled. Gary stopped the truck, heart beating steady. Combat-calm and calculating. Victoria looked down her nose at the two, shaking her head as if she had nothing to do with it.

Ellie-Mae broke loose. A swift kick to the ribs kept Martin on the ground. She screamed like a caged puma, tugging at her wet hair until she pulled a handful free from her scalp. Ellie-Mae sprinted away, barefoot and zig-zagging into the forest until she disappeared among the trees.

Martin lay in the fetal position on the ground, crying. Mother stepped closer to her youngest son with her head held high. She knelt beside him.

With the window down, Gary could just make out her words from the distance as she spoke to him. "I forgive you for what you've done, but I don't know if God will."

Gary was numb, stuck in that seat, unable to make a move. The axe was lodged in the hood of the truck, but he wished it was wedged into his own skull.

"I'll go fetch Ellie-Mae," his mother said and headed toward the end of the driveway.

"She didn't go that way!" Martin said.

"But we all know where she's gonna end up."

"There's something wrong with her." Martin struggled to his feet, clutching his ribs and following on her heels. "Something is wrong with that water. It made her—"

Mother turned and jabbed a finger into his chest. "I *warned* you about that water. I warned all of you."

"I know, but . . . what're you gonna do? She ain't gonna listen to nobody."

"She'll listen to me."

CHAPTER NINE

VICTORIA FORSYTH

FOR OVER A HUNDRED YEARS, her family had cared for the land in the holler. Her house was the only one this close to the Devil's Backbone back then. The ridge of treacherous terrain was well hidden from most explorers, but those who could find the land closest to it would reap the bounties—fertile soil, copious wild berries, plenty of fish, and wildlife for hunting. But those bounties came with a price. Victoria's parents knew that nuzzling too close to this stretch of mountain was dangerous. Stories passed down from generation to generation told of stolen children in Tennessee and witches to the north in Kentucky. Evil presented itself in many ways along the Devil's Backbone, but one thing was certain. No happily-ever-after ever came out of living so close to evil. So, Victoria's parents got in good with the folks at church down in Blackmoor, thinking God would keep their family safe while the mountain kept them fed.

But during the Great Depression, that all changed. While the folks in Blackmoor struggled to get by, the Forsyths continued to prosper. Berry farmers and huntin' folk got the idea to head up into the holler to claim lots of their own. There's a give-and-take with the mountain, and too many people were taking, giving nothing in return.

When Victoria Forsyth was a teenager, she and a neighbor friend—June Marie Anderson—hiked the woods behind her home. It was the part of the forest that her parents forbade her from venturing into. Where the water was said to be poisoned.

"Is all the water poison?" Victoria had asked.

"It doesn't look poisoned." June-Marie stepped from one exposed stone to the next, navigating the stream crossing on their path into the woods.

They'd stolen June-Marie's brother's pants from the line to make the trip into the forest. All they'd had was dresses in their closet, hardly the attire for two explorers.

"We're like Lewis and Clark!" June-Marie said.

"Who are they?" Victoria asked as she leaped from a rock to the soft soil. Her foot slipped on the landing and sank ankle-deep into the water. Victoria screamed and pulled her foot from the mud, while June-Marie fell down laughing on the trail.

"It's just a little mud."

Victoria checked her ankle, certain her skin would be boiling off, but it was all intact. No sizzling. Nothing happened and she began to question the stories her folks had told her.

"I don't feel right being here." June-Marie stopped as a clearing came into view ahead. "This feels wrong."

It was too late to back out now. Victoria had ventured into the lair and could see the glistening hint of water ahead. It sparkled and tempted her to take a peek. She'd come this far. She hadn't realized it, but she was still walking toward it as if being pulled against her will.

"Victoria!" June-Marie called from behind.

She didn't look back. Her eyes filled with dazzling greens and blues as she neared the end of the trail. Nothing so beautiful had ever been seen.

June-Marie's footsteps caught up. "Is this it?" she asked. "Is this the Devil's Bathtub?"

Victoria shrugged. "I don't know. Looks like a regular water hole."

They carefully navigated slabs of slick rock and climbed above the water hole to get a better look at the shape from above.

June-Marie wiped her wet hands on her pants. "The water isn't poisoned. Knew it."

"I don't think this is it . . . "

"But *that* might be!" June-Marie pointed to the opposite side where a wall of rock lined a smaller pool of turquoise water.

The bathtub-shaped hole in the earth had depths unknown. The turquoise color deepened to a dark blue, and then black at the center, like a liquid geode.

June-Marie sat on the ledge and sank her bare feet into the water.

"No—"

It was too late. June-Marie's head threw back, eyes bulging wide. The caramel brown irises turned to pale ash. Victoria grabbed her friend by the arms and dragged her out of the water as she trembled and thrashed. She kept her hands under June-Marie's head to keep her from bashing it into the rocks.

Tears spilled from Victoria's eyes and splattered in little puddles at the edge of the Bathtub. "I'm sorry! I'm sorry! I'm sorry!" she chanted, rocking back and forth until her friend's body relaxed and she regained consciousness.

They didn't speak the entire trek back. And with each passing day, June-Marie was drawn back to the water, and with each plunge, she lost more of herself. Her parents locked her in her room to rest, but Victoria knew—somewhere deep in her marrow—what needed to be done. June-Marie took from the mountain, and it was time to pay up.

On an evening when the moon could guide their path, Victoria covered herself with her father's cloak so as not to be identified and helped set June-Marie free from the confines of her locked room.

She followed June-Marie and watched as she stripped herself naked to soak in the tub.

As she waited for June-Marie at the edge, toes flirting with the temptation to dip into the pool, a noise drew her attention to the thick brush beyond. There was a dark opening beckoning her to enter the forest.

A splash startled her attention back to the Bathtub, where June-Marie had emerged, cold wet fingers wrapped around Victoria's ankle.

The water found a way in, and her vision tunneled to darkness. She stood at the mouth of a great chasm with a child in her arms. She didn't know how, but she knew the child to be her own flesh and blood. A baby was in her future. The bony spine of a mountainous ridge loomed above. It was a strange mountain range that she'd never seen before, but she'd heard the stories of its existence. She cradled the child against her chest as she fell backward into—

Victoria gasped back to reality, doubling over to sop up the water from her ankle with her father's cloak. "No, no, no, no . . . "

June-Marie shook as she rose to her feet. Her eyes were lost, her balance weak. She staggered the way her drunken father did after downing half a bottle of bourbon.

Victoria backed toward the opening in the brush, branches snagging on her cloak. Her heart told her everything she was doing was wrong. That God could never forgive her, but it was the only way. The mountain's water showed her what would happen—some future that must be avoided. It owned them both now and Victoria had to pay up.

"This way, June-Marie," she summoned her friend down the black path.

Victoria Forsyth hadn't expected Gary to come home at all, so when she pulled up alongside him today in Blackmoor, it took her heart a minute to stop racing. The mountain wanted him—it had always wanted him—and she'd do anything to keep him safe. She whispered a prayer to God to forgive her for her sins. To understand why she had to do the things she'd done. God, above all others, would understand why extreme measures had to be taken.

Ellie-Mae was on her way to the Devil's Bathtub again, just like June-Marie, just like Rebecca, and just like Victoria's husband . . .

Victoria swung by her chicken coop before making the trek into the forest to find the girl. The late afternoon sun sank behind the mountain, leaving the holler in a wash of gray and blue. In the field beyond the fence, the dying saplings were crisp tan. Grasses and berry bushes shriveled. The mountain needed sustenance, and despite all it had taken recently, it yearned for more.

Greedy Devil.

Chickens scattered. Typically, there were dozens flocking to her as she approached the coop, but today, there were only ten remaining.

Greedy Devil takes and takes.

Victoria entered the coop, checked over her shoulder to be sure her boys hadn't followed her home and to be sure she'd closed the door behind her.

She knelt on the creaking floorboards, pressed her trembling hands together, and then raised them to the sky. Her hands came back to the floor, where she slid a file from under the nesting box. The loose board pried up easily, revealing her secret hiding place.

So many secrets were kept for the mountain. She was tired of it.

Guilt and shame fought for control, but Victoria couldn't give way to those feelings. Not when her child's life was on the line. God would have to understand that a mother's love transcends the rules of right and wrong.

All she'd done was give, give, give to this greedy mountain, and it continued to take. Her gifts to the mountain had been more frequent than ever. Lately, despite all her offerings, the mountain gave up no fruit in return.

Victoria gently lifted the ash-gray cloak from the hidden compartment, sticks clicked together like a wind chime. Bits of twig and chicken bones snapped and fell to the floor, but most of the protrusions stayed in place. The cloak had evolved over the years as she added more branches, mimicking the jagged ridge of the Devil's Backbone. Victoria slipped her arms inside and lifted the heavy hood up over her head to conceal her identity.

Before opening the door to the coop, she peeked outside to be sure the boys hadn't come home, and Victoria darted to the fence and into the forest, because Ellie-Mae—like many who lost their mind to the mountain—needed help finding their way home.

CHAPTER TEN

MARTIN

ELLIE-MAE'S KISS REMAINED as a ghostly touch against his lips—or maybe that was the cool caress of water absorbed into his skin. That sweet, sensuous tincture from the water hole hadn't left his mind. Nor had the images of time and space that flashed before his eyes. He wanted to see it again. He wanted to see it all.

"Martin!" Gary's voice finally registered through his fantasies.

Martin looked at him, sitting in the cab of the truck. His great hero of a brother was shattered inside. Broken and lost like everything else on this mountain.

Gary's hands were clenched on the wheel. "What the hell is wrong with Ellie-Mae?"

Sparks of pain shot through Martin's side as he approached the truck. "I think you know."

His brother sat unmoving from the driver's seat. A statue frozen in this moment, mind probably racing with fury, betrayal, and heartache. But Martin didn't have time to talk about his brother's problems.

"Come on," Gary said.

Martin got into the truck. "Are we leaving?" His desires split in two. He wanted to run away from the holler forever with his brother—Captain Kirk and Spock off to another frontier. But a new side of him, the scientist, wanted to go back to the water and investigate its wonders. There was much to learn.

Gary didn't head down the hill, he pulled the truck deeper into the holler and headed home. A deep sigh of relief bloomed from within Martin's soul.

They parked the truck at the back fence near the chicken coop. Gary's head tilted back like the weight of the world had filled it right up and he couldn't manage to hold it above his shoulders any longer. "Let's go get Ellie-Mae and get outta here."

They'd hiked in silence halfway to the water hole when Gary finally spoke up from behind. "Wait up."

Martin turned around and paused. Gary's attention was sharp, checking side to side, twisting around to check behind. The man hiked like he was being hunted, and for a moment, Martin considered telling him about the thing he'd seen in the forest earlier, but he kept it to himself.

The trail wasn't wide enough to walk side by side, so Martin took the lead, slowing his pace.

"Why are you still here?" Gary asked. "Why didn't you go to college?"

"Because Mama asked me to stay."

Gary huffed under his breath. "She's a piece of work."

"What do you mean?"

"She's selfish. It's always about *her*."

Martin laughed.

"What's so funny?"

"It's not about her. It's always about *you*."

"Me? She sent *me* away."

"Because she knows what this mountain does to people. She knows it wears people down. Notice she didn't let *me* go? Only her precious Gary is allowed to escape this place. The rest of us have to endure it."

"Endure what? Mountain life? Beats the fucking jungle hell I was in!"

Martin saw his draft card burning in his mind. He had regretted doing it every day. Not because he wanted to fight, but because it was a one-way ticket out. "I would've preferred to take my chances in the jungle."

Gary grabbed Martin's shoulder and twisted him around with a jerk. His lip curled like a growling dog. "It was a living Hell . . . "

Martin put up his hands in surrender. "Okay. I'm sorry."

"A living, fucking Hell, Martin."

"Okay! I'm sorry." Martin left it at that and marched ahead, letting Gary fall behind. Silence returned and with each glance back, his brother looked smaller and smaller.

His regrets for not leaving Gray Hollow began to diminish as they got closer to their destination. The remnant sensation of cool water against his lips multiplied and spread across his body. If a few drops had shown him the universe, what would full immersion do? He longed for the feeling of submersion—of floating in a lake on a hot summer day, every inch of his body comforted and cooled by the water. The Bathtub lured him in like a succubus, urging him to come and indulge in the pleasures within, open his mind to the sights it could show him. There were secrets to the universe held within its waters, and with each step down the path, his speed picked up until he was running the last leg of the trail.

As he reached the first water hole, the sky had already darkened. He glanced back to see that Gary hadn't yet rounded the last corner, so he hurried ahead, slipping and stumbling over the slick rocks. His eagerness was a hazard and he tried to contain his excitement. The water of the Bathtub may as well have reached out and carried him to it. He gravitated toward it, like a meteor destined to collide . . . like a rat to a forgotten meal . . . like his lips to the nape of Ellie-Mae's neck.

His eyes shut, wondering what the mountain would show him next—he wanted to see it all. He wanted to know about the Earth's beginnings. The Big Bang. The expanse of space and time. He wanted to see into the depths of the universe, farther than any man would ever have the privilege to see.

There was no hesitation, no reconsideration, no fear of what may happen. Martin did not stop at the edge of the water hole. His pace remained steady, and he was propelled forward, eyes closed, as he dropped into its embrace.

Toes, ankles, calves, hips . . . his testicles should've retreated at the icy grip of water, but every cell of his body sparked warm & alive. His chest submerged, heart rate placid, calm. His head went under and the last strands of his hair floated at the surface for only a second before sinking into the water with the rest of him.

When he opened his eyes, he did not see the tree canopy or clouds, but instead the night sky. Black and speckled with glittering stardust. The cold emptiness of space lapped at his skin, undulating waves across his flesh, rolling and writhing. Martin's body floated through the void, beyond Earth and the moon and the entire solar system. His body was a ship across the vast cosmic sea, riding the gravitational waves Einstein theorized. Nebulae condensed and formed into stars. Supergiants exploded in violent ends, which blasted particles and radiation across the fabric of time and space.

But tucked deep within that fabric of space were pockets of darkness. Far darker than the blackness of space. Anomalies in the continuum lured him like the Bathtub. It was the Unknown inviting him to come hither.

Peeking into these pockets felt wrong. He wasn't meant to see this far into the universe. He wasn't meant to uncover these secrets. But its gravity pulled him in, and as he fell beyond the cusp of darkness, he discovered people inside. Humans and creatures untold. Starlight blinked out, replaced by viscera. Blood and sputum and semen. Flesh and bone snapped. Screaming and tortuous cries. Monstrous roars rumbled within. Martin's blood boiled and his hair singed as he blasted through the pocket of hellfire. Surrounded by molten rock, Martin was spewed from the pocket of Hell. Stardust and rock had traveled through pure evil and carried it to a young solar system where it would birth new pockets of unholy vileness within a small rocky planet.

Martin stood at the edge of the Devil's Bathtub, ejected from the water without knowing how. Not a single ripple was in the water below. Dark clouds loomed overhead, and Hell summoned him below. Something sinister had laid its seed on earth long ago, and now he stood on a mountain range forged from that primordial evil. And it wanted him to climb inside. It lured him to fall into it, to let his soul be one with the universe once again. One with the bits of meteor rock and stardust that had penetrated places in the universe that are not meant to be found.

"Martin?" Gary's voice came from behind, distant and sheepish in the encroaching night. His palm landed upon Martin's soaking-wet shoulder.

Yes . . .

Now the moisture would absorb into Gary's hand and show him a glimpse. He would behold the awe-inspiring nature of the mountain.

His brother's hand pulled away, but Martin couldn't let him go. The mountain demanded souls, and an instinct as natural as breathing compelled Martin to supply all he could.

CHAPTER ELEVEN

GARY

GARY BLINKED AND FELT the dry heat of the desert on his shoulders. An amber bottle of Bud dripped with condensation as Enrique lifted it to his lips, hesitated, and set it back down without taking a drink. He stood alone on a porch overlooking a rocky front yard. Vast sandy flat land for miles. Enrique lowered himself into a wicker chair and the tears began to fall.

Gary snapped his hand away from Martin, who stood facing him. Thick rivulets of water drooled from strands of hair and saturated clothes. Martin's eyes were wide, his body tense and rocking with eager anticipation.

"Did you see it?" he asked, reaching for Gary.

Gary jerked away from his water-logged hands.

"Tell me you saw it!"

Gary had seen Enrique at his home in Arizona. A cold beer on the porch—a sunset on the horizon. Gary's heart plunged into his gut as his brother raved before him. He'd seen too many brothers lose their minds, lose their sense of morality, lose their lives . . .

"Martin . . . " he said. "I know a place we can go that's far away."

"If you asked me that yesterday, I would've gone." Martin's arms hung to his sides. Water spilled from his hair over his face. He opened his mouth to drink it. "But today . . . Do you know what I've seen? What I know? Where I'm going?" Martin raised his eyes to the sky overhead and for a moment he was his baby brother again, head in the clouds. Dreaming of taking off to the final frontier.

Martin's attention snapped to the brush beyond the dark pool where a narrow passage opened, vines and brush folded back to reveal obsidian stepping stones. Gary had seen this path before. It was a trail most people only hiked once in their life. And Gary, Martin, and his mother were the only souls he'd ever known to come out alive.

Gary was in kindergarten at the time, but the memory was clear. His mother stood at the edge of a great void in the side of the mountain—where the trees stopped growing. Where no life dared to take root. Mother stood on the edge of a cavernous hole, holding his little brother over the ledge. She sobbed, body retching with despair.

"Mommy?" he'd said.

She'd staggered away from the edge, clutching Martin to her chest.

He couldn't remember her words precisely, but she was angry and scared, screaming at him to go home, but he was frozen with fear. Mother stepped away from the ledge that day and brought her toddler home safely in her arms, but Gary worried that she might have come home empty-handed had he not followed her. She made Gary promise never to speak of it, or the mountain would take them all. With each passing year, the memory grew as foggy as the holler, and if he were to speak of it, he worried his mother would claim that it was nothing but a bad dream. So, he kept her secret locked in his memory, hoping it would disappear like everything else in the holler, but it never did.

CHAPTER TWELVE

VICTORIA

VICTORIA HAD FOLLOWED her friend June-Marie along obsidian stepping stones, through a narrow path that eventually opened to a desolate slope of rock. A bare mountain ridge devoid of growth towered over them. Along the slope, a narrow pathway was carved into the incline leading to what at first appeared to be a cave, but as she drew near, a great chasm opened in the cave floor. June-Marie stood at the edge, and even though Victoria didn't know what was going on inside her scrambled mind, she felt the mountain's hunger trying to pull her in. It wanted them both.

Brought to her knees with crippling fear, she regretted ever going to the Bathtub.

"It's not fair!" she cried. "She touched me with the water. I didn't do anything wrong! I don't deserve this."

The lure of the chasm had its hooks in her chest. Its core tried to reel her in. Her feet defied her and she staggered up the stone steps. The mountain's sharp peaks stabbed the sky overhead as she approached the wavering June-Marie.

Victoria whispered a prayer, not to God, but to the force within the depths of the great void. "I'll give you anything you want. Anyone! I promise . . . I'll do anything." Tears spilled to the dry rocks at her feet and saliva strung between her lips. "Spare me," she begged.

June-Marie turned to face Victoria and was startled, as if she didn't recognize her own friend. Victoria adjusted the hood over her head and stepped to the edge of the drop-off. She placed a hand on June-Marie's back. All it took was a gentle nudge, and her balance was lost. June-Marie vanished into the depths of the mountain.

She'd promised the mountain anything—*anyone*—but she never expected it to be so greedy to ask for her firstborn. Years passed and a second child was born, and she withheld them both. No matter how many out-of-towners or neighbors were gifted to the mountain, no matter the fact she sacrificed her own husband to its needs, Victoria knew what it really wanted. Then, in a time of desperation, she sneaked away and offered the mountain her second-born child—Martin—and she reneged on the deal when Gary had seen her.

All souls tempted by the gifts of the water belonged to the mountain. But often, in their declining mental states, they had trouble finding the passage. Lured to the core of the mountain, it only took a little nudge from The Gatherer to send their weakened minds up the black steps carved into the side of the mountain and, eventually, over the edge.

Ellie-Mae staggered along the black stones to the steep incline of the Devil's Backbone and Victoria followed, her cloak hiding her identity. As Victoria followed, she heard the soft whinny of a horse ahead. Ellie-Mae wandered off the path and found the old Appaloosa tangled in the ebony thorns.

Last night, in Victoria's desperation to stave off the mountain's insatiable appetite, she'd sneaked into Stillwater's stall and set him on the path toward the mountain, but he never made it. Knowing there would never be enough chickens, horses, or people to keep the Devil sated, Victoria's heart plummeted to her gut upon seeing Gary had returned to the holler.

"You can't have him," she whispered.

Ellie-Mae grabbed Stillwater's mane and jumped, swinging a leg over and straddling his bare back. He spooked, bucking slightly to shake his rider, but the old horse was too weak. Ellie-Mae held his mane and whispered in his flicking ears. She guided him out of the tangle of black thorns and onto the path leading up to the ledge. Stillwater stopped, snaked his head, and stomped his hooves. The animal's instinct knew better than to proceed.

Victoria hunched her shoulders, pricking her branched hood upward, and ran toward them, forcing them along the path.

Stillwater swung his hind quarters back and forth, then took off, up the narrow trail, back on course.

When she caught up with them at the ledge of the great chasm in the mountain, Ellie-Mae sat atop Stillwater, stroking his neck. Her body lay against him as he stomped the ground with anxious hooves. Ellie-Mae was a kind soul. Much like her mother, Rebecca, had been. Surely, offering a mother *and* daughter this week would make up for her failure to deliver her own child.

Victoria extended a hand toward the chasm.

"Take them, and give us peace," Victoria said.

Martin's voice came from behind. "Ellie-Mae?" He stood several steps below, staring up with eyes that had seen sights not meant for him. The light was fading from his eyes. He was poisoned now, and Victoria couldn't help but feel a swift rush of relief. Finally, the mountain could be appeased with an offering of her child.

But then her gut lurched as Gary rounded the switchback and came into view behind his younger brother. Her heart sank to see her oldest son standing so close to death. "Not him," she whispered. "Anyone but him."

CHAPTER THIRTEEN

MARTIN

MARTIN, DRIPPING WITH knowledge of all that had been, stood a few black steps away from The Gatherer, its ashen cloak adorned in long talon-like spikes. He recalled it hovering over his body when he was very young. Moonlight at its back, silhouetted face a dark emptiness. Beside the creature tonight, was a horse aglow in the wash of the moon, and on its back, Ellie-Mae was clothed in a pale gray dress, draped over the horse's back. She whispered to Stillwater and he stepped forward, toward the vast hole dug into the mountainside. Ellie-Mae looked back to Martin with a smirk and waved for him to follow before she and Stillwater disappeared over the edge. The horse's tail was the last thing he saw before they vanished without a scream or a whinny. No tumbling of hooves on the rock walls of the cave. Nothing.

Gary shouted from behind, his voice a distant thing not to worry about.

"Gary!" The Gatherer yelled. "Go home!"

The voice was familiar, but even in his mind's altered state, Martin recognized it as his mother's. The drugging effect of the water wasn't strong enough to maintain the terrifying image of the beast. Instead, his vision focused. The veil lifted and he saw his mother's face under the cloak's hood.

Gary dropped to his knees, hands around his mouth, tears streaming, and Martin struggled to understand his brother's reaction.

Gary whispered from behind, "We can turn around now and leave this mountain forever. Let's go, little brother."

Martin inspected his brother—the big man on campus, the star player, the town hero. Now, the broken man floundered on the ledge of insanity. The mountain wanted Gary. It wanted all of them.

Martin stepped backward, up the staircase to the ledge, and took his place beside his mom.

Gary approached cautiously, but Martin held up a hand to him and shook his head.

"Martin, no," Gary said, choking on his tears. "You can still go to school . . . learn about space."

The concept of going to college or doing anything on earth seemed so trivial now that Martin was enlightened. "Go ahead, Gary. I'll catch up with you later." Martin approached the vast cavernous void. Black as pitch, the vacuum within drew him toward it. The darkness wrapped its tendrils around his heart, into his crevices, and enticed him to step inside.

The Gatherer stood by his side, gesturing for him to enter.

"Martin, no!" his brother's voice gained distance.

The Gatherer placed a hand on his shoulder and leaned in. "You were born to do this. This was the reason I had you. To protect your brother."

Gary charged toward him, but Martin knew that Gary needed a break from being the hero. It was time for Martin to step up to the plate for once.

He locked eyes with his brother. "You've seen enough . . . *Run.*"

Martin took one giant leap backward and the void swallowed him. The tunnel of light overhead shrank to a pinpoint as his hair whooshed and his clothes grew ice cold against the wind . . . until there was no more wind. Only the freezing cold vacuum of space surrounded him. Martin fell bravely, fearlessly into the mountain that was once stardust, and he became one with the universe.

CHAPTER FOURTEEN

GARY

GARY COLLAPSED AT his mother's feet, arms reaching for the cold dark hole that swallowed his brother. A great beast rose within him. A monster worse than the fabled Gatherer. A creature unlike anything that lived in the Hellish pocket deep within Devil's Backbone. It raged in his heart and wanted to be released as it had been in Vietnam. He wanted his mother to pay for what she'd done. He imagined shoving her into the great abyss, or wrapping his hands around her neck and squeezing until she was blue. He imagined the face of the young man whom he'd fought to escape by ripping into his neck with his bare teeth—blood pulsing through his mouth. He pictured bullets and bombs and dismemberment and wished it upon the woman who claimed to love him.

Gary released his rage in a guttural screech and the mountain devoured the sound without so much as an echo.

Mother stood unfazed, not a single tear on her cheek. "It had to be done, Gary. It was the only way . . . "

He'd seen enough death and had taken enough lives for one lifetime. Despite the mountain's hooks being lodged deep into his flesh, he turned his back on his mother and the mountain and walked away, leaving her with her sins. As he reached the switchback, he twisted around to look at her one more time.

A black, nebulous cloud surrounded her. Smoky tentacles rose from the void and wrapped around her. She pawed at the ghostly demonic strands of darkness as they lifted her high above the abyss. The darkness dispersed and Gary's mother dropped into the nothingness.

Run.

He didn't pack a bag or try to sell the house before leaving the holler. The mountain would devour the abandoned homes. Gray Hollow and the Devil's Bathtub would become a whisper in the fog. A legend forgotten to time, so long as nobody was stupid enough to try to live so close to evil again.

As he drove west, the hook of the mountain slowly eased from his heart. For some reason, it released his tortured soul. He supposed not even the Devil wanted him after what he'd been through.

After days on the road, he made it to the porch of a house that overlooked a rocky flat landscape. The door opened, and his good friend Enrique stood before him. No words were needed. He threw his arms around him in a welcoming embrace.

They sat outdoors as the sun set. No mountains for miles. The stars shone overhead, unobstructed by trees and clouds. Here, he could try to forget about the things he'd seen and the things he'd done. Here, under the clear skies, he could imagine a new life ahead of him. And he could imagine that his little brother Martin was up there now, at peace among the stars.

THE END?

Not if you want to dive into more of the Dark Tide series.

Check out our amazing website and online store
or download our latest catalog here.
https://geni.us/CLPCatalog

We always have great new projects and content on the website to
dive into, as well as a newsletter, behind the scenes options,
social media platforms, our own dark fiction shared-world series
and our very own webstore. Our webstore even has categories
specifically for KU books, non-fiction, anthologies, and of course
more novels and novellas.

ABOUT THE AUTHORS

Born and bred in Tennessee, **Ronald Kelly** has been an author of Southern-fried horror fiction for 38 years, with fifteen novels, twelve short story collections, and a Grammy-nominated audio collection to his credit. Influenced by such writers as Stephen King, Robert McCammon, Joe R. Lansdale, and Manly Wade Wellman, Kelly sets his tales of rural darkness in the hills and hollows of his native state and other locales of the American South. He was a mid-list writer for Zebra Books from 1990 to 1996, and his work has been published by Pocket, Berkley, Pinnacle, Dark Harvest, Cemetery Dance, and Thunderstorm Books, among others. His novels and collections include *Fear, Undertaker's Moon, Blood Kin, Hell Hollow, Hindsight, The Buzzard Zone, After the Burn, Midnight Grinding, Mister Glow-Bones, The Halloween Store, Season's Creepings, Irish Gothic,* and *The Saga of Dead-Eye* series. His collection of extreme horror tales, *The Essential Sick Stuff,* won the 2021 Splatterpunk Award for Best Collection. Kelly lives in a backwoods hollow in Brush Creek, Tennessee with his wife and young'uns.

Laurel Hightower grew up in Lexington, Kentucky, and after forays to California and Tennessee, has returned home to horse country where she lives with her husband, son, and a rescue pitbull. She's a fan of true life ghost stories, horror movies, and good bourbon. She is the Bram Stoker-nominated author of *Whispers in the Dark, Crossroads, Below, Silent Key,* and the short story collection *Every Woman Knows This,* and has more than a dozen short story credits to her name. *Crossroads* was the recipient of an Independent Audiobook Award in 2020 in the category of Best Horror, as well as the This is Horror Best Novella Award for 2020. She has also co-edited three anthologies: *We Are Wolves,* a charity anthology released in 2020 by Burial Day Press,

The Dead Inside, an anthology of identity horror released in 2022 by Dark Dispatch, and *Shattered & Splintered*, a charity anthology released in 2022 to benefit the Glen Haven Area Volunteer Fire Department, who saved the historic Stanley Hotel from wildfires in 2020.

Red Lagoe is the author of the forthcoming novella *In Excess of Dark* (DarkLit Press 2024) and the novel *Bloodstains by Gaslight* (Brigids Gate Press 2024). She has authored three horror collections, including *Impulses of a Necrotic Heart*, *Lucid Screams*, and *Dismal Dreams*.

Red was the editor of the anthology *Nightmare Sky: Stories of Astronomical Horror*, she worked as a staff writer for Crystal Lake Publishing's *Still Water Bay* series, and her stories have been published in several anthologies. Amateur astronomy is her first love, so Red can often be found lingering in the inky shadows among the beasts of the night for a better view of the stars..

Readers . . .

Thank you for reading *The Devil's Backbone*. We hope you enjoyed this 13th book in our Dark Tide series.

If you have a moment, please review *The Devil's Backbone* at the store where you bought it.

Help other readers by telling them why you enjoyed this book. No need to write an in-depth discussion. Even a single sentence will be greatly appreciated. Reviews go a long way to helping a book sell, and is great for an author's career. It'll also help us to continue publishing quality books. You can also share a photo of yourself holding this book with the hashtag #IGotMyCLPBook!

Thank you again for taking the time to journey with Crystal Lake Publishing.

Visit our Linktree page for a list of our social media platforms. https://linktr.ee/CrystalLakePublishing

Follow us on Amazon:

Our Mission Statement:

Since its founding in August 2012, Crystal Lake Publishing has quickly become one of the world's leading publishers of Dark Fiction and Horror books. In 2023, Crystal Lake Publishing formed a part of Crystal Lake Entertainment, joining several other divisions, including Torrid Waters, Crystal Lake Comics, Crystal Lake Kids, and many more.

While we strive to present only the highest quality fiction and entertainment, we also endeavour to support authors along their writing journey. We offer our time and experience in non-fiction projects, as well as author mentoring and services, at competitive prices.

With several Bram Stoker Award wins and many other wins and nominations (including the HWA's Specialty Press Award), Crystal Lake Publishing puts integrity, honor, and respect at the forefront of our publishing operations.

We strive for each book and outreach program we spearhead to not only entertain and touch or comment on issues that affect our readers, but also to strengthen and support the Dark Fiction field and its authors.

Not only do we find and publish authors we believe are destined for greatness, but we strive to work with men and women who endeavour to be decent human beings who care more for others than themselves, while still being hard working, driven, and passionate artists and storytellers.

Crystal Lake Publishing is and will always be a beacon of what passion and dedication, combined with overwhelming teamwork and respect, can accomplish. We endeavour to know each and every one of our readers, while building personal relationships with our authors, reviewers, bloggers, podcasters, bookstores, and libraries.

We will be as trustworthy, forthright, and transparent as any business can be, while also keeping most of the headaches away from our authors, since it's our job to solve the problems so they can stay in a creative mind. Which of course also means paying our authors.

We do not just publish books, we present to you worlds within your world, doors within your mind, from talented authors who sacrifice so much for a moment of your time.

There are some amazing small presses out there, and through collaboration and open forums we will continue to support other presses in the goal of helping authors and showing the world what quality small presses are capable of accomplishing. No one wins when a small press goes down, so we will always be there to support hardworking, legitimate presses and their authors. We don't see Crystal Lake as the best press out there, but we will always strive to be the best, strive to be the most interactive and grateful, and even blessed press around. No matter what happens over time, we will also take our mission very seriously while appreciating where we are and enjoying the journey.

What do we offer our authors that they can't do for themselves through self-publishing?

We are big supporters of self-publishing (especially hybrid publishing), if done with care, patience, and planning. However, not every author has the time or inclination to do market research, advertise, and set up book launch strategies. Although a lot of authors are successful in doing it all, strong small presses will always be there for the authors who just want to do what they do best: write.

What we offer is experience, industry knowledge, contacts and trust built up over years. And due to our strong brand and trusting fanbase, every Crystal Lake Publishing book comes with weight of respect. In time our fans begin to trust our judgment and will try a new author purely based on our support of said author.

With each launch we strive to fine-tune our approach, learn from our mistakes, and increase our reach. We continue to assure our authors that we're here for them and that we'll carry the weight of the launch and dealing with third parties while they focus on their strengths—be it writing, interviews, blogs, signings, etc.

We also offer several mentoring packages to authors that include knowledge and skills they can use in both traditional and self-publishing endeavours.

We look forward to launching many new careers.

This is what we believe in. What we stand for. This will be our legacy.

Welcome to Crystal Lake Publishing— Tales from the Darkest Depths.